THE KER AT
THERMOPYLAE

Belinda Harrison

Available titles in the Thermopylae Bound Series
(In reading order)

DEDICATION

For my wife Renee – it took me all of about 20 seconds to fall in love with you, but another 20 years until we could legally be betrothed… it's a pity one of us wasn't a princess in Ancient Greece whose father could make up whatever rules he wanted to about who his daughter could marry! Our wedding may not have lasted as long as Alexis and Skylar's, but it was filled with just as much love xoxo

ACKNOWLEDGMENTS

First of all, thanks to you – the reader, I'm glad you're still with me on the journey to Thermopylae. As we get further through the series I think it's obvious that each book is different in its own way, but the most important part – the characters and their story are always at the heart of it all. Book 4 will be different again, and the heat gets turned up even more, so stay tuned for that!

Thank you also for the reviews and comments on Goodreads and Amazon you're leaving, and make sure you encourage as many others you know have read it to do the same.

Don't forget to connect with me online on Instagram at: belindagharrison, on Twitter at: beharrison78 on Facebook at: Belinda Harrison Author through my website at www.belindaharrison.com or via email at: belinda@belindaharrison.com

To my editor Kristie – this is probably the fastest turnaround on the 'final edit' we've done (go us!). It will be interesting how we go with the last 3!

To my new wife Renee (January 2019 was the official date she became my wife) thank you for everything you have done and been through our years together, and for those yet to come. My vows said everything else, but you mean so much to me and I love you just as much now as I did 20 years ago when we met. It's funny to think that this book and the wedding between Alexis and Skylar was written before I even got to propose to you, and before we were allowed to get married here in Australia.

For our daughter Ava, I haven't forgotten about you – thanks for being your awesome self, Mummy and I love seeing the amazing young woman you're becoming.

Book Four of the Thermopylae Bound Series *Dark Thermopylae* will be out in February 2019.

1

Trachis, Thermopylae
Later 10th, Moon of Gamelion, 508bc

Pressure at my forearm pulled me from the darkness. Hot fingers gripped me, nails digging into my skin. "I have only just found you, you changed my life. Do not make me walk alone in this world. I cannot do it again. Come back to me, Skylar. Please, I beg it of you. I cannot do this without you."

Alexis. Fear laced her pleas. I opened my eyes, panic fluttering in my stomach. My neck ached and my chin rested against the smooth leather armor covering my chest. *How long was I unconscious?* I attempted to move my arms, but they were bound, holding me tight against a wooden chair. Pain stabbed at my shoulder blades, reminding me where I was, and what was happening. Ares. The Keres. The baby.

Images returned with frightening clarity and other sounds emerged as I fought against my bindings. I raised my head and the circle of Keres came into view. We were no longer in the courtyard of the palace, but in the room Alexis and I shared. The women all had their eyes closed. Hands clasped together, fingers of the two either side of me wrapped around my upper arms to form an unbroken circle. Their black wings flapped silently, moving the fire-warmed air in the room.

Alexis sat within the circle, grimacing.

The Keres chanted words, almost melodic in their repetitiveness; soft, encouraging. I did not understand the language, but I felt their meaning.

They were going to bring the baby inside Alexis into the world. The power swirling about our bedroom intensified. It would not be long now.

I bucked against the ropes, finally breaking free of them, and the hands holding me. I jumped to my feet. Alexis screamed, grabbing at her swollen belly and I sent up a prayer that Artemis would protect Alexis, as well as our child, as she entered the world. I unsheathed the sword at my thigh, driving the metal blade into the Ker to my left. Her eyes grew wide as she grabbed at her injury, dropping to the floor as I wrenched my sword from her suddenly lifeless body. I had no sooner retrieved my weapon than Ares was beside Alexis, his face a mask of concentration as he continued the chant of the Keres. He shouted the foreign words as though attempting to mask the loss of the Ker I had slain.

I turned to the next Ker, slicing her head from her neck in a spray of blood. Ares' voice heightened in response. I rounded the circle, cutting and slashing at the monstrous women before they could mount defense against me. I had counted twenty back in the courtyard, but that number had swelled since I lost consciousness. Sweat trickled down the back of my neck as I drove my blade into body after body, and I only stopped at Alexis' cry of "No!"

I turned. Dianthe held a small, pink child in her arms. She stared in surprise at the bare patch on its left shoulder. Ares too, looked on in disbelief, taking the baby and inspecting every inch of her. My baby girl.

The wispy smattering of hair atop her tiny head matched the dark shade of my own. She cried at Ares' rough treatment and I sheathed my weapon, crossing to them in two strides and snatching my daughter from him. Her howls quieted as I drew her to my chest.

"She is not one of you. Leave this place. Do not return. Ever," I growled.

"She does not carry your mark. She is not your Chosen One," Alexis panted, reaching her hand up to me. I helped her across to the bed, handing her our child and settling them both on the covers.

"She does not wear the completed mark," Ares murmured.

"It must be there. Eir told you she would," Dianthe replied.

I turned and drew my sword on Ares and my grandmother. "Get. Out," I snarled.

"She is powerful, Granddaughter," Dianthe said. "With your tainted blood and lack of wings, you may not have felt it, but she is of the line. She *is* the one."

"No!" I screamed. I charged at Dianthe and slammed my sword into her stomach. Blood spilled from her mouth, dripping to the floor to pool with the blood from the wound. I retrieved my weapon again as she grabbed at her insides, choking on the mucus in her throat before she fell to the ground.

I levelled my weapon at Ares, but he only howled in response, disappearing in a flash of light and leaving Alexis and I alone in the room with the bodies of my kin. I put away my sword and returned to her side, taking our daughter and checking for the mark myself. There was no three-sided shape on her shoulder as there was mine. No indication at all that the blood of the Keres, of Ares, ran through her.

Her eyes matched Alexis' in their greenness. She looked up at me with those familiar orbs, innocence and openness written across her small, pink face. I smiled. My daughter. Our daughter. Strong and healthy.

How could I have wanted to end her life before she could show me that she did not belong to them; that she belonged to us? No matter what Ares believed, I would always protect her from him, teach her to be strong and resist whatever he offered her. She would know what I had not when she was old enough.

I kissed her forehead and handed her back to Alexis, crossing to the door and lifting the timber lock. My father and Thaddeus burst into the room, swords and shields in hand, eyes wide as they surveyed the scene in front of them.

"Where is Ares?" Father asked.

"Gone," I replied.

"You killed them all?" Thaddeus added, kneeling beside each Ker, searching for signs of life.

"Yes."

"Even Dianthe?" Father queried.

"Yes," I said again, pointing out her lifeless body.

Father's eyes held mine for a moment before he turned his attention to Alexis. "Are you alright?" he asked. "The child?"

Alexis managed a smile for him. "I am well. Come, meet your granddaughter."

The smile that split my father's face could have lit the room on a dark winter's eve. He dropped his weapons and crossed to Alexis, taking the child and wrapping her in a long length of material when Alexis offered it to him.

His eyes found her shoulder, as ours all had, and his grin widened when he saw she bore nothing there. "My darling girl," he crooned, drawing in the smell of the small child as he cradled her against his large body.

"How are you?" Thaddeus asked quietly, a hand on my arm.

"Alive," I replied. "Go see our child," I added, gesturing in Alexis' direction.

One side of his mouth lifted in a grin and he gave me a curt nod, making his way to the rest of my small family.

With the three of them occupied with the child, I slipped out of the room. Leaning against the cold stone wall, I blew out a deep breath.

"She is perfect, Alexis," Thaddeus said, his voice carrying through the still-open door. "Welcome to Trachis, sweetheart."

Welcome indeed, I thought. *What shall await you as you grow, daughter of mine?*

6 MOONS PREVIOUSLY...

2

"You do not have to. I would accept your request without it; you must know that," King Agrias said, pacing across the Throne Room.

"And I appreciate the sentiment, but you should not. The council shall not accept me without further proof I am to remain, and that I am worthy of calling Alexis my betrothed. It is how it must be," I argued.

Alexis and I had returned from the Heraion at Pera Chora early that morning and after I had asked Agrias' permission to betroth Alexis, he had requested a special meeting with his small council. It was that meeting he and I had just come from, his announcement of the upcoming betrothal between Alexis and me met with words of congratulations and excitement by many of the attendees. Unfortunately, a small number had also voiced their concerns or spoken their outright refusal to support the suggestion; it was those later men the king and I disagreed on now.

"The council does not have the final say in the matter, that decision is mine, and mine alone," Agrias snapped.

I drew a deep breath, blowing it all the way out as I nodded. "I understand that but consider what an alliance with Cleomenes could provide your people with ... *our* people with. You speak of wanting to turn from your brother's ways, from your Macedonian heritage. What if, as Melina fears, Amyntas does not take kindly to such suggestion? With the Spartans behind us, we would have fiercer, more experienced soldiers to aid us should we find ourselves in battle. We would have access to much coin for new armor or weapons against them, or any southern Greeks who wish to attack if they learn we are no longer part of the mighty Macedonian empire. It also sees us protected against Andreas and the Molossians should they become a threat. Agrias, I love Alexis with all my heart, but she is a *Princess*, and anyone who wants to wed her *must* prove they deserve her."

"Hmph," the king grunted. "In my eyes you have already done so."

"I appreciate that, but you know it is how it must be."

"I sought an alliance with the Epirotes all those winters ago, and look what that led to," he said, holding his hand up to halt my attempt to protest. "I know it may still have come to the same end, what with Basileios' wish to leave them, but I am not convinced another alliance is the smartest way to persuade the council to believe you have our best interests at heart."

"Allow me to at least speak with Cleomenes. He may not even agree to join me, and if that is the case then I shall accept it and find another way to convince the council, and you and Melina, that I can be all Alexis deserves, that you all deserve."

"Thaddeus tells me the council was less than receptive to the announcement," the queen noted, entering the room and crossing to us. "Many of them still mourn for the sons, husbands and fathers who were killed in the battle with the Illyrians. A battle they hold Skylar responsible for."

"I am well aware that I bear the responsibility for the Illyrian attack," I agreed with a nod. "I aided them in sending their loved ones to the afterlife, though it appears that was not enough."

"What are your plans to quell such murmurings?" Melina asked.

"I need to gain not only their trust and support, but their respect and acceptance," I replied. "I want to ask King Cleomenes of Sparta to ally himself with me, that way I would bring to our union the wealth and power befitting the betrothed of a Princess."

"I have told her it is not necessary. Her remaining here with us and the kind and fair treatment of Alexis is all I need to allow the union to go ahead. Our daughter's happiness and health is all we want."

The queen did not reply immediately but nodded as she looked between the two of us. "Both of you speak with truth. Whilst I agree with Agrias that simply having you here day after day, winter after winter, would elevate you to many, the prospect of being able to call on a power such as the Spartans could hold appeal to others. Permit Agrias and I a discussion before a final decision is made on the matter. Alexis would benefit from your company, she is feeling poorly this afternoon."

I frowned slightly, concerned that Alexis had found herself confined to bed since we returned from the Heraion. "I shall leave you to your words and return to speak with you both before the sun sets," I nodded.

Agrias returned my nod and offered his hand to Melina, leading her to her throne beside him.

*

A week later, Thaddeus and I waited on the shores of Lake Copias outside the village of Orchomenos – which was roughly halfway between Trachis and Athens – for Cleomenes to arrive. The Spartan King had eagerly agreed to the meeting, attempting to pry information from my messenger about the nature of our intended discussions. I could only assume he believed I had reconsidered helping him with the archon situation in Athens. Though I knew I would be disappointing him, I hoped he would put aside his disappointment and agree to what I asked of him.

As we sat beneath the shady trees, I told Thaddeus what I knew of how Lake Copias had been formed – a feat attributed to our favored hero, Heracles. "Heracles had left and returned to his hometown of Thebes many times before his eighteenth winter, aiding those with his feats of strength when they asked it of him, or using his height to deter enemies from approaching small villages who could not defend themselves," I began.

"Are you certain you speak of Heracles?" Thaddeus asked with a grin. "I notice a few similarities to your own upbringing."

I returned his smile with a shake of my head. "No, it is definitely *his* story, for on one such return to Thebes, Heracles met a group of Minyan emissaries from Orchomenos who were also making their way to Thebes. He asked them why they travelled there and learned that the Thebans had to pay a tribute of one hundred cattle to King Erginus of Orchomenos every winter for having been defeated by him.

"When the emissaries shared the story of how the defeat came about, Heracles became enraged and vowed to end the Thebans' debt to Erginus. He cut off the ears, noses and hands of the men, hanging their body parts from their necks and telling them they would be the only tributes their King would get that winter."

"Uh … should I ask what the significance was of their facial features?" Thaddeus asked.

"The Minyans had told Heracles that was the punishment that awaited the Thebans if they failed to produce the cattle when the emissaries went to collect them."

"I see," Thaddeus muttered.

"As you might imagine, King Erginus did not take kindly to the mutilation of his men and declared immediate war on the Thebans. Heracles stood beside the Theban soldiers, arming them with weapons which had been dedicated in temples and blessed by the gods. The Minyans had reputation as dangerous enemies when faced on horseback, and when Heracles heard this, he dug the river we followed here called the Cephissus and flooded the plain, leaving behind Lake Copias and effectively unseating the riders from their steeds when they attempted to cross. When King Erginus was killed, the Thebans declared victory and forced the Minyans to pay double the tribute they had been. In return for Heracles' aid, the king of Thebes – Creon – rewarded him with his daughter Megara."

"Megara – as in Heracles' wife whom he killed, along with their children, when Hera sent the fit of madness down upon him?"

"The very same," I nodded.

"We find ourselves in yet another legendary place," Thaddeus murmured.

"We do," I agreed, waving to the Spartan King as he arrived. I got to my feet and pulled Thaddeus up as Cleomenes slid from his horse.

"Greetings, my friend," the king said, offering his arm.

"It is good to see you again," I nodded, gripping him tightly in return. Thaddeus and Cleomenes exchanged pleasantries and I indicated we sit by the water to speak.

"I was pleased to receive your messenger," Cleomenes said. "You shared words with King Agrias on your return to Trachis and he wishes to lend aid to my cause in Athens?"

"Unfortunately, it is not your business in Athens which I have sought you for," I replied, sitting beside Cleomenes as Thaddeus took his other side.

"Oh?"

"No. I wish to ask for *your* assistance in a rather more personal matter."

"I see. Do I dare hope it is a request that would once again see us side by side?"

"In a manner of speaking," I nodded. "When we saw you at Corinth, I spoke of Princess Alexis and I being lovers. If you recall, I noted that I wished for no other to ever warm my bed again."

"I remember," the king acknowledged with a smile.

"We were on our way to the Heraion in Pera Chora and when we were there, the great goddess Hera favored Alexis to carry a child for us."

"Indeed?" Cleomenes said, his eyebrows raised.

"Yes. I owe much to Thaddeus and his wife, who assisted, but I want Alexis, the child and I to be a family in all sense of the word. I have asked King Agrias to betroth Alexis and me."

"I did not believe I would ever hear those words from your mouth, given your history and upbringing. Though having met your Princess I am not surprised, for she is beautiful and appears kind hearted. Which begs the question of why she has fallen for you. I would imagine she has the choice of any Princess or soldier her heart desires," he laughed, bumping my shoulder.

"That she would, though I am happy to say she is content to make do with *this* particular warrior," I replied, returning his grin.

"There has never been anyone Alexis has favored more than Skylar and we are thankful she came to us and makes Alexis so happy," Thaddeus noted.

"So, what is it you request of me?" Cleomenes asked. "Has the king denied your request for betrothal to his daughter? Do you require me and my army to convince him?"

"Not at all, indeed he and the queen welcome it with joy, though there are some who would oppose it," I replied. "To convince those others, I wish to offer more than just my love to Alexis. As you say, she is a Princess and as such the one who calls her their betrothed must offer something in return. An alliance or position is what is called for and unfortunately, I possess neither. That is where I ask for your help."

"In what manner?" Cleomenes asked, leaning forward with interest.

"I request a personal alliance with you, with Sparta. I understand there are a number of towns who are allied with you. I have heard it referred to as the Spartans and their Allies. I imagine it is akin to the city-states Athens calls theirs to command."

Cleomenes regarded me a moment before nodding. "There are similarities between our alliance and those of Athens certainly. I require those under *my* rule to seek permission from me before they carry out large or small battles with their enemies. In return, they receive protection and assistance from my own soldiers for their battles, or at home if anyone dares attack them there. There are some larger towns, such as Corinth who, though we are allied, work under considerable freedoms. I allow them to battle those they wish without question, though I would send men if it was asked, just as they would send soldiers to me if I requested it of them."

"If you would agree to stand beside me when Alexis and I are betrothed, you would gain Trachis and the entire region of Thermopylae as your ally. At this time, we are still tied with the Macedonians, so you would have another powerful tribe as ally – and it is one best to be alongside rather than against," I said.

Cleomenes nodded, his eyes finding the lake before returning to mine. "Your request intrigues me, and it appears I have much to gain by agreeing to stand with you ... and in all fairness I owe you more than just a slave girl for the evening for your aid with Hippias in Athens, to say nothing of your assistance in Stratos," he paused before continuing. "If I was to grant your request, perhaps I would set you the same freedoms as Corinth; both of us requesting aid or soldiers from the other only when necessary, rather than as a given. For I could no sooner demand the King of Macedonia assist me, than he could in return."

"I believe those terms would please King Agrias," I said with a nod.

"Tell me, what customs do you intend to observe when you betroth

Alexis? Macedonian? Greek?"

"A little of both, I hope. Nothing has been confirmed as yet. I told Agrias I wanted to speak with you first, and when my father returns, I hope for his guidance in the matter also."

Cleomenes nodded again. "Perhaps as a favor to me you would observe one particular Spartan custom I am fond of?" I nodded to indicate he explain. "Two nights prior to the celebration, the husband gains approval from the bride's parent or guardian and then seizes her, taking her to a secret place where the two of them spend the night creating a child," he held his hand up to halt my question when I opened my mouth. "Given what you spoke of earlier, I understand this is not necessary for the two of you, but for those who would oppose your being with the princess, the act could allay their fears that it is not what is best, if they are not aware that she already carries a child."

"They are not," I confirmed.

"Then if it appears that the two of you are able to produce a child through your union, clearly the gods themselves have blessed you, and who would dare go against what the gods approve of?"

I drew another deep breath. His reasoning was sound; we had told no one other than my father, Agrias and Melina of the child growing inside Alexis, wanting to wait until we had carried out Hera's test to find out if she was carrying a boy or girl before we did so. Adding that knowledge to the alliance with Cleomenes could certainly help silence those on the council who had their doubts.

"I shall speak with Agrias on our return and arrange it," I agreed.

"Good," Cleomenes smiled.

"When we have chosen a time for the wedding, you shall come when I send word?"

"I would be most pleased to do so. Perhaps if all is not settled in Athens, I shall speak directly with King Agrias on the matter."

I grinned. "I would expect nothing less."

"Good," Cleomenes said again, pushing himself to his feet. "Well, I must take my leave. I am certain you are also eager to return to Trachis."

"Indeed," I nodded, following him to his feet. "I offer my deepest thanks to you."

"Allow us to consider ourselves even now for past aid and deeds," he replied.

"See you at the betrothal."

Thaddeus and Cleomenes shook and the king climbed back onto his horse. "Until then," he waved, turning the dark mare back towards Athens and taking off at a quick trot.

"If I had to guess, I would say either Isagoras or Cleisthenes is holding a banquet tomorrow night that Cleomenes is eager to attend," I laughed, watching the red himation of the Spartan King flap behind him as he pressed the horse on.

"Indeed," Thaddeus agreed with a grin.

"I would suggest we attempt to catch our dinner before we leave, but there are more eels than fish in the lake here, and the slippery beasts are not my most favored of dishes."

"Nor mine," Thaddeus laughed, climbing up onto Darko as I settled myself atop Skotos. "Perhaps we shall find something more suitable as we journey through the mountains."

"Race you to Mount Parnassos?" I grinned.

"Absolutely," Thaddeus replied, digging his heels into Darko's side and taking off before he had even finished speaking. I shook my head and started after him, glad our return journey would be even quicker than our one to the lake. I *was* eager to return to Trachis to see Alexis and ensure she was feeling better than when I had left her. She had spent a good deal of time in bed since we returned from the Heraion and, though I had been assured that was perfectly normal, I did not enjoy seeing her so unwell.

Once I had looked in on her and ensured she was well, I would tell Agrias what I had achieved, and what Cleomenes had asked I do in return regarding the seizure of my future wife. I grinned and tightened my grip on Skotos' reins, gaining on Thaddeus and Darko as we raced through the fertile plain of Orchomenos.

3

Hesper escorted me into the room, remaining silent as I surveyed bunches of flowers in vases and lying loose on surfaces, their petals scattered on the floor and the heady scents adding to the beauty of the colors. The bed was covered with coins for prosperity and rice to symbolize the putting down of roots and the following day, Alexis and I would return together and officially call it our home.

I turned to Hesper with a grin. "It is perfect. Thank you."

"You are most welcome, my friend," she replied, squeezing my hand affectionately. She led me back outside where my father waited.

When she had made her goodbyes he asked, "You are satisfied with the preparations of the bridal chamber?"

"Very much so. Hesper, Melina and the women did a wonderful job."

"Good."

"It shall be a little strange to call Agrias and Melina's apartment our own once Alexis and I are wed though," I added as we walked beneath the entrance of the palace and down into the town.

"I can imagine, but with the impending arrival of your child, it makes sense you would all be housed in the central chamber area, as Alexis and her parents have been since her birth," Father replied.

"It just does not sit well with me to send Agrias and Melina from their lodgings."

"They shall not be far away. The apartment Thaddeus and Hesper occupied is almost the same size, and *their* re-housing to the two apartments on the north side of the palace shall suit them better with the expansion of their family."

"True enough," I agreed.

We headed towards Ophelos and Aspasia's home in the center of Trachis. Alexis' grandfather, whose life I had saved five moons ago after he was stabbed, had insisted I use his home for part of the wedding celebrations and I had gladly taken up his generous offer.

Usually, the bride and groom had separate houses as the young woman still lived with her parents, the groom an older fellow with his own home, which he would take his new bride to when the celebrating was done. But as with much of the life I had lived in my nineteen winters, the usual conventions did not apply to my situation; for one, Alexis and I already lived together at the palace. But I had insisted that for certain activities we would celebrate our marriage in a traditional sense with the two of us segregated the night before. I also intended to play the part of the groom in the days leading up to the betrothal, sacrificing and celebrating as all men do before they take their new wife.

Our wedding itself was to be a combination of both Macedonian and Greek customs. There were a number of similarities between the two ways, not least of which was the length of the wedding itself; three days in all with celebrations and feasts to take place between the palace and Ophelos' house.

At the palace, Alexis, many of her friends, Queen Melina, Aspasia and Hesper were busy making flower decorations and singing and dancing to encourage good luck for the upcoming nuptials. They would also participate in a feast and ceremony where Alexis would cut some of her hair and sacrifice it to Artemis in recognition of the transition from her old life to her new.

She would also sacrifice fruit to the goddesses Hera and Aphrodite in thanks for their assistance and to ask for successful child-bearing in our partnership. Though it was not required, I had made my own sacrifice to Hera giving my thanks once again for her assistance in Pera Chora.

In comparison, it was far less busy for the men and I. Thaddeus and Moeris, along with Cleomenes, and his favored general, Demosthenes, were staying with Ophelos, me and my father, who had recently returned from Konitsa, to help me prepare for the celebrations. I was glad for the humor and relaxed atmosphere they provided – the six men enjoying a great number of amphorae of wine on my behalf. I was keeping my wine intake to a minimum, wanting not only to recall and enjoy the whole process, but to keep a clear head in case anything unexpected happened. I did not want to dampen the mood, but I had known of plenty of attacks to occur while a king was celebrating his wedding and I wanted to be able to protect those I loved if the need arose.

Despite all that had happened the past five moons, I had not forgotten Agrias' words that Andreas may arrive after the summer fighting season was done. There had been no word it was to be so, but I did not believe it would be long.

My father had not been pleased to learn I had secured an alliance with Cleomenes and the Spartans to aid in the union of Alexis and myself. I had pressed him once again on his aversion to the Spartans, but he would not speak of it, telling me it was not the time for such conversations. I kept at him, but the named man had entered the room and the discussion ceased. My father had not mentioned his reluctance to the king and the two of them had been enjoying one another's company and tales without incident, just as they always had.

"So, tell me of Nasrin's return with you. I was surprised and yet glad to see her again. She appears well," I said, nudging Father's shoulder.

"She is," he grinned. "It was a surprise to me as well that she wanted to come, though I am pleased. Unfortunately, my visit to Konitsa was not as uneventful as I would have wished for. Trouble found us, taking with it a number of innocent casualties."

"Oh?" I enquired.

"Nasrin's daughter, Ava, was one of them I am sorry to have to tell you."

"What happened?" I asked, silently sending up a prayer to the young woman I had last seen almost four winters ago.

"As I travelled to the north, I met a group of young men I later learned to be from a Thesprotian tribe of Epirus. They told me they were travelling to Tricca on the opposite side of the Pindos Mountains and wanted to avoid the tribes who called Konitsa and Tymphae home near Mount Smolikos. They asked where exactly they were to be found and I told them, not realizing their true intent was to attack the Molossians at Konitsa."

"Why?"

"They already have a presence on the west side of the Molossians in central Epirus and wanted one on the east."

"Central Epirus – you mean Andreas' tribe?"

"Yes. Their intention was to catch the Molossians unawares as they attacked from both flanks. They had already joined with the Tymphaioi tribe at Tymphae and were on their way to meet them and take Konitsa."

"Did they succeed?"

"No, but they arrived with such stealth there was no time to get the women and children to safety. You recall I spoke of Theron and Irina; my friends from Thrace?" I nodded. "Ava was married to their eldest son, Origenes. She was outside with their child and was cut down in the first wave of the attack. The young boy was unharmed, saved from certain death by Origenes who heard his wife's cry."

"You killed many of them in response?"

"Yes, though it did not prevent Origenes for placing blame with me for his wife's death. I could not fault him for the thought – I did unwittingly give the Thesprotians their location. I believed Nasrin would also place blame with me, but she did not and when I received your messenger, she wanted to accompany me back here."

"She did not wish to remain to look after her grandson with Origenes?"

"No. Irina shall see he is well cared for and send messengers to tell of his progress as he grows."

We entered the front gates, heading directly for Father's room so we could continue to speak uninterrupted, though the rest of the house was quiet. He poured us each a skyphos of wine and I joined him on a klinai.

"Do you believe you love Nasrin, or could love her?"

My father did not reply immediately, consulting the swirling wine in his cup as though it contained the answers he sought. "Perhaps. But as it always has been, my heart remains in the past with your mother."

"There is much in the past that leaves permanent marks on us, but is it not time you found out if you could love another? Give yourself and Nasrin the chance to be happy together. The past must remain there, else it holds us back from all we can do in the present and future. You must live in the now and enjoy what is bestowed on you."

My father looked up, grinning. "Is it not I who is supposed to offer such sage advice about love on this day?"

"And if you had any to share, I am certain you would," I replied, returning his smile and bumping my shoulder to his.

"Indeed, indeed," he laughed. "Perhaps your words ring true. Ava's early demise, just as my Zita's so long ago, proves a reminder that life can be but fleeting and we must ensure it is the happiest it can be." I nodded and we both sipped our wine. "When we first found ourselves in Trachis, I would never have believed we would be here almost a winter later … or that I would be celebrating your betrothal," he mused.

"No. I was certainly not seeking love or any sort of attachment. But it found me anyway and I would not change it."

"I do not believe we are ever ready for love when it comes to us. It is always a surprise which both excites and frightens. Nasrin told me she has cared for me all these winters; that I have held a special place in her heart since we first met."

I nodded again. "I felt something for Alexis that first day in the Spercheios Valley. I was drawn to her. The way she smelled, the way she held herself, her fragility as she stood before Melanthios. I wanted to know who it was hidden beneath the material that covered her eyes. She took the breath from my chest. When I woke later at the palace, she was there again, tending to me in her quiet manner. At first it was only lust that saw me dream of her, but the more time we spent together, the more my feelings grew and changed. I did not expect to want to spend time with her, so determined was I to re-join the soldiers and you. But I found I wanted to see her smile, to make her smile, to hear her laugh, to make love to her …" I trailed off, embarrassed at my speech.

"I believe *that* is how you know it is love. That it is meant to be," Father smiled. "You speak of your love for Alexis in the same manner I have always spoken of it for your mother. I am so happy you have found the love of another in this world, for there are few things worth more. Care for her. Love her. Allow her to love you in return. Every day," he said, wrapping an arm around my shoulders.

"I shall. I do," I replied, doing the same around his waist. "And you shall give of yourself the same? Allow yourself to receive it in return?" I added as I released him again.

He continued to grin and nodded. "I believe I shall."

"Then those are words we should drink to," I said, raising my skyphos to his. He pressed his cup against the side of mine and we both took a large mouthful of the sweet beverage before he spoke again.

"I am truly glad to be back in Trachis. You and I have both found special women to call our own and I look forward to remaining here until I am old and find myself greeting Hades in the Underworld."

"I believe this shall be a special place for us all. It is home."

"Indeed. Now come, it is time we sacrificed wine and fruit to Aphrodite, just as the women shall be, then you must attempt to slumber. The morning brings another long day."

"It does," I agreed with a nod.

4

The following morning began with my ceremonial nuptial bath in the palace bathing area. I was in the first room, and I knew Alexis to be in the second, though we were not allowed see one another yet. The water for our baths had been drawn from the Spercheios River; the place we had first saw each other. It was collected by Hesper and Thaddeus' eldest son Nikomachos and his best friend, Lysistratos, the two of them to be further involved during our betrothal.

I had named Thaddeus as my koumbaro; my main attendant, and it was a task he had been more than happy to take on, until we arrived at the bathing area. He had never been comfortable seeing me naked and I had taken pity on him – allowing him to remain outside until after I had bathed and Moeris had adorned my skin with oils and perfume and settled my tunic and bronze cuirass in place.

Thaddeus entered the room again as Cleomenes fastened the pair of bronze greaves he had gifted me to my shins. Father handed Thaddeus a dagger and he cut a lock of my hair for us to offer the gods.

When Demosthenes belted my xiphos around my waist, I nodded to my father. "I am ready," I told him. He inclined his head in return and the six of us left the bathing area for the Throne Room.

Agrias, Melina, Ophelos, Gnosidicus and two men from the small council waited for us, their faces breaking into wide grins when we entered. I bowed to each in turn before approaching Agrias and Melina, who sat on their thrones.

"Skylar, welcome," Agrias said, reaching out to take my hands. I placed mine in his and knelt at his feet as we had discussed.

The room fell silent and waited and I did not hesitate to begin. "King Agrias, Queen Melina, esteemed kin, and friends, I humbly request your blessing and approval to betroth your Princess; Alexis. To secure her hand, I offer not only my love and the promise to treat her with respect and honor, but my alliance with the King of Sparta."

Cleomenes stepped forward, placing his hand on my shoulder as he addressed the gathering. "Skylar has my complete support and I would proudly send my men to stand beside her should she seek their assistance. I too would hold my shield at her side, as she would mine, to protect and fight for those she loves. I make this alliance without hesitation and hope you shall accept the terms just as quickly." Agrias nodded and Cleomenes returned to his previous position.

I watched silently as the King of Trachis locked eyes with the men in the room, each nodding his approval in turn. The queen also gave her consent, unable – and unwilling – to conceal her wide grin as she inclined her head.

"It is agreed," Agrias said, his fingers tightening on mine. "I accept your alliance, and by extension ours, with Sparta and I gift my daughter to you to call your wife."

I bowed to Agrias and Melina as I stood. "Thank you, my King. My Queen. You honor me with your acceptance."

Agrias grinned and released my hands. "It is time the young women joined us," he announced, nodding to Thaddeus. The king's favored guard bowed and left the room, Agrias leaning in close to speak as he said, "You see the two men I invited from the council – Stavros and Antigonos?"

"Wise choices," I nodded. Stavros, a former Macedonian and dear friend to the king, had been a supporter of my intentions with Alexis from the moment Agrias spoke of them. Antigonos however, was not, and I had not forgotten that he had once called Dodona home as Melanthios had, or that he had spent time with Melanthios when he was here.

Further conversation between Agrias and I stalled as Hesper led Alexis into the Throne Room, my breath suddenly hard to catch. She wore a red, silk chiton dyed purple in patches, a girdle belted high beneath her breasts and a yellow veil covered her face and hair, held in place by a bridal crown made from the branches of a laurel tree called a stephane. I attempted to find her eyes through the material, but it was too thick and I had to be content with the knowledge that when she officially became my wife later in the evening, I would have the privilege of removing both the veil and the girdle. It was obvious the care Hesper had taken in preparing my bride and I smiled warmly at her and the attendants in thanks.

Thaddeus returned to my side, placing a stephane of my own onto my head. "Our women are particularly stunning this day," he murmured, giving my crown a final push into place.

"Indeed," I replied with a grin.

"Come," Agrias announced, taking his queen's hand. "Our celebrations continue in the banqueting hall."

Thaddeus offered me his arm and I looped mine through it as Alexis took Hesper's, following the king next door. Two tables had been brought in, Agrias directing Thaddeus and Hesper to settle Alexis and me on one side before taking their places beside us. The king, queen, my father and Nasrin sat opposite us and Stavros, Antigonos, Alexis' grandparents, Gnosidicus, Cleomenes and the soldiers from Trachis and Sparta took their places at the second table. Klinai were positioned around the room for the rest of the guests and slaves poured wine for everyone.

A large, circular, and freshly baked bread sat in front of my father and Agrias, each man taking a side and pulling. Agrias came away with the larger section, holding it up for everyone to see. "It appears Alexis shall be the more dominant in the union," he laughed as the room erupted into cheering.

Agrias had been eager to participate in the Athenian tradition between fathers of the betrothed when I spoke of it and my father said the outcome would never affect their friendship as it had some families he had been witness to.

Alexis shook her head and I chuckled as well, squeezing her hand and wishing again I could see her face – I had no doubt her cheeks would be dark. "I needed no bread to prove the truth of that," I told her, leaning close. "I am always helpless to deny you of anything you wish." She shook her head again, but I heard her laugh in reply.

With the entrance of the food, the rest of Agrias' small council joined us, finding klinai and enjoying not only the wine, but Hesper's famed honey-bread, and sesame seeds mixed with honey which was a delicacy at many Athenian wedding feasts. Professional singers arrived soon after, offering libation to the gods at the beginning of each piece of music, and to Alexis and me, for a long and prosperous union, before entertaining the guests.

*

Candlemarks later, as the sun began to set, Agrias stood, calling for quiet in the banqueting hall. He indicated for Alexis and I to stand as well and I swallowed a smirk – this part of the ceremony my favorite, given where it ended, when Alexis and I had practiced. I took Alexis' wrist, holding it up so all in the room could see.

Agrias cleared his throat and began to speak. "It is time for my daughter, Alexis, to be given to her new family. Traditionally, this is when a father must say goodbye to his child as she leaves his house and settles into her husband's. Thankfully, I do not have to say goodbye at all and am fortunate enough instead to welcome another daughter to our family. Nevertheless, I shall speak the words which shall see Skylar and Alexis joined officially. Then we shall partake of the traditional procession, making our way through the streets of Trachis and back here to the palace."

"And then we shall feast and drink some more!" Stavros called out, raising his cup in our direction. Laughter filled the room at his words and Agrias nodded enthusiastically.

"Indeed. Skylar, in front of witnesses I give this girl to you for the production of legitimate children and a long and prosperous union. Opa!"

"Opa!" came the thunderous reply.

Moeris and Thaddeus led us from the banqueting hall, their horses waiting outside the main entrance with a stable hand. They climbed up, taking the procession down into the town, my father and Agrias next, lighting the way on foot with blazing torches. Skotos and Calla were brought forward, a chariot attached behind them for Alexis and me.

I held my hand out, helping her up into the wagon. "Place your feet slightly apart and hold onto this," I directed, stepping up beside her and taking the reins from Brygos.

I gave him a nod, receiving a wide grin in return before he turned, lifting Nikomachos into the chariot as well. I settled the boy between Alexis and me, ensuring he too held onto the wooden front. He had been named as our amphithales and stood between us for our journey as a symbol of good luck and the expectation of our own successful offspring. He was not privy to the last part; believing only that he was our good luck charm, as he had constantly told anyone who would listen leading up to the day.

Hesper handed me a crown made of thorns and nuts for her son and I settled it carefully over his hair as far as his ears. "Ow. Why does it have to be made of thorns?" he complained as Skotos and Calla began to walk.

"It is to remind us of the threatening proximity of wild nature," I told him.

"But why?" he continued, unable to scratch at his head with the movement of the chariot.

"As we travel through life, there is much harm we may encounter, even on a short journey such as this one. It is to remind us that we must be ready for it at any time."

"It is not as though we need such reminders," Alexis said, bending her head towards me. "We met such creatures during our journey to the Heraion."

"Indeed," I replied. "I cannot imagine we shall meet any beasts here, but just in case," I placed a hand on the pommel of my sword. She nodded but said nothing further.

Lysistratos ran beside us, holding out bread for Nikomachos to throw to the gathered men and women who stood outside their homes in the hopes of seeing us as we passed by. In return, some showered us with flowers.

"Do not forget the words you must speak," Hesper called to Nikomachos from her place behind us with Melina.

"Oh, yes," he recalled, turning to Alexis and I as he said, "I fled worse and found better. I fled worse and found better." He repeated the sentence a number of times, barely pausing for breath between, his bread throwing becoming wilder with each rendition.

"Thank you, Nikomachos," I grinned, resettling the crown on his head.

Bringing up the rear of the group were young men who danced and whirled constantly to the lyres and flutes of the musicians, along with two torchbearers. I smiled and waved at the onlookers, catching a piece of bread Lysistratos had intended for Nikomachos' face. The two of them looked at me guiltily, and somewhat afraid. I stared them down a long moment before throwing the bread into my mouth with a grin. They visibly exhaled and kept the bread in the crowd for the remainder of the journey.

"I feel as though I am a triumphant homecoming victor from one of the Panhellenic Games," I laughed over the noise of the gathered crowd as we neared the palace again.

"This is the sort of welcome they receive?" Alexis asked.

"Yes, although they are often carried through the streets on the shoulders of friends, family, well-wishers or strangers. And they are never without a cup of wine in their hands," I replied.

At the entrance to the palace, a great cry of joy went up from those in our party, and the gathered witnesses who awaited us inside the gates.

"A successful, safe journey for our bride!" Gnosidicus' voice rang out through the open doors.

5

When we had passed through the entrance, Moeris and Thaddeus halted our horses on the path in front of the courtyard garden. I stepped down, lifting Nikomachos from the chariot and then Alexis, walking with her in my arms to where my father stood near the central chamber. It was customary for the mother of the groom to welcome her new daughter-in-law to the family home, but as my mother was no longer alive, Father had offered to do the honors.

I set Alexis down and he held out his hand to her, which she took without hesitation. "Welcome to the family, Alexis. I am honored to call you kin and wish you good health and a prosperous union with my daughter." He opened his arms and Alexis stepped into his embrace, his wide smile matching mine.

When they released one another, Nasrin stepped forward. "May I also share words?" she asked.

We had not previously discussed her doing so, but I nodded. "Of course."

The four of us joined hands as Nasrin began. "I hope the two of you will also consider me part of your family. Alexis, we have only just met, but I see you are a fine young woman, and more than a match for Skylar's fiery temperament." She turned to me. "And Skylar, I could never replace your mother, nor would I ever attempt to do so, but ever since I met you four winters ago, I have thought of you as another child of mine. I find myself overwhelmed with parental pride to see you standing here with Alexis today. I hope you shall feel comfortable coming to me if ever you have questions on motherhood or for anything in this journey we call life. I shall always be here for you."

I swallowed loudly, the lump in my throat preventing me from forming any words for a long moment. "Thank you," I finally managed, squeezing Nasrin's hand and hoping it could convey just how much what she had said meant to me. She smiled and nodded in return, taking me in a tight embrace. "Thank you," I said again, hugging her firmly in return.

"The welcome is complete," Father announced, giving me a wink and another grin as he took Nasrin's hand and stepped aside.

Hesper offered Alexis a plate of warm quince generously drizzled in honey. The smell was dizzying, though I knew not to take any of the fruit; Hesper had promised I would have some of my own the following day. I could not wait for she had told me it was even better than her honey-sweetened bread.

When Alexis had finished the quince, Hesper swapped the plate for a lighted torch and Moeris and Thaddeus set the axle from the chariot we had ridden in on at her feet.

"It is tradition at this point in the celebrations to have the bride burn the axle from the chariot to show she accepts her new home and family in place of her old one," my father stated. "Alexis, if you would step forward." She did as asked. "Are you willing to accept your place in my family? To cherish the kin who shall now surround you and give love to you in return?"

"I am," Alexis replied loudly. My father smiled and indicated she set the axle alight.

Alexis touched the torch head to the wood and it caught almost immediately; Thaddeus must have applied some sort of oil for it to catch so quickly. The crowd cheered again, and Alexis handed the torch back to Hesper.

My father handed Alexis a basket filled with dried dates, nuts and figs. "We have accepted Alexis, and Alexis has accepted us in return," he told the gathered crowd.

"And we have given Alexis to Skylar with our blessings and have accepted the offerings given to secure her," Agrias added, stepping forward and offering his arm to my father. They shook, their matching grins wider than I had ever seen as the crowd clapped and cheered the announcements. "It is time for the unveiling of the new bride and for the couple to retire to the bridal chamber where they shall consummate their union," Agrias continued. Another great cheer went up.

"I wish that did not have to be announced," Alexis whispered, and I wondered just how red her face was beneath the veil.

I chuckled and turned to her. "Do not fear, they shall not be privy to *exactly* what I intend to do with you when we go behind that closed door."

"Skylar," she scolded, but I heard the grin in her voice.

"I am so glad your father accepted the price I wished to pay for you," I added with a laugh.

"As if he would have denied you."

I reached out, taking the bright pins from her crown and the veil beneath, handing them both to Hesper when she stepped forward for the purpose. I lifted the sheer fabric up, revealing the sparkling green eyes and pink cheeks of my bride. "Hello," I murmured, smiling again.

Alexis returned my grin as I passed the veil to Hesper. I placed a gentle kiss on Alexis' lips, my hands finding their way to the girdle beneath her breasts. "Removing your clothing has always been one of my favorite past times," I whispered.

"Skylar," she groaned.

Three strands of rope had been twisted together, forming ribbons either side of the central Heracles knot, which was a symbol of protection for new brides. I took my time undoing it and went over the words I wanted to say once the task was done. The exact wording was my own and I hoped Agrias would approve.

I unwrapped the rope from around Alexis and held it aloft for the crowd. "With the removal of this girdle, I formally claim this woman as my own and call her my wife. In return she calls me wife and we shall be known as the same to all. This marks the final ties which bound her to her previous husband and his kin. It removes all ties she had with him and marks her once again as a maiden to be claimed by one approved by her father. Tonight Alexis, Princess of Trachis, in the region of Thermopylae becomes the bride of Skylar, Warrior of Thermopylae." The crowd erupted into cheering yet again, slaves appearing to refill their kantharos with wine which had either been drunk or spilled in all the excitement.

Agrias approached, taking me in his arms and clapping me on the back. "Well said."

"Thank you."

My father neared and Agrias released me and moved to embrace Alexis. "You now call Alexis your wife. Congratulations," Father said.

"Thank you, Baba."

"She appears to be handling the day well."

"She does. I thank the gods she has regained her health. Seeing her unwell all the time frightened me. I do not wish to lose her because she bears the burden of carrying our child."

"There is nothing to be afraid of. All women experience sickness when their child first grows inside them. Your mother felt the same with you."

"Alexis says it is so as well," I nodded. "She says she never experienced it with Basileios."

"You have your answer then. She shall carry your child to the day of its birth without incident."

"I hope it is so."

"It shall be. Now, allow us to turn our thoughts from such worries, you must go and celebrate your union. I shall find Agrias and discuss the timing of the announcement of your child to the small council and the people of Trachis."

"It shall be a girl," I told him.

"Indeed? How do you know that?"

"Hera told us of a test which we performed two days ago."

"You believe it to be accurate?"

"Hera said it would be, and after what she has done for us, I have no reason to doubt her."

"A daughter. A granddaughter," he murmured, his face splitting into a grin. "Do Agrias and Melina know?"

"I assume so. Alexis was going to tell Melina while they went about their preparations for the wedding. You may speak of it to Nasrin, though we would prefer to tell everyone else when the official announcement is made."

"Of course."

"Apologies for the interruption, Leandros," Alexis said, arriving beside us.

"No apology necessary, my dear," Father replied. "If I may be so bold, I would venture that you are eager to find yourself alone with my daughter."

"I am," Alexis laughed. "It has been a long day."

"That it has," he said, wrapping an arm around both our shoulders and placing a kiss on our heads. "I would wish you well with your slumbering, though I do not believe you shall be doing much of it, so I shall simply say; enjoy the rest of your night."

"Oh, we shall," I assured him. "Come, my bride, the bridal chamber awaits us." Alexis shook her head, her cheeks darkening at Father's words as she slipped her hand into mine. I signaled Moeris to join us. It was his honor to stand guard at our door for the rest of the night while Alexis' friends remained in the courtyard entertaining the guests with songs and jokes. "We are ready to leave," I told him.

"Very good," he said with a nod.

We made our way to the room which had, until so recently, belonged to Agrias and Melina. "I shall ensure you are not disturbed until the morning light of Helios greets us," he said.

"Thank you, Moeris," I replied, taking his arm in mine and squeezing firmly.

"Princess," he nodded, bowing to her.

"Goodnight, Moeris," Alexis replied. I shut the door behind us, grinning when Alexis headed directly for the bed, climbing up onto it and stretching out on her back.

"Gods, I am so exhausted."

"Allow me to undress you then," I offered.

"Please."

"You looked beautiful today," I told her, slipping off her sandals.

"Thank you. You looked quite handsome in your armor as well."

I grinned, removing the laurel wreath from my head and setting it aside before removing her chiton. "Moeris and Thaddeus prepared me well then," I murmured, placing feather-light kisses across her stomach.

"Indeed," she agreed.

I slid from the bed, quickly discarding my bronze cuirass and greaves, my tunic and sandals joining them a moment later. Alexis rolled onto her side to face me when I returned.

I pulled her to me and kissed her. "You are feeling well?" I asked.

"Tired, but not ill as I have been. I do not wish to disappoint you, but I am not certain I can fulfil the duties expected of a bride this night."

I smiled, my finger tracing the line of her jaw. "I am not disappointed. In truth, I have not slept well these past nights without you beside me, so I would be happy to find myself in Hypnos' realm rather than sating other desires if that is what you prefer."

"Tonight, yes. But when we find ourselves alone again later in the day … I shall reward you for waiting."

"I shall hold you to that."

"I hope so."

Alexis turned so her back was against my breasts and I pulled the light blanket over us, settling my arm around her waist. "I told you they would not know exactly what we were doing in here," I chuckled.

"It is not what they imagine, I am certain."

I placed a kiss in her hair. "Indeed. Goodnight, wife."

"Goodnight, wife," she replied, wrapping my arm tighter around her. I smiled, allowing the sounds of the singers outside to send me to sleep.

6

Alexis and I were woken on the third day of our wedding ceremony by singing from the Pannuxis – the women who had begun their songs the evening before after we had retired to our room and had not stopped since. Neither of us had moved from the positions we laid down in the night before; my arm still wrapped protectively around Alexis, her body curved into the front of mine.

"Good morning," I murmured, sliding my hand across the base of her stomach.

"Morning," she replied, stretching languorously as she turned in my embrace. "I have not slept so well in many nights."

"Neither have I," I agreed, placing a kiss on her lips. "I wish we did not have to leave this room for the rest of the day. I could quite possible return to slumber ... or other more carnal pursuits."

"And yet there are still a number of festivities we must be involved in. I believe it was *you* who wished for such traditions to be carried out."

"Mmm," I grumbled. "Perhaps then I should be allowed to call a halt to the celebrations so I may enjoy my wife in only the company of this room."

"Perhaps a present would persuade you to wait just a little longer for such alone time?" Alexis offered, sliding from my arms and off the bed, making her way to the table on the far side of the room.

"It may, though I thought my idea to be a better one," I grinned.

"I do not disagree," Alexis replied, carrying a covered package back to me. "Open it," she added, holding it out. I did as she asked, peeling back the outer wrapping of the parcel and revealing a light summer cloak. "Your father helped me selecting the material and gave direction how to weave it. He called it a chlanis."

"It is beautiful. I would not have thought he knew how to craft such an item. Perhaps my mother taught him many winters ago."

"He did not say, though it did not appear to cause him sadness to speak of it, so perhaps it was another who showed him." I nodded again and sat up, placing the chlanis around my shoulders. "A befitting item for the wife of the Princess of Trachis," Alexis noted, smoothing it across my back.

"It shall serve me well in the warmer moons here," I said, leaning forward and kissing her. "Thank you."

"It was a tradition I was happy to see continue."

"I apologize, I do not have anything in return for you."

"The dowry you offered to call me wife is more than enough, I assure you."

I slid my arms around her waist and pulled her against me as I grinned. "I am glad to hear you say that – I was not certain an entire Spartan army would suffice to secure you."

"I believe you know that if my father had not allowed it, I would have run away with you anyway. Now that I have found you, there is no way I am ever letting you get away."

"My thoughts mirror yours, Princess," I murmured, covering her mouth again.

Alexis and I had barely begun to enjoy one another when there was a knock at our door. "It is time for the bride to receive more gifts," Moeris announced. I growled, reluctantly disentangling my limbs from Alexis' and pulling on my clothing, allowing Moeris to escort us.

The Throne Room was a flurry of activity already. Agrias and Melina were surrounded by both sets of attendants, members of the small council and townspeople; their arms full of gifts and skyphoi of wine. With Alexis' fingers twined in mine, I led her to her throne, ensuring she had food and wine within easy reach as the first of the guests presented their gifts. I stood behind her, eyes roving the room, finding both friends and strangers enjoying the celebrations.

While Alexis was receiving gifts of jewelery, fragrant oils and perfumes, the musicians kept the guests entertained with more songs and dancing. It was difficult to hear everything the well-wishers said to Alexis as they handed over their presents, though it all went along the same lines.

When Stavros stepped forward, the musicians were between songs and I heard his speech in its entirety. "Princess Alexis, on the joyous occasion of your wedding, I offer you this token." He held out an amphora of perfume to Alexis. "Perfumes have always been used to enhance beauty, though I gift it to you now as a symbol only, for beauty such as yours does not require enhancement."

"Thank you, Stavros," Alexis replied.

The older man bowed and stepped aside. When he passed me, I placed a hand on his arm. "Well said, my friend. It is obvious this is not your first wedding celebration."

He grinned and shook his head. "It is not, and anyone who has been to one before and does not wish to offend either the bride or groom knows to pre-empt his gift with such words."

"Indeed," I smiled, acknowledging his bow before allowing him to move away.

My father and Nasrin were the last to approach, bowing to us as everyone else had. "I note we are not alone today in gifting you with the perfume you favor most," Father grinned, handing the amphora to Alexis.

"No, I believe I shall have enough to last me many winters," she replied with a smile.

"Perhaps this shall make up for our commonness," Nasrin added, handing over a much smaller package. I leant forward, watching over Alexis' shoulder as she undid it. "I have heard that husbands provide the only jewelry their wives are to wear, though I hope you shall permit us to provide something quite unique."

Setting aside the covering, Alexis held up a leather bracelet with the Heracles knot prominently displayed for me to see. "It is beautiful, thank you," Alexis said, slipping it onto her wrist and adjusting it. "Where did you find such a gift?"

"Leandros and I made it," Nasrin replied with a shy grin.

"You did?" I asked, stepping around the throne to get a better look. Alexis held up her arm and I ran my fingers across the leather, already warm from contact with her skin.

"Thank you," Alexis said again. Father and Nasrin inclined their heads and moved away. "What a thoughtful, and surprising, gift," Alexis murmured.

"It is," I agreed as Agrias called for quiet.

"Now that the presents have been given, it is time for our townspeople to leave us. Moeris, if you would see them beyond the entrance?" The named man nodded and led them from the room. "The doors shall be closed to all others for a time. The women shall prepare another feast for us and I ask you now to join me in the andron."

Alexis stood, pushing up onto her toes to kiss me. "I hope you enjoy what we are to prepare," she grinned.

"As long as you have made the quinces Hesper promised me, I shall enjoy it. But do not make it too grand for I am eager to be alone with you again sooner rather than later."

"You have had enough of exchanging stories with your friends?"

"Enough of the inane conversations with the small council members you mean," I replied with a roll of my eyes.

She laughed and kissed me again. "I shall do my best."

When we had eaten our fill and the wine was almost at its end, Alexis and the women returned, my princess joining me as Gnosidicus called for quiet.

"Esteemed members of the small council, friends and kin, on behalf of King Agrias and Queen Melina, we thank you for being here these past days to help witness and celebrate the joining of this young couple; Princess Alexis, and the newest member of the royal family of Trachis, Princess Skylar." The gathered crowd raised their cups with Gnosidicus in silent acknowledgement. "Traditionally, this last feast is held only with the groom and the male members of his family, who bear witness to the feats of his new bride's skill in preparing a delicious meal. And, while I am certain you shall all agree our princess has done a wonderful job in feeding us, there is another reason you have been invited along this day."

Gnosidicus paused, casting his eye over the council members, who appeared curious to learn what their secondary purpose in attendance was. "It is my great pleasure to announce, that our princess is with child," he held up a hand to halt the murmur sweeping the room. "I am certain you all recall the act whereby Skylar spirited away her intended bride for a number of days, in the hopes of creating a new life by their union?" Voices around the room acknowledged what the healer referred to.

I too recalled the time Alexis and I spent together camping by the hot springs. Alexis had thankfully begun feeling better by the time we arranged it and we had spent most of the time making love and enjoying the quiet time alone with only one another and the water for company. I found her hand and gave it a squeeze, her answering grin suggesting she too remembered our coupling at the spring.

"But how is it so?" one of the council members asked.

"Who is to say it is truly their own child? Was not a man with them?" another asked.

"He speaks true. They are two women, vessels only for children to grow inside once a man – a husband – places it there," Antigonos called out.

My jaw tightened. It was not the first time I had heard Antigonos' thoughts that women were nothing more than a place to store a child until it was born. Though I knew it was a common concept in the Molossian tribe he was part of, I could not understand how he could believe a woman was nothing more than a possession to use, fill and discard as he pleased. He did have a number of wives – and children – though which proved it. I would need to keep a close eye on him, for his words mirrored Melanthios' too closely.

My free hand clenched and Alexis covered it with her own, waiting until I met her gaze. She shook her head. "Not here," she cautioned. "Do not allow him to spoil our celebrations."

Before I could make reply, Gnosidicus continued, apparently unfazed or angered by the questions and statements his words caused.

"Please, please, I cannot give answers as to how it came to be. But I assure you, there was no man with them when they partook of the tradition. And if the gods see fit to bless this couple with a child, then who are we to question it? Who amongst us wishes to incur the wrath of the gods for the plan they have for our princess and her chosen lover?"

"In what moon shall we be fortunate enough to welcome this new life into our midst?" Moeris called, offering a wide grin to me when I looked in his direction.

"She shall arrive in Mounichion – the first moon of spring," I replied, giving him a thankful nod in reply.

"A daughter? How can you know this already?" Stavros asked.

"Hera, Goddess of Marriage and Childbirth has blessed us, and it was she who told us it would be so," Alexis replied. Another rippling murmur swept the room, though it was not confusion, but awe, I saw on our guests' faces.

"A fine moon indeed," my father shouted, effectively silencing the crowd. "My granddaughter shall make her entrance as Persephone returns from Hades and the Underworld to breathe life back into all living things in our realm. The bitter cold of winter shall be passed, and the flowers shall open to rejoice and welcome her with us," he grinned.

Agrias stood, placing one hand on my father's shoulder and the other lifting his cup high in the air. "Well said, my friend. As the springtime flowers return, so too shall we welcome new life, not only to our family, but to our beloved and prosperous town of Trachis. A child could want for no two better parents," he dipped his head briefly to Alexis and me, before addressing the rest of the men in the room. "And I know you shall all join me in welcoming her when she arrives." My father and I exchanged grins as Agrias raised his kantharos higher and drank down a large gulp of the sweet wine

"It appears Gnosidicus' words have calmed those who spoke earlier," Alexis murmured, leaning closer. "Perhaps it was the threat of incurring the gods' wrath which sees them accepting finally of our union, and my choice in you."

I searched the face of every council member and guest in the room. "Allow us to hope such peaceable relations continue for many winters to come," I agreed, not convinced Antigonos would be so easily satisfied.

Alexis wrapped an arm around my waist and pushed up onto her toes to whisper in my ear. "Now that the announcement has been made, do you think we could leave the men to continue celebrating the news whilst we do some celebrating of our own … alone?"

I grinned, my hand snaking its way down her back until it rested on her bottom and my lips finding her neck. "Mmm, you read my mind, Princess." I slid my tongue up towards her ear, my grin turning to a smirk as a shiver gripped Alexis' body.

"Skylar," she breathed, her hand tightening on my hip.

I chuckled and threaded my fingers through hers. "Impatient, sweetheart?" I rumbled, catching the soft flesh of her earlobe.

"You have no idea," she growled, my stomach instantly heating.

"Wait here," I told her, retrieving my arm as a number of carnal thoughts flew through my mind. I approached my father and Agrias, holding my arm out to each before addressing the king. "If it pleases you, Alexis is tired. I would request we take our leave now."

"Of course," Agrias replied. "Shall I announce your departure?"

"No, I believe it would only prolong it."

"Of course," he said again. "We shall see you again soon, though I would not be surprised if we were still here celebrating your betrothal and our new granddaughter with old friends and new." I smiled and returned to Alexis, the two of us slipping from the andron without another word to anyone.

Once inside our new apartment, I closed the door, locking it securely before hastily stripping the chiton from Alexis' body as she did my clothing. I took her to bed and we made love for the first time as a wedded couple.

My wife. My love. My everything.

7

"Good. Again," I directed Nikomachos as his wooden sword met mine solidly. I was with the eldest of Thaddeus and Hesper's children in the sparring area of the barracks. The mid-morning sun was warm but not overly so – the summer season drawing towards autumn. Small puffs of dust billowed around our sandaled feet as the boy defended and attacked under my direction.

Though he was not quite seven winters old, Nikomachos showed fair promise of swordsmanship. I intended to begin him with a shield after his birthing day, which was in another half-winter. Agrias had shown me the building which held a seldom used forge and anvil and I wanted the shield I presented to Nikomachos to be one I had made; I already had most of the items I needed to make it.

Alexis and I had been betrothed for a moon and the murmurings from those in the small council who originally opposed our union had been all but quelled. I received nothing but support and kind words from those men when I had need to speak with them. Antigonos was the lone man who did not greet me warmly, though neither did he speak words of disapproval. I kept close watch on him, asking Stavros to do the same when I was not around.

Cleomenes had returned to Athens after the feasting was done, intending to make his way back to Sparta soon afterwards. Demosthenes though had headed directly to Sparta, eager to get back to his duties with the soldiers and prepare them for the arrival of their king.

Nikomachos approached again as Alexis appeared in the walkway between the barracks and the palace. She wore a plain, white chiton which reached her ankles, her bare feet visible beneath the material. Her hair was loose and appeared freshly combed as it hung past her shoulders. Nikomachos' wooden sword connected with my thigh, but I barely felt it, the grin Alexis gave me heating the lower half of my body and reducing my awareness to anything but her.

Nikomachos rapped his sword on my bronze cuirass as Alexis made her way across the dusty ground. "You always tell me not to get distracted during a fight," he laughed.

"When the princess is around, I am often distracted," I replied, my eyes remaining on my wife as I rubbed absently at my thigh.

"You would not be the first to disarm Skylar when I neared," Alexis noted as she reached us, ruffling the boy's hair. "My father was also fortunate enough to do the same once." She lay a hand on my arm and pushed up onto her toes, kissing me. Her tongue teased my lips and I slid my hand around her waist, resting it against her hip as I pulled her to me. "You did not wake me," she murmured when we parted.

"No, I believed you needed the rest. I cannot say when you shall see your bed again tonight; there are many who wish to celebrate the day of my father's birth until Helios' light greets them in the morning, and we are expected to remain as well."

"That is true," she replied, appearing about to say more before she caught herself, turning instead to Nikomachos. "Would you mind terribly if I borrowed Skylar? I must send her on an errand."

"No," he said, motioning me to drop to his level. I took my arm from Alexis and knelt on one knee so our eyes were at the same height. "Errands are boring," he confided. "Can we finish our training later?"

"Absolutely. I shall find you when I am done," I grinned, giving him a gentle push as I got to my feet again. Nikomachos nodded eagerly and held his hand out for my training weapon. I passed it over and we followed him back through the walkway. Once he reached the courtyard, he gave us a wave and took off across the garden area towards the apartment he shared with his parents and brothers.

"He adores you," Alexis noted, watching him go.

"And I him," I agreed, taking her hand. "He shall make a fine husband for our daughter one day if she wishes to choose him."

"Is that so?" Alexis smiled, eyebrows high on her forehead. "You have given it much consideration already?"

I laughed. "Not so much, but I would not deny him if he asked it of us. Now, what is this terribly *boring* errand I must run for you, Princess?"

"That can wait. I have something else in mind first," she replied with a cheeky grin, leading me towards our apartment.

"Oh," I murmured, my heart skipping at her tone and my body warming even further.

"Yes. I sorely missed waking to find you beside me this day."

"I believe I know a way to make it up to you," I grinned, leaning forward to place another kiss on her lips.

"I hope so," she said, opening our door and pulling me inside.

I closed it behind us, turning to find my lover at the edge of our bed, her hand on the pin at her shoulder. I crossed the room, covering her fingers briefly before removing the clasp and allowing her chiton to fall to the ground. I stepped back slightly, my eyes running the length of her, noting the changes the child growing inside her caused; her slightly rounded stomach and full breasts the most prominent.

She reached out, hooking her fingers in the top of my cuirass and tugging gently. "The day is warm, this must be keeping you even more so," she teased.

"It is rarely my armor which keeps me warm when I am with you," I told her, not missing the sudden color in her cheeks as my eyes roamed over her naked flesh. "Shall I remove it? I do not believe I need such protection here with you."

"If you do not, I shall be disappointed," she replied, her voice barely above a whisper.

I swiftly undid the hinge at my ribs and ties at my shoulders, sliding the bronze over my head and laying it beside the bed. "Better?"

"A little, but there is more you need to discard."

I reached for the fibula at my shoulder, allowing it to drop to the floor on top of my tunic when it came free. "And now?" I asked, a smile dancing on my lips.

Her finger traced across my collarbones before sliding down between my breasts. "Much better."

With one arm around Alexis' waist and the other beneath her knees, I picked her up, carefully laying her on our bed, sliding in behind her and placing my hand on her belly. Drawing small circles on her soft skin, I kissed her neck and shoulders. "Good morning," I whispered into her ear.

She pushed back against me and I drew in a sharp breath. "Good morning," she replied. I heard the smile in her voice.

I smoothed my hand across her stomach again before sending it lower, gaining a contended sound and Alexis' hand at my hip to keep me close as she warmed to my ministrations. I pressed my lips to her shoulder and found the warmth between her legs, caressing her as my heartbeat increased and my body heated. Her hand tightened against my skin and I matched her movements, driving us both towards the peak of desire.

"Gods," she breathed, her hand covering mine and pressing me inside her. I gasped, close to my own release, and filled her again. Her bottom dragged across my flesh and I closed my eyes, praying I could finish her before she did me. "Harder," she directed. I obliged, feeling the shudders begin deep inside her, her hand sliding down to my thigh before slipping between.

"No," I gasped, wanting to give her all I had.

"Yes," she insisted, her fingers entering me.

"Gods," I growled, my teeth finding her shoulder.

"Skylar," she panted, her legs tightening around my hand as she found release. I did not reply, joining her in our pleasure.

*

"Thaddeus is going to the agora this morning. Would you help him bring the amphorae of wine to the palace for tonight?" Alexis asked from within my embrace, our need for one another sated for the moment. "Grandfather has set them aside at his stall for us already."

"Of course. I shall find Thaddeus now and we can leave together … after I assist you to re-dress."

Alexis tilted her head back and regarded me, the hint of a grin gracing her lips. "I have not often known you to help me dress. Your specialty appears to be in the disrobing."

"Hmm, you may speak the truth. Perhaps it shall require a lesson?" I asked with a smile of my own. "Perhaps I should attempt both so as to understand the complexities of the task."

Alexis laughed and pushed gently at my chest. "I fear you may never get to the agora if such a lesson begins." I pushed out my bottom lip and Alexis laughed again. She rolled closer and kissed me, her hand lingering at my breast as she spoke again. "Go. Meet Thaddeus. There shall be time for more of this after the festivities of the evening."

"Promise?" I asked, stealing another kiss.

"I would not wish for anything else."

I smiled again and rolled off the bed, dressing quickly and heading for the door before my body's incessant wishes overtook my head's sense of duty and assistance. "I shall keep you to that," I assured her, my eyes making another journey over her naked form before letting myself out of the room.

"You had better," she called as I closed the door.

8

Thaddeus and I made our way through the busy streets of the agora, waving and stopping to chat with the stall holders we knew. It appeared most of the town had gathered at the market today, no doubt ensuring they had all they needed for the celebration tonight as well as for the coming days when their heads were recovering from the wine and rich food.

I had always loved to walk through the busy trade section in Athens, with its hustle and bustle – a combination of slaves and mules crowding the pathways between the stalls. The owners of the merchandise shouted their wares and prices to the passers-by, while others bargained for the price they wanted, rather than the one the customer wanted to pay.

Though the negotiations were often drawn out, they were always settled amicably or lost without anger, and the presence of the soldiers here in Trachis ensured these ones remained so. Since Ophelos had been attacked the night of the banquet in town, a greater number of soldiers patrolled the market, though no further attacks had occurred. I expected none, having dealt with the offenders personally, and learning there were no others eager to take their places as would-be mercenaries.

I saw to it that the boys responsible for Ophelos' injury were not dealt harsh punishments or beatings, but rather with a guiding hand. Hektor, the youngster who had driven his crudely made sword into Ophelos' stomach, had returned to Sparta with Demosthenes. His parents had named him for the great Trojan champion and after a number of long discussions with the general, and the blessing of his family, Hektor requested to take leave from Trachis and atone for his mistake under the rigorous training schedule of the Spartan army.

He believed being pitted against boys who had trained seven winters longer than he, would test his skills and cunning. He admired the Spartan ways and with Cleomenes and Demosthenes' visit had learned far more than he had ever hoped to about them. I spoke in favor of his decision to both his family and Demosthenes and farewelled the boy with the knowledge that he would always be welcome to take his place among the soldiers in Trachis should he wish to return. He promised to aspire to the honor and achievements of his namesake and when he had done so, he would return.

The other two who had accompanied Hektor that night – Sander and Kleitos – I helped integrate into the barracks, with Moeris overseeing their training and ensuring they were welcomed and taught by the other men as well. They showed initiative and intelligence in strategy and I had them aid me in organizing and competing in challenges between the soldiers for different styles of battle. In my new role as joint leader of the army with Moeris, I taught the men the Greek phalanx formation, how to fight and be hidden in dense trees, how to lay traps for their enemies if they wanted to capture them rather than kill them outright and how to fight from atop horseback.

With my position with the soldiers, and the other responsibilities Agrias gave me, diversions such as Alexis and I had found this morning were rare, and I had welcomed the opportunity, vowing to myself that I would find more time to shower her with my love.

Thaddeus and I reached Ophelos' stall and Alexis' grandfather's eyes lit up immediately. He hobbled around to our side of his table and took both of us in a crushing embrace. "My friends, it is good to see you again."

"And you, Ophelos," I managed when he released us from his grip. His stomach may have still been healing, but his arms were as strong as ever.

"You are here for the wine for your father's banquet tonight?" he asked.

"We are," I nodded.

"I hope you have enough," Thaddeus added. "With the celebration open to all who wish to attend, I am doubtful there shall be."

"Do not fear, young Thaddeus, I have given word to all who have stopped by today that they must take some of their own wine should they hold the same concern you do. Most have thought it a truly wonderful idea."

"Inspired," I agreed with a wide grin.

Three more customers waited behind us and Ophelos nodded to them as he waved Thaddeus and me behind his stall. "All of these are for the palace. Whatever you cannot carry, I shall have my boy deliver to you."

"Do not bother him, my main task this day is to assist with preparations, I shall return as many times as necessary," I told him.

"They are my orders as well," Thaddeus added.

"As you wish," Ophelos nodded, turning to his new patrons with a grin and a firm slap on the shoulder for the oldest man in the group.

"Do not forget about Nikomachos – your interrupted training session this morning was all he could speak of when he returned to the apartment," Thaddeus grinned.

"I would not dream of it," I replied, matching his smile.

"You took your time finding me, your princess had another errand for you first?" he smirked.

"A *very* important one," I assured him.

"A husband's duty is never done, is it?" he chuckled as he shook his head. "Challenge you to the speed and number of amphorae you can carry back to the palace?"

"Shall I gift you a head start?" I laughed.

"Only if you want to lose."

"Come then, Favored Guard of the King. Prove the training you have done with our soldiers serves you well."

We eagerly attacked the pile of amphorae Ophelos had set aside, loading them into our arms as carefully, but as quickly, as we could. I stopped at six, knowing Thaddeus would attempt to carry more than me, which would be his undoing; the slight rise on the way up to the palace would only ensure the full amphorae felt heavier, and we could not afford to break any. I took off, dodging stalls and the angry tirades and raised fists of customers I almost knocked down in my attempt to reach the palace first.

Thaddeus was reaching for another amphora when he realized his error, shouting out his surprise at my sudden departure. It was not long before he was close behind me, puffing and panting as we reached the incline. I laughed and put on a burst of speed, racing through the open doors of the portico and entrance and skidding into the kitchen where Hesper and a large number of other women were working tirelessly to prepare the food for the evening.

"Skylar, careful!" Hesper admonished as I almost upended a tray of bread from her hands.

"Apologies, Hesper," I panted. "I bring wine."

"So I see."

Thaddeus burst through the doorway as well, almost crashing into me as he slid to a stop. Hesper looked between the two of us before shaking her head and rolling her eyes. "I should have known as much. The two of you rarely do anything together without it becoming a competition."

Thaddeus and I grinned at each other, knowing it to be the truth. Since our return from the Heraion, we had become close friends; indeed it was almost as though Thaddeus was my older brother as we competed and teased each other the way I imagined siblings would.

"Where should we leave these, my darling wife?" he asked, kissing her cheek.

She swatted him away. "Put them in the next room, we have nowhere to keep them in here."

"As you wish, my love," Thaddeus grinned, placing a hand on her rounded belly where their own child grew and kissing her again.

"Out!" she laughed, shooing both of us back through the door and into the rarely-used banquet hall beside. We stacked the amphorae into one corner, jostling each other through the door as we returned to the agora for our second load.

We made two more trips, Thaddeus beating me back on the second and I clearly leading in the third, when a woman in a hooded cloak with a hunched back stepped into my path. I managed to avoid knocking her down, but our collision sent her off balance. I was carrying only the two final amphorae in my left hand and reached out, grabbing at her himation with my right to halt her fall.

"Apologies," I said, still holding her cloak as I set the amphorae on the ground. "Are you hurt?"

"No, no, I am fine," she replied in a strangely rasping voice. "You travel hurriedly."

"Er … yes. Though for no good reason. I should have been more careful," I replied, itching at a spot high on my shoulder blade.

"Not to worry, no harm done, Skylar. It is in your blood to act rashly at times without thought for the consequences. Your mother was the same," she replied.

"W-What?" I stammered as Thaddeus arrived beside me.

"Is all well?" he asked.

"Yes, dear boy, all is well," the woman replied.

"I almost knocked her over," I managed in a distant voice. "Take my two amphorae. I shall see her safely to her destination."

"You realize I shall claim victory in our challenge," he murmured.

"Fine," I replied, turning back to the woman and wishing she would take down her hood so I could see her face.

"I shall tell Nikomachos you shall come for him after the noon-day meal," he added, picking up the wine I had set down.

"Fine," I said again.

When he was out of earshot, I spoke again. "What do you know of my mother?"

"Much. I knew her a long time ago."

"She is dead now," I murmured, uncertain why I felt the need to speak the words.

"Yes. But if you want to know the truth about who she was, meet me this night. Late, at the Temple of Anthela. You are familiar with it?" I nodded in reply. "Good. You shall first see your princess back to your apartment. She shall be weary after the day's events and your presence shall not be missed at your … father's celebration. The amount of wine you took to the palace shall see to that." There was something about the way she referred to my father which spoke of disdain or displeasure, but before I could reply she continued. "You do *want* to know about your mother, do you not?" I took in a deep breath, my eyes flicking back up to the palace momentarily. When I looked back, she was gone.

I frowned, turning in circles and scanning the crowd for her departing form. She was nowhere to be seen. She could not simply vanish, could she … not unless she was a goddess, and that was the only explanation I could think of for her sudden disappearance.

I blew out the breath I had been holding and started back up the path, lost in thought and questions I knew could only be answered by going to the temple and meeting the woman.

9

The rest of the day had passed with agonizing slowness and, though I attempted not to show it, I was anxious for the celebrations to be over and Alexis to speak words of wanting to retire to our apartment.

Nasrin sat in my father's lap, their hands entwined and sharing a kantharos of wine. The look of joy on both their faces spoke words they had not shared with me; not that it was required. I could tell Nasrin had taken deep root in my father's heart, and she in his. I wondered momentarily if we would soon be sharing their wedding feast.

I wanted to tell Father of the woman at the agora but decided it would not be tonight. Not when he looked so happy, and not until I heard what the stranger had to say about my mother. I did not know what his reaction would be if I told him she had spoken of her.

Antigonos passed by my chair again, glowering as he downed yet another kantharos of wine, and signaling for his cup to be refilled. It was the sixth passing I had counted, though so far, he had made no attempt to engage me in conversation – or argument – which was what I assumed we would have when we finally spoke. As so many men had in winters past when we found ourselves at a celebratory feast, Antigonos needed the courage of wine to approach me.

He passed again and I turned, pinning him in place with a glare. "What do you want?" I growled.

"How is it that a child grows within the princess?" he asked, keeping his voice low as he approached, taking another gulp from his cup as he added,

"It is not possible without a man. It is not *right* without a man."

I stood in a quick, smooth motion. "Careful, Antigonos," I warned.

"Or what?" You carry no weapons this night. You play at being a Princess in fine linen, but you are no Princess," he spat.

"I need no weapons to send you to Gnosidicus, or to Hades," I replied, towering over the smaller man, fists clenching at my sides.

Alexis had insisted I wear the long chiton I had worn to the first banquet I attended in Trachis as reminder of what I had spoken to her after Lasus' poem ended. In return she promised to show me what she did not know how to that night when Father's celebration was done. I had reluctantly agreed. I had known that Antigonos was to be at the palace tonight and was all too aware that my armor aided in keeping him far from me whenever I saw him in town. Without it, he believed I was no threat. But that was his first mistake.

"Gnosidicus is an old fool, his mind wanders in his old age."

"Do not show such disrespect," I rumbled. "The healer has attended your home on too many occasions; needing to assist any number of your wives after you struck them or harmed them in some other manner." Antigonos raised his brows but did not step back. "Yes, I know much about what goes on in your home. None of it *right* or respectful. You dishonor the men who have given you their daughters or sisters to call wife. You dishonor the women themselves," I said, my finger jabbing his chest with each word.

"The wife who has told you this shall pay for her words," he promised.

"You shall not raise a hand to them, nor your children, for it was none of them who told me what goes on."

"Gnosidicus then shall pay for speaking out of turn."

"Touch one hair on his head and you shall greet your first wife in the Underworld before you take another breath. Perhaps she has had time to find suitable punishment for you. Perhaps she has spoken of those punishments to the gods on the other side and told them of your treatment of her, of how it was you who sent her to their realm."

"My wife died attempting to birth our second child. They were both lost to me tha—"

"I have heard the story. I also know the truth."

Antigonos' blustering faltered as Moeris arrived behind him. "Skylar is all well here?" he asked.

"It shall be when Antigonos takes his leave," I replied, my eyes never leaving the named man.

"Yes, it is time I returned home. My wives wait for me to go to them," he smirked. "I have not yet decided which shall find my favor this evening." He drained his kantharos and threw it aside, the sound lost beneath the musicians and laughter in the banqueting hall. With a flourish of his himation, he turned, pushing past Moeris on his way out.

"Do not allow him t–"

I brushed past the commander, catching Antigonos as he reached the door. With a bunch of his cloak in my hand, I dragged him into the walkway and slammed him against the stone wall, his head cracking against it with a satisfying thud. Before he had the chance to, I reached beneath his himation and grabbed the dagger from the belt of his tunic. Pulling it free, I held it to his throat. "Your position on the small council is no longer required. Do not attend any meeting or be here at the palace again."

"You have no such authority," he panted.

"But I have the king's ear and he shall see it done."

"You are the one who is not wanted here."

"Oh? By who, apart from you? The townspeople have welcomed my father and me with open arms, as is attested to by the size of the gathering here. It is men such as yourself who are not wanted in Trachis. Perhaps I shall achieve that as well one day," I said, pressing the blade hard enough to draw blood.

"I have friends," he gasped, a drop running down his throat to stain the front of his tunic. "The princess shall not remain here forever, just as was always intended."

I slashed the knife across his throat deep enough to draw blood, but not enough to be fatal. He dropped to his knees, grabbing at his neck to stem the bleeding. I followed him, our foreheads almost touching. "You had best hope your friends are formidable warriors for if they come for *my* princess, I shall not waste words before I send them to the Underworld. And when I am done with them, I shall find you, you can be certain of that."

"Skylar, what are you doing?" Moeris asked, aiding Antigonos to his feet as I straightened.

"Sending a message," I replied, removing Moeris' hand from the wound. "He can find his own healer tonight. Gnosidicus is never to treat him." I placed my body between the two men, shoving Antigonos towards the entrance and following to ensure he did indeed leave.

"What was that about?" I ignored Moeris' question, sliding the dagger into my own chiton and returning to the banqueting hall.

"We need to talk," I told Agrias when I found him just inside the door. He nodded and took a step to follow me outside, halting when Alexis arrived beside us. I took one look at her face, recognizing the exhaustion written across it, and expelled a deep breath to calm the blood pumping through my veins. "Later," I nodded to the king. He returned it and found another cup of wine as he moved away. "You appear tired, sweetheart," I murmured, sliding my arms around Alexis' waist and pulling her close.

"I am. Would you be upset if I asked to leave?"

"Of course not," I replied, placing a kiss on her head. "Come."

"I know what I promised earlier, but I do not believe I coul–"

"Do not worry. I understand." I twined my fingers through hers and led the way to the central chamber. "There is always the morning – and I know how much you enjoy it then."

"I do," she agreed, leaning her head against my arm as I pushed open our door.

I stripped her chiton from her body and settled her beneath the covers, combing my fingers through her hair and over her forehead. Her eyes fluttered shut, her breathing deepening moments later and I knew she was asleep. I stood, quickly removing my own chiton and re-dressing in a tunic and belting my sword at my side. I would deal with Antigonos, and speak to Agrias, later. For now, I was due at the temple.

Closing the door quietly behind me, I left the apartment, running into Moeris just outside. "You are not going after Antigonos at this late candlemark, are you?" he asked, his voice only slightly blurred from his wine.

"No. I shall deal with him soon enough. I … er … my father. I was just seeing the princess to our room. I intend to return to the celebrations."

"With your sword?" he asked, eyebrows raised in doubt.

"I feel more comfortable with it in reach," I replied.

"Should you not remain here with your princess? A locked door would be advisable. It would not do to allow her to be taken advantage of, even though she finds herself with child, and betrothed to you."

"Would you take such advantage of her, if I asked you to remain outside our door until I returned?" I asked, narrowing my eyes and stepping forward.

"I would never disrespect my princess with such actions, nor you or my king and queen. You know this," Moeris frowned. "I stood beside you at your wedding celebration and have always believed the two of you are meant to be together. You offend me with your accusations, I was referring to Antigonos and what *he* may be capable of."

I backed up a step, shaking my head. "Apologies, Moeris. Perhaps I have had too much wine this evening and have forgotten my senses," I lied, having barely finished two cups. "You have always supported me and Alexis and what has happened between us."

He nodded. "*Do* you want me to stand guard until you return?" he asked, placing his hand on my shoulder.

"I do. If my words have not caused you too much offense."

He waved away my lame apology. "Think no more of it, perhaps I spoke out of turn with such morose thoughts. But please know I do not trust Antigonos any more than you do, to him I must appear to be on his side against you, just as I pretended when I spent time with Melanthios. He would not have been happy being bested by a woman this night, but my loyalty is to you, always. I give you my word."

"I know. And I thank you. I forget how you must act towards Antigonos now since I put you in that position. Hopefully, it shall not be for much longer."

"I hope that is the case as well. Shall you be gone until the sun rises?"

"I do not know. Perhaps."

"Go. Enjoy yourself. Whenever you return, I shall take my leave."

"Thank you, my friend and I apologize once again."

"Do not allow it to concern you any longer. I shall see you when you return."

I inclined my head and made my way back towards the main banqueting hall beside the Throne Room. I glanced over my shoulder, pleased Moeris did not feel the need to watch my departure out of the central chamber. I bypassed the almost empty hall and followed the path to the stables beyond. I took Skotos from his pen, readying him with no more than a covering of material over his back and his reins around his neck.

10

Though the moon was in its waning phase as it headed toward the new, there was still a large slice of its light to guide me across the plain and rivers to the temple of Anthela. I was grateful for its company and the brightness it afforded me, which ensured I did not need to light a torch and draw attention to myself.

The temple of Anthela lay a little over eleven stadia to the south-west of Trachis and twenty-two stadia of the hot springs. Had I been walking, it would have taken me less than half a candlemark to reach. With Skotos, it was even faster. Bright light emanated between the columns when we arrived and I quickly tethered Skotos to a large tree near the entrance.

It was not the first time I had been to the temple; in my pursuit of Melanthios after he took Alexis, my father, Moeris, Thaddeus and I had been ambushed here. I had been here since then as well, but I hoped my visit here tonight was not going to be as it was that first time.

I had barely pulled the reins tight around the branch when Skotos began to stamp his hooves and snort, straining to back away from whatever he could see over my shoulder. I turned, noting that the woman from the agora had appeared at the entrance to the temple, her hood still covering her face. I turned back to Skotos and attempted to sooth him with quiet words, but he would not be calmed and in the end, I simply patted him on the nose and made my way towards the woman, scratching again at my back as I walked.

"I am pleased you came."

"I do not believe I had much of a choice," I replied, though not unkindly.

"There is always a choice, Skylar, though I am glad you chose as you did. Come, allow us to speak inside," she said, stepping aside to allow me to enter ahead of her. I did so, finding the temple lit with torches that banished the shadows from its marbled corners and most of the high, tiled roof. There was no one else inside. "Do you know why this temple was built?"

"Yes. After the Trojan War, the Great Amphictyonic League was formed, some say by Amphictyon, brother of Hellen and common ancestor of all Hellenes, though after such a time, who can be certain?" I replied in a rush. "There were twelve founding members, all from north Ionian tribes, who agreed to protect and administer the temple of Apollo in Delphi, and the temple of Demeter here in Anthela. The representatives of each of the twelve members meet here in spring, and in Delphi in the autumn.

"Their main authority lies in their power to pronounce punishments in the manner of fines or expulsion against offenders who defile either of the temples, though they have also been known to sanction sacred wars and to set down the rules of such battles. The league's guidelines insist that no member is allowed to be completely wiped out should war befall them. The water supplies of all members must remain intact as well, even during wartime." I paused, uncertain why I felt the need to tell her *everything* I knew.

The woman showed no outward signs of displeasure or boredom, but with her face still hidden beneath her hood it was impossible to be certain. "I am impressed with your knowledge," she finally said. "Have you been here before?"

"I attended the council meeting with King Agrias last spring. It was he who supplied me with answers … and I was here once before that, though I did not enter the temple then."

"When you sought to free your lover from Melanthios last winter?"

"Y-yes," I stammered. "Melanthios had left Alexis' chiton here for me to find and when we returned to Trachis, I asked Agrias what the temple was used for. He spoke of it and then invited me to sit in on the meeting two moons later."

"Well, perhaps it is fitting then that I chose this place to speak with you. Though we shall not be proclaiming wars or dealing out punishments, it is where truths have and shall come to light and secrets banished," she said with a nod.

I made no comment, waiting for her to continue. She too waited a long moment before crossing to a marble bench and motioning for me to join her. When I was seated, she spoke again. "What do you know of the Keres?"

"The what?"

"In all your travels, and with all you have ever learnt, your father never spoke of the Keres with you?"

"No. Should he have?"

"Yes. Though it is not a surprise he did not. He has long feared them I am certain."

"If you wish to tell me of them then do so. I am not interested in hidden words."

"Very well," she said, her dark hood dipping and raising as she nodded. "There were originally five Ker women, all daughters of Nyx, Goddess of the Night who is one of the oldest goddesses. Their names were Anaplekte, Akhlys, Nosos, Ker and Stygere. Each name spoke of what they would gift to the mortal realm; Anaplekte gave quick, powerful death, often when the death was caused by accident. Akhlys provided the mist which covered the eyes of those upon death's door so that their suffering came to an end. Nosos sent disease to claim the lives of many others, Ker herself brought nothing but destruction in the form of murder and Stygere ensured hate was the cause of many deaths, often in battle."

"They do not appear gentle of spirit."

The woman laughed. "No indeed they were not. But their tasks were important to the mortals, and the gods, for without their specific talents what reason would mortals have to pray to their gods for revenge or healing? They were called demons, misunderstood by many, but they ensured mortals found Hades in the Underworld just as often as their brother – Thanatos."

"Thanatos? You speak of the God of Non-Violent Death?"

"Yes."

"The two are kin and yet their ways are so different," I noted.

"True, but Nyx had many children who assisted in the two realms, each bringing their own talent to the worlds, not all good, but all necessary. She bore Aether and Hemera; brightness and day. The Hesperides and Geras; who provide the evening sunset and old age. Hypnos and the Oneiroi; the God of Sleep and the dream givers. Philotes; who ensured there was friendship and love, and the Moirai who determine the length of each mortal's life.

"In addition, she gave birth to Moros with his penchant for driving men to their own destruction, Momus who incites blame and Oizys who causes nothing but woe, pain and distress to those he meets. Nemesis and Apate gave the world retribution and deceit and Eris, the Goddess of Discord caused strife amongst those who encountered her. There is one deed in particular I am certain you have heard of to which Eris is connected." I frowned, attempting to recall the name of the goddess she spoke of, shaking my head when I could not. "It was Eris who caused the Trojan

War," the woman supplied.

"I thought that was Aphrodite," I said, my frown deepening.

"Aphrodite played her own part, but it was Eris who cast the golden apple amongst the wedding banquet Zeus held in honor of Peleus and Thetis. Eris had not been invited and so sought to cause disruption." The woman lifted her head, though her face remained hidden. "May I share the tale with you?"

I hesitated, not wanting to offend her by refusing to hear the story, even though I was more interested in hearing of the Keres and why she had wanted me to meet her. "Go ahead," I nodded.

"Peleus and Thetis – parents of the hero Achilles – were thrown a wonderful wedding feast by Zeus. As was so often the case, Eris had not been invited to celebrate with the gods, for she would have made it an unpleasant affair for all involved. The goddess was angered and went anyway, taking with her a golden apple from the garden of the Hesperides. She had inscribed the fruit with the word 'kallisti' which meant – for the fairest.

"As you may imagine, the other goddesses clamored to ensnare the apple for themselves, with Hera, Athena and Aphrodite each claiming they had been first to lay hands upon it, and each believing without doubt that they were the most beautiful. They asked Zeus to name the one he believed to be the one, but Zeus would not, having allegiance to each woman and not wishing to incur the wrath of the two he did not choose.

"Ares too was at the banquet and suggested to his father that a mortal be allowed choose from the three women. He named a Trojan called Paris, whom he had recently bested in a contest between Paris' prized bull and the war-god himself, in bull-form. Ares told Zeus, and the gathered immortals, that though the odds had been against Paris from the beginning, when Ares defeated his animal and revealed himself, Paris still awarded the prize to the god without hesitation.

"Zeus agreed and with Hermes' guidance, the women bathed in a sacred spring at Mount Ida before appearing to Paris as he herded cattle. Each goddess disrobed so the young man could make his decision, but he was unable, as all were so stunning. As Hera re-dressed, she decided to offer an added incentive to secure the favor of the mortal; she told Paris she would make him a king. Not to be outdone, Athena offered wisdom and skill in war. Aphrodite then promised that the most beautiful woman in the world would be Paris'.

"Paris did not hesitate and awarded the apple to Aphrodite. The other goddesses disappeared in fury and Aphrodite spoke to Paris of Helen of Sparta, the woman she intended to give to him. Aphrodite spoke of Helen's beauty and her many suitors but told Paris that Helen would choose him if he went to her. Paris left immediately, only learning Helen was already married to Menelaus, the King of Sparta, when he arrived there. He was undeterred by this knowledge and stole Helen away, returning to Troy and inciting the start of the Trojan War."

I knew it was not the only time Helen had been stolen away from her home – Theseus having done so after she found herself in Troy, but I kept the story to myself. "Did Helen ever attempt to leave Paris?" I asked instead.

"Perhaps she would have, but she fell in love with Paris when she set eyes upon him. Some say that too was Aphrodite's handiwork, though she has never admitted as much."

Both of us were quiet for a long moment before I spoke again. "You began by speaking of the Keres. What is it you want me to know about them?"

"Ah," she smiled. "The Keres had no specific purpose until their sister Eris gave them one. She enjoyed destruction and death, almost as much as Ares, the God of War, and she encouraged her sisters to fly, hidden, above the battlefields and draw strength from the felled warriors by swooping down and drinking their blood before carrying the men off to Hades in the Underworld.

"They continued in this manner for many winters, until Eris allowed Ares himself to take charge of them and become even stronger. Ares called upon the Moirai for further assistance, assigning each Ker to mortal warriors who were destined for a violent death. They watched over the warriors until their lives ended and fed on them before delivering them to the Underworld. This they did for many more winters, until a son of Zeus altered their fate. I believe you are well familiar with Heracles."

"A great hero," I nodded.

"He is perceived as a hero by mortals, but because of his actions that day, he almost caused the Keres to disappear from the mortal and immortal planes," the woman said. I noted the same disdain for Heracles in her voice as she had for my father earlier, but before I could question her on Heracles' involvement in the supposed fate of the Keres, she continued. "Some have described the Keres as fanged, taloned women who dress in bloodied garments, but that is not always the truth. Their clothing *is* often covered in the blood of their chargers, but not until after they feed, rather than when they fly above the battlefields."

"You speak of fangs, talons and flying. Are the Keres birds?"

"Of sorts. Though their faces and bodies resemble that of women, great black wings sprout from their shoulders and their hair is as dark as raven feathers. Fangs fill their mouths, though they extend from their teeth only when required. In this way they can appear quite mortal."

"So, they walked among their chargers?" I asked. "They still do?"

"No. It has always been forbidden for them to reveal themselves."

"You appear to know a lot about these Keres, yet you remain hidden from me, even here when we are alone. I can only presume you are one of these supposed bird-women, are you not?" The woman laughed, a grating sound, as though it was an unfamiliar gesture. "Show yourself. Prove the truth of the creatures you speak of," I insisted, drawing my sword as I got to my feet.

"As you wish," she said with a nod.

The woman reached for her hood, her sleeves falling away to reveal fingers with hooked black claws extending from the end of each. I drew in a quick breath as the fabric fell away, revealing long, dark hair the color of my own, though knotted and loose where mine was neat and held back from my face with a single hairclip. Her face was white, as though barely touched by Helios' rays and her eyes were red with black centers when she raised her face to mine. It was impossible to tell her age for she appeared neither old, nor young.

"Satisfied?" she asked, grinning and revealing two rows of pointed teeth.

I swallowed, attempting to gather my thoughts. "Are you assigned to me? I am destined for a violent death?" I asked.

"No. As I said, Keres are forbidden to reveal themselves to their charges. It has only happened once."

"You said you would speak of my mother if I met you. What do the Keres – your people – have to do with her?"

"Everything."

"Ho–?" I paused as a thought struck me. The night I told Alexis of my love for her, Father had shared the tale of how he and my mother met in Thrace. He said her hair was the same shade as mine but long and tangled. He cited the breeze around them as the cause, though perhaps it had always been the same. The same as this Ker's. He said too that her eyes were bright – did they mirror the red before me as well? "You expect me to believe that my mother was a ... a Ker? A creature? If that were true, my father would have spoken of it with me."

"Would he?" the woman challenged, allowing the cloak to fall from her body entirely. She wore a white chiton underneath which was free of blood and dirt. She was not beautiful, but neither was she unpleasant to the eye. She did not appear anything other than a mortal woman either – if you did not see her eyes or the folded wings at her back. She straightened, extending the dark feathers. I took a step back, inhaling as they lengthened and billowed in a light draft behind her. "Tell me you do not recognize this," she said, turning so her left arm faced me.

My heart beat faster but I shook my head as my eyes found the three-sided shape that resembled my own. "No. How can it be ... what trickery is this?" I murmured.

"No trickery. You belong to the proud line of the Keres, Skylar. You are one of us, just as your mother was before you."

"How? Wait ... my mother ... is she, is she alive?" I asked, a distant hope flaring in my chest. If my mother truly was a Ker, then perhaps the night I was born she had had to return to her kin. Perhaps the Keres were akin to the gods; often called back to Olympos soon after creating children with mortals.

The woman replaced the himation as I put my sword back in its sheath. Her eyes dropped to the ground as she shook her head. "No. I am sorry. I felt her passing deep within my soul the night she met her end."

"Tell me what happened," I said, my words gentle.

"That is enough revelation for this night, Mortal."

"Wait. At least tell me your name."

"I am Dianthe," she replied.

"How can I find you again?"

"You wish to meet again, to share words?"

"Yes. Tomorrow around this same time. I want you to speak of the night my mother died. And I want to know how my mother and father met. You said Keres were forbidden to appear to their charges, but you did not say they could not appear to others – as you have to me. I want to know how it came to be."

Dianthe hesitated only a moment before inclining her head in my direction. "I shall come and speak of what I know. We can meet at the area known as the west gate of the Pass of Thermopylae. Late again, when the moon is high in the sky. Until then, do not speak of our conversation with anyone."

I nodded. I had no intention of sharing what I had learnt with anyone – not even Alexis – until I knew more. "Thank you."

"Until we see each other again," Dianthe agreed.

I nodded again and when I raised my head, I was alone, save the faint flap of wings echoing around the temple. I blew out a deep breath and exited the building, the torches extinguishing behind me.

*

I delivered Skotos to his pen, ensuring he had enough to eat and drink before I left again, silently making my way up the path and through the walkway on the south side of the palace.

"Skylar?"

"King Agrias!" I jumped, having been so consumed by my thoughts I did not hear or see him approach.

"If you intend to re-join the festivities for your father's birthing day, I am afraid everyone has retired to their rooms, homes, or simply fallen asleep where they lay."

"I was not seeking to do so," I replied with a shake of my head.

"Is all well? Is Alexis feeling poorly again?"

"The princess sleeps, but I could not, so I went to visit Skotos so I did not wake her with my tossing."

"Did the banquet frighten him?"

"No, he has never appeared disturbed by such gatherings."

"I am glad to hear it. What then troubles you enough to keep you from slumber? Is it what you wished to speak with me about earlier?"

I frowned, attempting to recall what he spoke of. Antigonos, I realized. "Oh, no, it is not that."

"Do you wish to speak now? We could go to the Throne Room."

"No," I replied, having no room in my head to deal with Antigonos and what that might entail at the moment. "I shall come find you tomorrow to speak on that matter, if it pleases you?"

"Are you certain?" Agrias asked, regarding me with a tilt of his head reminiscent of his daughter.

"Yes." It did not feel enough to simply leave it at that, not after all Agrias had done for me, and the kindness and acceptance he had shown me since I arrived in Trachis. "I suppose I have questions and concerns, as any expectant parent does, about what it shall mean when their son or daughter arrives," I offered, not a lie, as those thoughts *had* been at the back of my mind for some time.

Agrias stepped close, taking my shoulders in his hands. "Do not allow fears to trouble you for you and Alexis shall make excellent parents, and you have Melina and I to aid you, as your own father and Nasrin shall," he hesitated, then added, "You know if you ever want to speak about anything I shall listen. Even though Leandros has returned, I do not hesitate to offer."

"Thank you and perhaps one day soon I shall take you up on that," I said, taking the king's hands when he dropped them from my shoulders. "But for now, I should return to our apartment in case Alexis wakes and finds I am not there."

"Of course." I squeezed his fingers and nodded before letting go. "Goodnight."

"Goodnight," I repeated. I took a step towards my room before pausing and turning back Agrias. "Apologies, I did not ask; is all well with you? What finds you out this late if the feasting has finished?"

"I am well. I was just settling Leandros and Nasrin in their room. They were in no position to see themselves there safely or quietly," he replied with a grin.

"Why am I not surprised to hear that?" I chuckled.

Agrias raised his hand in a wave and I continued towards the central chamber, hoping the king had not seen Moeris stationed outside our door, or at the very least had not had words with the soldier if he did.

Moeris nodded to me when I arrived. "Thank you for remaining here as I asked," I said.

"Of course. How was the rest of your evening?"

"Enlightening," I replied with a tight grin. "The banquet is finished and my father and Nasrin are back in their room, no doubt they shall wake with sore heads in the morning."

"It is time I found my way to bed also, if you do not need me for anything else?"

"No. Go, rest."

"Very good," he nodded, turning on his heel and heading for the barracks.

11

"I took this from Antigonos at last night's celebration," I told Agrias, handing him the dagger as we stood in the Throne Room the following morning.

"Antigonos? What reason does he have to carry a weapon? What threat does he believe awaits him?"

"I do not believe he was carrying it for protection, rather to cause harm himself."

"Oh? To whom?"

"Me. Alexis. Gnosidicus perhaps. Whoever he deems to have wronged him." The king stiffened at the mention of threat to his daughter. "I have seen a similar weapon once before," I said, taking it back. "Melanthios carried one. I killed him with it."

"Could the dagger be Melanthios'?" Agrias asked.

"No. His was sent back to Epirus with his other weapons and body," Moeris replied, entering the room. "Apologies for the interruption, I came to find Skylar. Few are yet to wake after the festivities last night, but I knew you would want to train so sought to offer my weapons. Alexis told me you were here. Is there anything I need to be aware of?"

Agrias' gaze slid to mine and I nodded. "He knows I had words with Antigonos during the celebrations last night."

"Very well," the king murmured, motioning the commander to join us. "Yes, Come. Skylar believes Antigonos may have greater allegiance to his original tribe than to us here in Trachis, what are your thoughts on the matter?"

I passed the dagger to Moeris when he held his hand out for it. "Before Melanthios arrived, and even when he was here, he gave no indication of that, but after Skylar killed Melanthios and his brothers, there have been signs that it could indeed be so," Moeris nodded. "Antigonos is the only one who remains obviously opposed to their union, whereas all others have accepted it either quietly or with outspoken support, such as Stavros has shown."

"You believe Stavros to be sincere?" I asked, though I had no reason to think otherwise.

"I do. He is as loyal to you as he is to our King and Trachis."

"Who does Antigonos speak with? Do you think he is gathering together others who are opposed to the decision I made to allow Skylar and Alexis' betrothal?" Agrias asked. Moeris shrugged, but I nodded.

"He spoke of friends, though I am not convinced they live here," I replied.

"I shall have a man trail him in case there *are* others here we need to keep an eye on," Moeris offered.

"Have one watching Gnosidicus' home as well, in case Antigonos decides to make good on his threat to hurt the healer," I added. "And tell no one about this. Allow just the three of us and Gnosidicus to know of Antigonos' threats."

"Should we not at least speak of it with Thaddeus?" Moeris asked. "He can keep an eye on Alexis whilst at the palace."

"No. I do not want her to worry and if Thaddeus knows, he may speak of it with Hesper, who would then tell Alexis. The two of them share everything."

"I agree, allow it to be just the four of us for now. If the time comes when we need to inform others then we shall do so," Agrias nodded.

"Could I suggest it be five? Leandros would be an important addition to our number," Moeris asked. I nodded again in response.

"When he wakes, I shall speak to him of it," Agrias said. "I have other business I must attend, but keep me informed of any developments," he added, heading for the doorway.

"We shall," I agreed. "It is time we went to the barracks as well." I waited until the king left before addressing Moeris again. "I want you to stand guard outside our room again tonight."

"Of course, though with the lock on your door, and yourself, I do not believe you need me as well," he replied.

"I shall not be there, not the entire time."

"Where are you going?"

"I am meeting someone."

"About Antigonos?"

"No, though it is of no less importance."

"Then speak of it."

"Shall you guard our door and keep your princess safe or not?" I snapped.

"Of course. But I expect answers in return."

"And when I have them, you shall get them," I said, turning on my heel and stepping out into the courtyard. "Are you coming?" I asked, realizing Moeris had not followed me. He hesitated before nodding, joining me as I passed the statue of Artemis.

12

Dianthe and I sat on the ground in the Pass of Thermopylae, our backs against the dilapidated wall. "You say I am of the line of the Keres, as my mother was before me. Yet I possess none of the same features as you – I am perfectly mortal, with no wings or talons on the ends of my fingers. I do not understand how you believe I am such a creature without these obvious signs," I told her.

"It is true, you do not outwardly show your Ker heritage. I must assume it is because of your father's blood which has made it so. But I am in no doubt you possess the skills of my kin."

"What skills? I cannot fly, nor can I stomach thought of drinking the blood of fallen warriors."

"Your talents are yet to reveal themselves. But it shall not be long before they do, of this too I am certain."

"How can you be?"

"You asked me last evening to speak to you of how your parents met. Do you wish to hear the tale now?"

"I want you to answer the questions I have asked tonight." My shoulder blades itched beneath my cuirass and I wished I had a stick to relieve the prickling. I squirmed inside the bronze instead, though it did not alleviate it much.

"I shall do so. When the time is right," she replied.

"And when is that?"

"That is for those who know to know, and for us to find out," she said cryptically. I growled. The woman was as frustrating as every other immortal I had ever met; joyfully content to speak in riddles. I drew in a deep breath, just as eager to hear the story of my parents' meeting as I was to receive answers about all she had begun to tell me.

"Speak of it then," I grumbled.

She nodded. "The Keres had long been under the command of Ares, God of War, committing their assigned mortals to Hades in the Underworld when their time came and growing strong on the blood they consumed. Heracles was a young man, his feats of strength and cunning becoming known throughout the world, even though Hera had attempted on many an occasion to quell his popularity, and to end his life on many more.

"She had sent down a fit of madness, during which Heracles killed his family, and he was sent to his uncle to atone for their deaths. His deeds would be of little interest to you or me this night, were it not for the sixth task he was set."

"His defeat of the Stymphalian Birds," I offered.

"Indeed," Dianthe acknowledged with a nod of her head. "What do you know of it?"

"What does it have to do with my parents?" I asked instead.

"What do you know of it?" Dianthe asked again.

I frowned, blowing out a deep breath as I recalled the story. "Heracles was sent to a lake near the town of Stymphalos. His task was to drive away the flock of birds gathered there. It was said the birds were man-eaters with beaks and feathers of bronze, sacred to Ares ..." I paused as the thought came to me. "There were Keres?"

Dianthe nodded. "Only some had beaks of bronze, though it was the birds who lived at the lake who possessed them, not the Keres."

"What were the Keres doing there?"

"Continuing their line. Until that particular winter, they travelled to Stymphalos each winter to mate with the local birds who were fierce and secular. When they returned to Ares, a new generation of Ker children grew inside them."

"It did not continue after that?"

"No. As I am certain you are aware, Heracles was provided a rattle made by Hephaestus, brother to Ares." I nodded in acknowledgment. "With the rattle, Heracles scared the flock from the trees, shooting many out of the sky with his bow and arrow when they took flight. The arrow tips had been dipped in the poisonous blood of the hydra and those it came into contact with died a slow, painful death. The few who were left vowed never to return to Stymphalos – or Greece – lest they suffer the same fate. Instead, Ares settled them far from Heracles' presence to the north on an island in the Inhospitable Sea, and the birds visited *them* for the continuing of the line."

I raised an eyebrow. "The Inhospitable Sea, east of Thrace?" I recalled the name from a map Agrias had shown me.

"Yes. Though our island was not the closest to the Thracians, we spent much time there. It is how your mother became assigned to your father. How the entirety of the line was changed."

"She was assigned to him? Then … then that means he is destined for a violent death." *And that* she *was the Ker who broke the rules and appeared to her charge.*

"You are surprised at this?" Dianthe asked, regarding me with the hint of a smile playing at her lips.

I blew out a deep breath, shaking my head slowly. "I should not be I suppose, given how we have lived all these winters."

"And the tribe he was born into," Dianthe reminded me.

"You know of the Bessoi?"

"Of course. I too was given one of their number to watch over."

"Were you alive when the Keres were placed near Thrace? Was my mother?"

"I was. But it was many winters before your mother was born."

"How old are you?" the question burst from my lips before I could find a way to soften it.

Dianthe smiled. "Old enough to have seen much and experienced even more."

"Are you immortal?"

"No, though we Ker do not age as you are used to. We begin as mortal children do, growing older until we reach the age where we can bear children to our line. When that is done, and the next generation arrives, we do not age more than a few more winters. We remain at this age for a long, long time."

"So you shall die eventually?"

"Eventually. If I am fortunate enough to grow to a great age, I shall return to Stymphalos and change to my bird-form and remain there until my death. I do not know how long I shall live in that manner, but I hope it shall be many more winters."

"So … if you were alive when Heracles was, are you not already at a great age?"

Dianthe smiled again. "There are many older than I am now and they have not made the change as yet. I know of others who have been allowed make their transformation earlier. Perhaps when I have finished all I was sent here to do, I too shall be given that choice."

"When you have finished here – do you mean here in Trachis?"

"Here, as in what my master has always expected of me." Dianthe replied simply.

"Your master? Is that Ares?"

"When it is time, you shall come to know of whom I speak. Now, shall I tell you what I know of your parent's meeting?" I frowned, frustrated again by what Dianthe did not tell me, but eventually nodded. "From the day your father was born, he was named as Zita's responsibility. She was to watch over him and ensure he did not die before it was his time."

"How did she know when that would be?" I interrupted.

"We are told when the day arrives, not before," Dianthe replied. "Your mother remained his protector for many winters as he grew. But as she came to know him and watched him share his home with one whom he did not love, she began to have feelings for him. She battled those feelings for a long time, but finally she could bear it no longer and she appeared to him."

"Was it as my father said; beneath a silver birch tree as he slumbered one night?" I asked.

"I believe so."

"Did she appear in a mortal form? Were her eyes as red as yours?"

"Yes, to both your queries. Her wings she would have kept beneath her skin, her talons clipped to resemble mortal nails, but her eyes remained their natural color. From the moment your father returned words of affection, Zita's loyalty to her kin was tested. And, as it so often is when love is involved, her family loyalty was not able to win out over her love for the mortal. We did not know of the child – of you – who grew inside her belly, but I often wondered if it was that knowledge that finally drove her to leave us."

"Father said they did not know I was within her when they left Thrace. They only wished, along with Irina whom my father was bonded with, to be allowed live with the ones they truly loved."

"Mmm," Dianthe murmured. "Be that as it may, it was foolish of her to remain with him, out of contact with us when she learned of it. She should have known a child of the line could not be safely brought into the world without our involvement. Had she spoken of it to me, I could have ensured no harm came to her that night."

"You could have saved her? She would not have died giving birth to me?" I asked, my heart beating faster at the thought.

"There would have been no need for her to die, if only she had confided in me," Dianthe murmured, and I wondered how much the words were to herself, rather than to me.

"You were close with my mother?"

"Until she left, yes. I am certain she spoke with your father of who she was, of where she had come from. Still he did not convince her to return or to speak with me. He must have known how it would end if they attempted to birth you."

"So you have known about me since I was born? Why did you not appear to me sooner?"

"I did not know of your birth. The first time I felt you was the day you made your first kill in Anticyra. I felt then our blood coursing through your veins, of the strength you possessed."

"You did not appear to me then either. Why?"

Dianthe hesitated. "Not everyone was convinced you were who I claimed. We had to wait until you were older. Until he felt you were ready to learn of your past, of your mother."

"Who wanted to wait?" Again, Dianthe did not answer. I let out an exasperated grunt. "Another secret you keep from me? With such secrecy perhaps I have reason to question the truth of all you have said. If I was to ask my father, would he confirm what you have told me?"

"Though I asked you not to speak of what we had discussed, you could have gone to him. Why did you not? I am certain you wanted to," Dianthe said, regarding me intently.

"It was not the time."

"Or perhaps you are afraid he shall confirm what I have said. You do not want to face the truth that he has lied to you all these winters." I made no response, for she did speak with some truth. "With what I have told you this night, you now understand that *he* is the reason your mother is not here with you today. Because they hid from us, she died the night you were born. And it is his fault you have never known your mother's family, that you have never met his as well I suspect."

"He ... he said he can never return to Thrace," I stammered. "Why? Are his family dead?"

"Not all of them. I gather he has never returned for fear that we would find you there. He must know it is near our home ... Did you never want to know where your mother was from? Who her kin were? Did you never yearn to meet them, to have them shower you with love as you had witnessed so many other children receive from the bosom of their families? Did you never harbor rage that your father did not speak with you of her?"

Her words pulled at something deep within me. I had always told myself I did not care to know more about my mother, about my parents' families or where they had been born. Until I spoke to Father when I realized that I was falling in love with Alexis, I had never pressed him too hard for answers about her. I did not believe it to be important. We had one another and that was enough. It was everything.

"He did what he believed was right," I replied after a long pause.

"She would not have died that night had she been with us. You would have been safe. You could have grown with your mother's love all this time. Without our kind with her to witness your birth and bring you into the world ... well, you know what the outcome was. It was his fault. It was hers; she knew the consequences of her actions."

My hands clenched and my breath grew short. "So you keep saying, but it cannot be changed. My mother, my father, they made choices which saw them birth me and lose her. Nothing you say can alter that so why do you continue to speak of it?"

"Because it is time you knew the truth. If your father had not spoken words of love to Zita then she would not have fled from us. The line would not have become blurred with mortal blood and she would still be here today, reveling perhaps in the knowledge that her existence and the expectance on her was more important than the touch of some mortal!" Dianthe cried, her voice heightening with each word.

"You are jealous of her? Of the knowledge that she left you all? Was that something you once wanted but never achieved?"

"I am far from jealous of her. She was selfish in a way you are yet to understa—"

"Then speak of it with me. Tell me why you hold such anger for my mother and why you seek to goad me into an argument with my father."

"I seek only to speak to you of who you truly are. Of who your mother was and the proud line you carry on."

"We are done here. I do not wish to see you again," I said jumping to my feet.

"I do not accept that, nor do I believe it. You are yet to learn of your true role in our lives. You are yet to learn of the Chosen One and the prophecy that goes along with it, and once you do, you shall not be so quick to dismiss me."

"I need no more of your tales. I have my family and I do not need another." I turned on my heel, stomping my way along the path and across the wider grassed section of the Pass of Thermopylae.

"If you find yourself curious, you need only speak my name and I shall meet you wherever you wish to," Dianthe called.

"I shall not call on you," I assured her.

"We shall see. It is best you return to the palace now anyway, your princess sleeps restlessly. She would benefit from your presence."

I paused and turned back to Dianthe. "You seek to threaten with your words? To allude to knowing how Alexis is though you are here with me?"

"I allude to nothing. You should hurry, she shall soon wake." With that, Dianthe extended her wings and pushed up off the ground in a puff of fine, sandy particles, momentarily hidden from my sight. By the time the dust had settled once again, she was but a speck in the light of the moon.

With my head full of questions, along with a heavy dose of anger, burning deep in my stomach, I returned to the palace. Moeris paced outside the door to our apartment, relief flooding his features when he caught sight of me.

"Alexis woke a short time ago. She wanted to know where you were."

"What did you tell her?"

"The truth; that I did not know where you went, only that you asked me to remain until you returned. She did not care for my answer."

"I cannot imagine she did. You may go."

"She has not slept well this night. I have heard her crying out, but I did not go to her."

"Fine," I said with a nod.

"Skyl–"

"I am certain you require at least a few candlemarks rest before we begin training in the morning," I cut over him. He said nothing further but gave a curt nod and turned on his heel. I considered his words a moment, gathering an amphora of water from the bathing area and taking it back to our room.

I closed the door and quickly shed my cuirass and sword, managing to set them aside before Alexis stirred.

"Where have you been?" she asked rubbing at her eyes as she sat up.

"Fetching these for you. You have not slept well tonight." I poured the water into the basin beside the door, immersing a length of fabric in it and wringing it out before crossing to her. "Lay back," I directed, settling the cool material across her forehead when she did so.

She closed her eyes, laying her hand over mine on the bed. "Thank you. I cannot recall all the details, but I believe I dreamt of birds. Of our child having wings." I drew a sharp breath and was thankful Alexis had her eyes shut so she did not see my reaction. She smiled and shook her head gently, careful not to dislodge the cloth. "It sounds so silly when I say it out loud. Hesper says dreams are often strange when a new life grows inside you."

I swallowed and squeezed her hand. "I am certain that is all it is. You should attempt to get back to sleep." I stripped off my tunic and lay down beside her, cradling her in my arms when she snuggled into me. "Sleep now and know I am here. Nothing shall harm you when I am close," I promised, placing a kiss in her hair.

"I know," she mumbled, already drifting back into Hypnos' realm.

I closed my eyes, tightening my arms around Alexis and wishing Dianthe's words did not remain at the front of my thoughts. I had told her I would not call on her again, but I was not certain that would be the case. I had so many questions, and something told me she was the only one who could give me the answers.

13

4th rising, Moon of Pyanepsion

I sat on the narrow track between the Phoenix River and the temple of Anthela. The grass grew sporadically between the deep wheel ruts made by the merchants who brought their wares to the agora in Trachis. Mount Kallidromon towered behind me, its rocky outcrop giving way to the narrow path and the steep drop to the Malian Gulf below. I had my legs over the side of the cliff, occasionally dislodging small pebbles from the face and sending them towards the crashing waves and large boulders below.

Dianthe's words to me about a Chosen One and the prophecy gnawed at my waking, and sleeping, thoughts. I could not deny I was curious what role (if any) I would play with the Keres, and if they truly were my mother's family. My family. I wondered if I would finally have the opportunity to meet my grandparents if I asked Dianthe to arrange it. Were they both of the Ker line, or was my grandfather one of the bronze-beaked birds from Stymphalos?

I had not found the courage to question my father on what Dianthe had told me. Some of my reluctance was as Dianthe believed – my uncertainty at how he would react if it was true, and how I would in response. I held back also though, confused as to why Dianthe would tell me such a fanciful tale if it was not the truth. I could see no reason for her to want to cause conflict or distance between my father and me. Perhaps she appeared on behalf of another. Ares? Or perhaps it was one of the goddesses she spoke of – Aphrodite, or even Eris.

The familiar, frustrating thoughts swirled in my head, setting my jaw clenching with the continued unavailability of answers that I could blame on no one but myself. I picked up a small rock and threw it into the water far below.

"Though the morning is not cool, I hope you are not considering cliff jumping from here. It would not be wise when we find ourselves far from the clear, rock-free waters of the Heraion," Thaddeus' voice interrupted my musings.

"I have no intention of jumping, I assure you," I said, offering him a grin as he held out his hand.

"Good, for I am not certain how I would explain such an action to Alexis – nor the king," he replied, pulling me to my feet. He placed one hand on his chest as he continued, the grin still firmly in place. "Friends, I am sorry to inform you that the newest Princess of Trachis believed she was skilled enough to run across the wagon track and jump out *over* the rocks in the Gulf to find clear waters beyond and satisfy her love of daring and adventure."

I laughed in spite of the remnants of my brooding thoughts and pushed at his shoulder. "You would hardly go to them with such humor; I suspect you would barely get the words 'she is dead' from your lips before you were overcome with sadness."

"Perhaps you speak true. I certainly would not want to be the bearer of such news to any in the palace," he said, his smile fading. "I shall admit, I was somewhat concerned to see you leave Trachis for this place again."

"You have followed me before?" I asked, a touch of gruffness entering my voice.

"A few times," he nodded. *Astute as always*, I thought.

I should have been angry, not with Thaddeus, but with myself; I had never been aware of his presence, and knowing my surroundings was something I had always prided myself on. It appeared my absences the past half-moon had not been as inconspicuous as I had believed, and it appeared that the more I turned my thoughts inward, the more oblivious to anyone around me I became.

"What troubles you so? Do you wish to share it with me? I cannot guarantee I can provide answers, but if nothing else, I would listen."

I placed my hand on his shoulder and gave him another tight grin. "I appreciate the offer, truly. But in this, I must consider all alone."

"You have not shared it even with Alexis?" he asked, his eyebrows disappearing momentarily beneath his hair. "She shall not be pleased when she learns you have kept something from her."

"Do you not keep secrets from Hesper?"

"Some, though not matters which keep me from slumber or from her side because of their disturbing nature."

When I had first encountered Melina alone, she spoke of my directness in seeking answers, and yet in this matter I did not. I blew out a breath. "Perhaps it is time I approached the one I seek answers from, no matter the consequences," I murmured.

"A sensible decision," Thaddeus said, his smile returning. "Now come, Agrias asked me to fetch you and Alexis. Finding her was easy – she was with Hesper – but you spoke to no one of your destination after we trained earlier. It is fortunate I saw you leave, though I would have come here to check anyway."

"What does Agrias want?" I asked.

"He did not say, though I do not believe it is bad news, he appeared almost excited."

"I wonder what has made him so." He shrugged in reply, the two of us falling silent as we followed the Asopos River, turning north towards Trachis when the palace came into view.

My father, Nasrin, Agrias, Melina and Alexis were already gathered together in the Throne Room when we arrived, Thaddeus taking his leave when I entered the room.

"Finally," my father muttered when I passed him. "If your princess was also missing I could hazard a guess as to what kept you, but she has been here almost half-a-candlemark." I ignored him, continuing on and placing a kiss on Alexis' lips as she slid an arm around my waist.

"Is all well?" she asked quietly when we parted.

"Yes. And you?"

"I am well also." I nodded and turned as Agrias stood, addressing us all.

"As you may recall, before Alexis and Skylar went to create a child for themselves, I spoke of travelling to Macedonia to my brother's palace. I wished to discuss with him the possibility of breaking further from the ways of our upbringing. I believe now, before Alexis is too far along to travel comfortably or safely, it is time we made the trip."

"What a wonderful idea. I would enjoy spending time with my uncle and his family. We have not seen them in many winters," Alexis said.

"Much has changed for us all since last we were together," Agrias agreed. "The chance to have my brother meet the newest members of our family and to give his blessing towards my decision, would be of great comfort and joy to me."

"It sounds a fine idea, Agrias. Nasrin and I would be delighted to join you. When do you wish to leave?"

"Andreas intends to be here in a few weeks – around the new moon or so. I would allow him his wish to see the site of his sons' deaths and when he leaves for Epirus once again, we shall begin our own journey."

"Very good," my father nodded.

"Is that wise – to leave when he does? What if he returns and attempts to take Trachis for himself while you are gone?" I asked.

"He need not know of our intention to leave," Agrias replied, waving away my words. "Now, Thaddeus told me of the fun you had jumping from the cliff at the Heraion and south of Aigai is the town of Edessa, the first capital of Macedonia, which is well known for its large waterfalls and where I know many young men do the same from their great heights."

"Indeed?" I asked, my curiosity momentarily overtaking my worry about Andreas. I could not deny the excitement at the thought of jumping from the top of a waterfall rather than a slab of rock.

"Oh yes. There are actually seven waterfalls in Edessa. The most famous is the great waterfall known as Karanos and the multi waterfall called Diplos. It is said the Diplos is almost three hundred feet high and plunges down into the waters of the Edessaios River which flows through Edessa year-round," Agrias continued with a grin.

"Perhaps it is best not to use the waterfalls as enticement for Skylar," Alexis said sternly. "I do not wish for harm to come to her by such activities."

"Of course, of course," Agrias smiled. "I only speak of enjoyments to be had to give her something to look forward to until it is time to leave. For I cannot imagine the visit by Andreas shall be particularly pleasant."

I inhaled deeply, scratching at my back. I did not want to leave Trachis. Not now. With all I had learned so far, and all Dianthe must still share, I could not leave. It was time I sought direct answers. My earlier hesitation at seeing her again was gone. It was clear Dianthe could travel wherever she wanted, and would find me wherever I was, but finding time to meet with her alone as we travelled would be a challenge. I would call for her as soon as this meeting was done, and then I would speak with my father and learn his reaction.

"Alexis and I shall not be joining you. We shall remain here in Trachis," I finally said, holding a hand up to halt Agrias' protests. "You speak of her travelling now before she is too heavy with child but given her … problems in the past with carrying a child to term I would not have her far from a healer or midwife these next moons."

"Gnosidicus is aging, though his son, Podaleirius, along with the midwife could accompany us," Agrias countered.

"I do not believe journey is what is best when my wife is carrying our daughter. To find ourselves far from home and without proper means to tend her should she fall ill would not be prudent," I persisted, finding my father's eyes and challenging him to disagree. I could not read the look on his face, though I could tell I had hit a nerve and he was working hard not to respond in kind.

"But …" Agrias began.

"Perhaps she has a point," my father conceded. "None of us wish to see harm come to Alexis or the child she carries. Perhaps once she is born, we can all go to Macedonia and introduce your brother to his newest kin."

"Perhaps we should continue onto Thrace afterwards. To the mountains you once called home," I suggested, my gaze still locked with my father's. I could not help but goad him, though I did not know why I felt the need when I still sought so many answers from Dianthe. I had no intention of confronting him until I knew everything that she had to tell me. "Your family did not come looking for you after you left so perhaps it is time you returned to them and show them you are still alive. That you have a daughter and granddaughter as well."

"There is no need to go to Thrace," he replied coldly.

"You do not believe your family remain in Thrace? Perhaps you fear they have … passed on?" Agrias asked gently.

"Perhaps," Father agreed. "But there is nothing there for me now. I call Trachis home and it is where I shall remain."

"What if it is not just *you* who wants to see the place you were reared? The place you were once betrothed to a woman named Irina," I pressed, unwilling to allow my father to dismiss the subject as readily as I always had.

"If you have words you wish to speak, then speak them, for I do not understand your continuation of this questioning," he replied through gritted teeth.

"I simply do not understand your reluctance to return to your homeland, even if you have no intention of calling it home once again. What memories, other than those happy ones of when you met my mother, could it have for you?"

My father was silent, though our eyes pinned each other in place in a stubborn standoff.

Agrias cleared his throat. "We have a number of moons to decide our exact path. Andreas' approach appears to have us all on our guards. Allow us to put the discussion aside for the time being."

"A good idea," Nasrin said, placing a hand on my father's arm. "Leandros? You promised a visit to the agora with me today, shall we go now?" His jaw clenched, but he took his eyes from mine, giving his lover a single nod and allowing her to lead him towards the doorway.

"Perhaps you could speak with my daughter and ask why she seeks to draw me in such a manner," he murmured as he passed Alexis and me.

"Of course," she replied.

"I am standing right here. Do you think I cannot hear you?" I asked. He looked at me again but made no reply. Taking Nasrin's hand, he bowed quickly to Agrias, Melina and Alexis and left the room.

Alexis squeezed the hand of mine she held between her own until I met her gaze. "What causes you to speak to your father in such a manner?" she asked.

"No reason. I wish to continue the walk Thaddeus interrupted me having when he was sent to fetch me. I shall return before the sun fades behind the mountains," I replied, attempting to disentangle our twined fingers.

"Skylar, wait. Perhaps I could join you? It would be nice to walk along the sand with you as the sun fades."

"No. I would prefer to be alone. You should remain here anyway. I am certain there is much to be done before the banquet to celebrate you and your mother's birthing days tonight."

"There is little else I can assist with," she said.

"Well perhaps you should rest then, it would do no good for you to have to leave your own celebration early."

"I–" I cut her off with a quick kiss on the mouth.

"I shall return before the banquet begins," I promised, seeing myself from the room before she could protest further.

14

"Show yourself," I demanded, catching a slight fluttering off to my right. I stood outside the temple of Anthela once again, waiting for Dianthe to appear, squirming beneath my cuirass as I had so often the past few moons.

"You wished to speak with me again, Child?" she asked, shimmering into view, her lips upturned to reveal those pointed teeth.

"I have questions," I replied simply.

"I am glad, though you have kept me waiting."

"I have conditions to this meeting. There are things I want from you. Things you must agree to before I decide to remain."

"Oh?" Dianthe asked, eyebrows raised and the infuriating grin still plastered to her face.

"Yes," I held up my hand, checking off the items on my fingers. "One; you cannot simply decide we are done and leave whenever you feel. I have asked you to meet so you shall honor the request and remain until I decide I have had enough. Two; I want you to answer whatever I ask. I have no patience for hidden words or meanings. Three; you shall not challenge me to approach my father about what we have spoken of, and neither shall I take all you say as the truth. When I choose to speak with him, and how I approach him shall be at my own discretion and not yours. Are we clear?"

"Of course. I agree. All happens when it is time, a truth I often forget," Dianthe nodded. "I pushed you at our last meeting. You feel that I attacked you, provoked you, to reveal the words we had shared before you were ready. I apologize for that. I do not wish to fight with you. I find myself impatient at times." I was surprised at Dianthe's quick agreement to my proposal and wondered how much she too had replayed our conversations since we last met.

"Alexis and my father both accuse me of the same," I admitted.

"Perhaps then that is something we can begin with – a common ground if you shall permit the phrase," Dianthe said. "Come, sit by me and allow me to answer your questions." I hesitated a moment before joining her at the edge of the Phoenix River. "What is it you wish to know?" she asked, her gaze meeting mine steadily as she awaited my response.

"You said my mother was born a Ker. Did she have siblings? Did she live with both her mother and father? Did they love her? Did they teach her all she needed to know as she grew, of what was expected of her as a Ker? Was she happy? Why could my parents not remain together with your people? Was it just because he was a mortal or was it because he was also her charge? Why are you not allowed to appear to your chargers?" The questions poured from me before I could catch a breath and when Dianthe held up a hand to quiet me, I immediately fell silent, inhaling deeply.

"You want to know where you come from. Who your kin are," the older woman said, a small smile creeping onto her face.

"If you speak true about who I am, and who my mother was, then yes."

"I speak with truth," she assured me. "At the risk of incurring your ire, may I ask *why* you have not asked your father about what I have already told you?"

I shrugged in reply, drawing my fingers through the soft sand and allowing it to slip between them to be taken away on the slight breeze. "Perhaps I wish to know all there is before I go to him."

"Are you afraid of the answers he may give?"

"No," I replied too quickly. "Perhaps. He has been all I have had for so long. To believe he kept my mother's true identity from me ..."

"I understand. It is never easy to accept that others are not who we believed them to be," Dianthe said gently.

"You appear to know much about my mother and the events which shaped her life, and her end. You and she were close?"

"At one time, yes."

"Did she disappoint you when she wanted to leave with my father?"

"No, I was proud of her. But ... birthing you and not confiding in me, that was where she made her mistake. I know now I should have been there the night she died. I should have been the one, not my mother ... but I could not bring myself to attend."

"What do you mean?" I asked with a frown.

Dianthe inhaled and exhaled a long breath before she spoke again. "I could not bear to witness my daughter's demise."

"Your daughter?" I asked, my mind spinning at her words. "Then you are …"

"Your grandmother, yes. We are kin, Skylar."

"And you did not consider telling me that when we first met? You intended to keep such knowledge from me?" I asked, jumping to my feet. Dianthe was beside me before I could take two paces, her hand firm on my shoulder.

"Hush." She indicated I sit again and when I was settled, she re-joined me. "I did not know if I should reveal who I was to you right away. I suppose I wanted to learn who you were first. I needed to know it was something you would be interested in. Then you asked me to meet you again this night and the questions you want answers to; they showed me it was the right decision to make. That it was time to share it with you."

"So you shall answer my questions? You shall tell me of my mother?"

"I shall tell you much more than that. I shall speak to you of my own history."

"You spoke of the Chosen One and a prophecy. I want to know about that as well."

"As you wish," Dianthe said with a nod. She drew another deep breath and blew it all the way out. "I hardly know where to begin now I have the chance to tell you," she admitted with a grin. "I was not certain I would ever have the chance. At first, I did not know if we would ever meet, then I wondered if it would be your father who spoke to you about it first."

"I want to hear it from you," I told her.

"Then you shall," she said, nodding again. She took a moment to compose her thoughts and began. "Long ago, Ares received an amulet and a prophecy. It was foretold that one specific line of his Keres would bear a great warrior. She would be different to all the others of the line. Special. She alone would have the ability to wield all four elements of the amulet – fire, water, wind and earth. She would stand at his side to bring about whatever it was she desired. The line who would bear this chosen child was marked with the sign of the Delta; the one on your shoulder, and on mine."

"What does it signify?" I asked, my gaze falling upon the symbol I had never before had a name for.

"Change. It is fitting, do you not agree?" I only nodded in reply. "When my mother, Rizpah, birthed me and my sister, my kin wondered if finally, the time had come for Ares' chosen child to be born into the line. You see, each woman in our family had only ever birthed one child for our master. It was always a daughter, never a son. But I arrived barely half-a-candlemark before my twin, Ptolema."

"The line was changed."

"Yes," Dianthe nodded. "An event akin to no other in our history. It was an exciting time. Well, to all but me. You must understand the scrutiny

Ptolema and I were under from the moment of our births. Every waking – and no doubt sleeping – moment we were watched over and protected, to ensure nothing untoward happened to us and that we would grow to show our potential to our kin and to our master, Ares.

"Ptolema reveled in the attention, but I despised it. I did not want to be so … known. To have that sort of expectation placed upon you at such a young age is crushing. I wanted nothing more than for Ares to announce that Ptolema was the Chosen One. I knew the attention she would receive and I would be left alone. I would not be seen in the same reverence as she. I would just be the 'other' child, the same as the rest in the line who were not the Chosen One. I wanted it so badly.

"But, when Ares felt we were ready, as he had with all the girls of our line, he announced our tests. He gave us the amulet and demanded we prove our power. I went first and easily called forth the fire element, sending a blazing inferno through a forest. But when Ares asked a second test of me, I was unable to produce anything further. I did not protest when Ares took the amulet from me and handed it to Ptolema.

"Unfortunately for my twin, she was unable to call on any element to bend to her will as she so desperately wanted. She was devastated, certain there was a mistake and she begged Ares to test her again. He would not, turning his back on her and announcing that the line would continue through me. He did not appear disappointed that I was not his intended one, giving me – and my eventual child, Zita – his full protection."

"From Ptolema?" I guessed.

"Yes, and her daughter, Canace, when she was born. After our tests, the closeness Ptolema and I had shared was lost. We may have been sisters, but after that she treated me as an enemy rather than kin. On the one occasion we managed to speak openly, and alone, about the line and how badly she wanted it, I told her she could have it, that I had no wish to be the holder of any Chosen line. She planned to kill me – that I already knew – and I told her I would not stop her if she attempted it. Of course, that action, as with the attempts I made to end my own life, were thwarted by Ares and the protection he afforded me.

"I gave my word to Ptolema instead that I would never birth a child of my own. We believed that if I never gave another to the line, that the power and the responsibility to bear the Chosen One, would fall to Ptolema. We did not know if it would happen when I died, or if Ptolema simply bore a child first. But Ares had other plans for me and I was taken to lie with a male Ker.

"Canace was born before Zita, but Ares remained firm that the responsibility of the line was still with me. Canace was taught to want the title of Chosen One from the moment she was born, just as Ptolema and I, and all the girls in our line, had. She was given added incentive; to take it by any means necessary. When Canace reached Ares' required age, there was no test. Ares said he did not feel the need to do so as her power was so weak, the line so removed from her. That made her hate Zita even more.

"Canace's hatred of Zita did not abate with her cousin's death. Indeed it was inflamed again when she had a child of her own. The child was a boy – no clearer indication that Canace would never be Ares' Chosen One than if he had made her unable to conceive altogether. I believe it was your secret existence which prevented the line from reverting to Canace upon Zita's death, though I cannot be certain."

"So, my mother was the Chosen One?"

"No, she could only ever command the element of water. She did so by ensnaring a small boat in a harbor, sucking it up through the funnel before crushing it within. Ares tested her a second time, but she was unable to bring forth another element. He was not perturbed, believing the line was evolving and that his Chosen One was getting closer. None of us had ever brought forth the water element before. And now you are here. I believe it is *you* who is the Chosen One."

"Me?" I gasped. "No, it cannot be."

"Of course it can. Do you not see the signs? You are different. You were born to a Ker and a mortal man, yet you still carry the symbol of our line. Your lover is a woman and yet you have been given a child within your union. It is as it was foretold. The change is complete."

"I …" I stood once again, pacing across the sand. Dianthe did not attempt to return me to her side this time. "As I told you when we last met, I bear no resemblance to you or the Keres. I have no wings. My nails do not extend to mirror your own. Neither are my teeth pointed or my eyes the same red as yours."

"That is true. You have your father's eyes. It is but another change to what has always come before." Now Dianthe stood. She rested a hand above my left shoulder blade. She smiled. "Your wings remain hidden beneath your skin. I feel them, and your power swirling inside you."

I reached around quickly, attempting to feel the wings for myself. Nothing. Just the smooth skin of my back. Just as it had always been. "No," I said again, though my tone held no conviction.

Dianthe smiled wider. "Yes," she insisted. "The time for you to meet your master, Ares, draws nearer. He shall have you perform the tests, and then there shall be no question for you – or us – that you are the one we have waited so many generations for."

I swallowed, uncertain what else to say to refute Dianthe's claims. She appeared so confident. So certain of who I was. "Do my skills in battle come from my mother?" I asked finally.

"Perhaps, though your father is skilled also. He would not have been chosen for Zita's watch if he was not a warrior," she replied, her voice a mixture of reverence and discontent. I nodded, dropping my eyes to my sandaled feet.

"When we learned of your existence for the first time, we learned also that your father was still alive. We had believed him dead as well as your mother. If I had been there the night of your birth, I would have recognized him. I would not have mistaken another for him and I would have known the truth about you." She paused, giving her head a shake before she continued. "I watched you with him in Anticyra. I heard him speak of his tribe of the Bessoi to you – it was how I knew for certain that was who he was."

"Though he spoke to me of his tribe then, he obviously did not share everything about why he left."

"No. But I doubt you would have been ready to hear such words. Your father has always chosen his moments to share certain knowledge with you. He is akin to Ares in that manner – our master having always known when the right time was to test those in his line. Even with you there was no exception. He now feels your time has come. Now you are ready to become who you are destined to be."

I shook my head. "You are so certain I am your Chosen One, but I do not know if I believe it."

Dianthe grinned. "When I returned to Ares after watching you in Anticyra, he was not so easily convinced either. It was only when he accompanied me and we watched your father teach you to fight atop the horses, you knocking your father from his, that he began to believe. No child, no warrior, who had so recently picked up sword or spear should have been able to fight as well as you did. But it flowed through you so naturally that there could be no mistake."

"But you have waited so long to come to me," I frowned.

"As I said, Ares knew you were not ready yet. Your wish to aid anyone who needed help. Your witness to Kuria's tragic suffering in Corinth and the responsibility you felt for it. Your acceptance of the love of your Princess. The child you assisted to create inside her. You needed to experience, overcome and accept each and every one of those tests. They shaped who you are, what you want to achieve with your life. Without them, you would not know what was truly important to you. You would not know what help to ask of Ares when you stand beside him as his Chosen One."

"But why would Ares need me to stand at his side? Why would he want to stand at mine? Is he not powerful enough already? Does he not simply want the amulet's power for himself – he is the God of *War* after all, certainly it could only benefit his love of death and chaos."

"No, no. Ares can of course wield immense power, some of those same elements from the amulet even. He can cause much war and death, just as you suggest. But in this matter alone, he would assist you in whatever your heart desires. If you wish for kingdoms to call your own or his favor in war, then he would give it. If you wish for his protection for your family, your friends, then he would give that to you without question. The Chosen One holds the key to immense power, Ares simply wishes to guide you and aid you in its use. He shall give his allegiance to you, just as you shall pledge yours to him.

"You cannot know this, but it was Ares who healed you when you first arrived in Trachis. He could not allow one he suspected of giving him what he had waited so long for to die when it was at the hand of such an insignificant mortal."

"Then it *was* a god who healed me when I first arrived here," I murmured. "I wondered later if it was Asclepius. I … I heard talking. That was you speaking to Ares, was it not?"

"Yes."

"I believed it was a dream. I did not know then that I wanted to meet any grandparent I may have."

"You are glad now that you have?"

I thought about it for a long moment. "I am."

She smiled and settled an arm around my shoulder. "As am I."

"My father told me my mother's family did not approve of him being with her; that was why they left Thrace, but that is not true, is it?"

"Not entirely. I thought well enough of him, but he would not have been accepted by the Keres. He was a mortal and as I told you, we only ever mated with male Ker from our tribe, and the Stymphalian Birds prior to that. Perhaps if I had known then that he would allow the change in the line we had waited for … well."

"Do the other Keres have the ability to command fire or the other elements?" I asked after a short silence.

"No, it is only our line or those Ares favors to use *his* gifts at certain times. The other lines gain their strength by feeding on their felled chargers. They exclusively bear strong, male children, who are then chosen as mates for the women of our line."

"Oh. Is your mother still alive, and Ptolema?"

"My mother, yes. She is eager to meet you when you are ready. Ptolema, sadly no."

"What happened to her?" I asked.

Dianthe drew a deep breath. "A wayward arrow found her chest a few winters back. She was flying down to feed on her dying charger when another warrior loosed his weapon. I attempted to deflect it, but the angle of my shield caused it to ricochet off Canace's armor and find the only unprotected part of Ptolema's body – her neck."

"I am sorry," I said quietly. "What about Canace?"

"Oh yes, she still lives. I hold no love for my niece, though I understand her desperation at wanting that power for herself. She too is eager to meet you, though I would advise you not to see her alone."

"I am not afraid of her," I said, straightening to my full height.

Dianthe smiled. "I am certain you could handle yourself against her … for a while. With the birth of her son, it was clear she could never hold the power of the Chosen One's line, but that does not make her any less of a threat to you. Ares protects you, but I would wager she would still attempt you harm if given the opportunity."

"If she was such a threat to Zita, to the line of the Chosen One, why did you not end her life winters ago, when she made attempt on my mother's life?"

"Just as we are forbidden to take the lives of mortals, so too are we forbidden to take the life of another Ker. Unless it is specifically sanctioned by our master."

"You are akin to the gods in that manner," I noted. "Zeus forbids the gods to kill one another, though there are many who would gladly dream up cruel and painful ways to do so."

"I suppose we are, though it is not surprising, given that we fall under the care of one of the greatest there is."

"If Canace attempts to harm me then I shall have no hesitation in repaying the favor," I said with a grin.

"Allow us to hope it does not come to that. Once she witnesses your intent to take the title which is rightly yours, and you have proven your skill with the amulet, I am certain she shall assist you in whatever way she can. She always bows to a higher power, and you would be far higher than she." I only nodded again, settling my eyes on the darkening sky over the Malian Gulf.

"It is time I left you," Dianthe said.

"No. We had an agreement." Dianthe was gone.

"Skylar?" a new voice called. I turned; Moeris hurried towards me. "Thaddeus said I might find you here."

"What are you doing here?" I snapped. There was so much more I wanted – needed – to know from my grandmother. The amulet for example; what did it look like? When could I meet the other relatives Dianthe spoke of? When would I meet Ares? Would I meet him? What would he think of me? The last question gave me pause, I had not always cared what others thought of me, but the God of War? If I was the one that he had waited for, if I truly was the one, I wanted to be everything he had hoped for. I wanted to make him proud, just as I had always wanted to make my father proud. My father. I frowned. He lied to me.

I stood and straightened my tunic, my eyes boring into Moeris' as he hesitated with his answer. "Well?" I prompted.

"The princess requests your return. The banquet has already begun," Moeris finally replied.

"It is too early yet," I said with a shake of my head.

"You know the queen enjoys a banquet – especially when it is held in *her* honor. Her guests have been arriving since the sun reached its highest point."

"Where is my father?" I asked, making my way across the sporadic grass.

"I heard about your confrontation with him earlier. What has you so determined to upset him? Or do you intend to make apologies?" Moeris asked, halting my progress with a firm grip on my forearm.

"It is of no concern to you," I told him with a frown, attempting to shake myself free of his hold.

"Skylar?" he asked again.

"I have no words to share with you in the matter, Moeris. I suggest you do not pursue it," I replied, finally freeing my limb.

I hastened my pace, leaving behind Moeris' questioning shouts and the man himself. Sensibly, he did not attempt to stop me again, or catch me up so he could hound me for answers. He knew what I was capable of when angered, and I was certain he would not tempt me to turn my anger on him.

How would my father react when I questioned him on what Dianthe had told me? Would he lie? Deny what she claimed my mother was – who I was destined to be? If so, how could I tell which of the two were telling the truth?

I suspected it was my grandmother, and I did not know how I felt about that.

15

I had hoped to return to our apartment and change before I encountered Alexis, but clearly she had been awaiting my return and held open the door as I entered. I stripped off my tunic, replacing it with the burgundy chiton she had selected for me.

"You promised you would be back before the banquet began," she said, taking the ends of the material to tie at my shoulder.

"And I would have if it was anyone but your mother hosting it," I replied.

"You knew she would begin celebrating as soon as her guests arrived," Alexis persisted.

I drew in a deep breath, eager to avoid an argument with Alexis as I was in no doubt that one was brewing between my father and I. I turned, smoothing the green fabric covering Alexis with one hand and cupping her chin with the other. "I know. I am sorry if I upset you," I said, kissing her. "Allow me to escort you now to your banquet."

She pressed her body the length of mine, holding me close as she pushed up onto her tiptoes for another kiss. I leant down, capturing her lips, the tip of her tongue running the length of my bottom lip. She sighed, her fingers teasing a slow line up over my ribs and across my breast, hardening my nipple beneath the material. My body heated at her touch and when I deepened our kiss, Alexis allowed the untied ends of the material to fall, effectively disrobing me once again.

"None of *my* guests have arrived yet. I believe we do not need to attend just yet." She gave me a mischievous grin, backing up until she was at the door and sliding the wooden lock down into place.

I raised an eyebrow, smirking. "It was not your wish for me to return to escort you to the banquet, but to enjoy far more pleasurable activities with you. Do I understand correctly, Princess?"

Her grin widened. "You do." With a slowness which guaranteed the temperature of my body to rise to a dangerous level, Alexis drew the pin from her shoulder, stepping out of the material pooled at her feet and back towards me.

I swallowed, mesmerized by her approach, the promise of pleasures to come written across her face. As much as I wanted to confront my father, the sight of my princess, my wife, standing naked before me with the visible swell of our child in her belly, effectively pushed thoughts of him, my grandmother and the Keres from my mind. I forgot about them all – about everyone outside our apartment as I surrendered to my lover.

*

Two candlemarks later, Alexis and I arrived at the banquet, having enjoyed one another and a number of skyphoi of wine in our apartment. It was customary for men and women to do their celebrating separately, but as with much in Trachis, Agrias was apt to discard those traditions when the occasion suited him. Thankfully, tonight was one of those times.

Alexis was at the opposite side of the room with her mother, father and a number of young women who appeared around the same age as her. I was relieved Voleta was not with them, though I had barely seen her since the night in town when Ophelos had been stabbed. I could not imagine she had been pleased to learn of my relationship with Alexis; not when she had made such a showing of wishing for me to share her bed, but she had not confronted me on it. I had since learned her husband was Epiktetos, a member of Agrias' council, and he and I had shared words on many an occasion. He had never spoken displeasure at my refusal of his wife's offer, though he had hinted he knew of its existence, and he was not a man known to keep his opinions to himself.

I turned my thoughts from Voleta and took an amphora of wine, pouring a generous amount into a kantharos and sighting my father across the room. His arm was draped casually over Nasrin's shoulder, hers around his waist. They were both laughing hard; high spots of color on their cheeks suggesting they had already enjoyed much wine.

I finished my drink and immediately poured another, draining half of it as I attempted to put my thoughts in order. Father would not deny me the answers I had about my mother. Not this time, and perhaps with the amount of wine flowing throughout the room, he would be less inclined to keep his knowledge to himself.

With the kantharos still in my hand, I made my way across the banqueting hall. Another round of laughter burst from Father's group – a number of the soldiers we trained with each morning – and they made room for me to join their gathering.

Father eyed me coldly. "Skylar."

"Father," I replied in a similar tone. The men appeared to sense the tension between us and made their excuses to leave. Beside him, Nasrin stiffened, though she remained tucked beneath his arm.

"So, come to make your apologies, have you?" he asked, his words a little slurred.

I clenched my jaw, his words stirring a sudden, fiery rage in the pit of my stomach. "No. I came to see if you would speak the truth with me after all these winters."

"The truth? What truth do you believe I have not shared with you?"

"Tell me about my mother. Who she was. *What* she was."

He blinked and his mouth hung open for a long moment before he gathered himself again, a frown deeply creasing his forehead and his eyes narrowing. "Who in Tartarus have you been speaking to?" he asked, his words no longer running together.

"What does it matter? Do you intend to keep up the pretense that she was a mortal woman?"

"Lower your voice," he hissed, stepping closer and grabbing my arm.

"For what purpose? Should not everyone know of your lies?" I shot back, shaking off his grip.

"Do not make me ask you again," he rumbled.

"Then deny what I have spoken of. Tell me it is not the truth."

"I do not have to answer you anything. I am your father and you shall show me respect." He raised his hand to strike me, the one and only time he had ever done so outside our sparring sessions. I blocked his attack, shoving him backwards. He crashed into two of the soldiers he had been speaking with when I arrived and they aided him to regain his balance.

"Tell me it is not the truth," I demanded again.

Father drew in a deep breath. "I cannot," he replied, dropping his eyes from me.

For a moment I could do nothing. Could say nothing; disbelief, hurt and betrayal chased one another through my heart and mind. Dianthe had spoken true. My father kept knowledge of who my mother and I were from me. I had always held him in such high opinion. Had believed all he had ever told me of the world, of the night my mother left us. And now ... Now ...

Fury bloomed to life in my chest, flooding my arms and legs. I charged forward, grabbing father by the top of his tunic and shaking him as I yelled.

"You lied to me. You kept kin from me. Ensured you were all I ever knew."

He did not attempt to free himself from my grip, though he wrapped his hands around my wrists painfully. "I kept you safe. Taught you and supported you as you grew. What do you think they could have given you that I did not?"

"I shall never know, shall I?"

"There is much you do not know," he said, freeing my hands from the material at his neck. I rushed him again, dealing blows against his arms and chest. He made no move to stop me or defend himself against my attack.

"Stop it," Nasrin ordered. I ignored her, continuing to pound my fists against my father's body, crying out in rage, but speaking no discernible words. Tears pricked the backs of my eyes, but I allowed none of them to fall, concentrating on the anger I felt to keep them at bay.

Two soldiers stepped into our affray. One wrapped his arms awkwardly around my chest from behind, pinning my hands in place as the other protected my father.

"Skylar, your kantharos needs refilling," Nasrin said loudly and I realized that most of the guests in the banqueting hall had stopped their conversations and were staring openly at us. I calmed in the soldier's grip. "Come then, your father and I shall see to it," Nasrin continued.

The soldier released me. Nasrin clasped my forearm painfully, her other wrapped around my father's upper arm and she led us both unceremoniously outside to the courtyard. A large number of the revelers had already spilled into the gardens, so she directed us towards their room in the north wing of the palace. As soon as we were inside and Nasrin had shut the door, my father and I burst into accusations and questions.

"Quiet! Both of you," Nasrin commanded. We fell silent. "You each have questions, though unless you wish for the entire palace to know the answers, I suggest you ask them in a far calmer fashion." Nasrin crossed her arms over her chest as she held each of our gazes with a pointed stare.

My heart pounded in my chest, breaths coming in short bursts. I was too furious to speak so it was my father who did so first, his voice even. "Who told you about Zita?"

"My grandmother."

"Your grandmother? D-Dianthe is here? When did she speak to you? You should have come directly to me when she approached you."

"So you could lie to me again?" I said, unable to keep my voice from rising. "To deny me the chance to know my mother's family?"

"They are not who you believe they are."

"I know exactly who they are – people you did not ever wish for me to meet."

"Do not be fooled, Skylar; they are not people."

"No, they are Keres. I know. That does not change the fact that you kept their existence from me. You kept my true heritage from me. Who my mother was. Who I am to be."

Father closed his eyes and drew in a deep breath, keeping them shut when he spoke again. "What did Dianthe tell you about yourself? About your mother?"

"She told me I am the Chosen One. That my mother's line carries with it the prophecy of Ares."

"Your mother never wanted that for you."

"No, she never wanted the responsibility for herself. But it is mine now and I shall take it gladly to protect the ones I love. My mother aided you and watched over you, ensured you were not harmed as you fought your enemies and protected those in your tribe. Why would you deny me the same assistance? Why would you hide me from them when they could have ensured I was not injured as I fought for those who needed aid?"

Father laughed derisively. "Ha! Is that what she told you? That they *protected* me? That that is their aim in this world? The Keres are bloodthirsty creatures who feed on the blood of the dead, on the ones they watch over from the beginning of their lives until the end. Had your mother not fallen in love with me then that would have been my fate also. They also do the bidding of their Master when he asks it of them."

"You would say anything against them. You hated that someone else could have watched over me and kept me safe. You took me away from those who call me kin. Those I would have called kin. You were determined to be the only family I knew."

"They are not as innocent as you may believe. Do not take all Dianthe tells you as truth. Ask her of the night your mother died. Ask her where *her* mother was when Zita drew her last breath."

"I am done with your lies. With your secrets. I am done with you." I crossed to the door and opened it, one foot outside as I turned back. "I do not want you to remain here in Trachis with Alexis and me. Take Nasrin and leave again."

"Skylar, no. Please. Allow us to speak of all this," Nasrin said. "Allow your father to expl–."

"No," I cut her off, wondering how long she had known what my mother was.

"Skyl–"

"No, Father. I do not want to hear anything else you have to say." I slammed the door behind me and headed across the courtyard towards the apartment Alexis and I shared. Though I knew Alexis would wonder at where I had gone, I had no wish to return to the banquet, especially when I saw Voleta and her husband Epiktetos entering the hall, their grins almost predatory as their eyes found me.

16

Discarding the long chiton I had put on for the banquet, I replaced it with a tunic, adding my armor and sliding my sword into place at my thigh. I ordered two soldiers to keep an eye on Alexis and stand guard at our door once she returned for the night before leaving the barracks and heading south-west.

I would have taken Skotos with me to hasten my departure, but I had decided not to go to the temple or the Pass as I had so often recently. It appeared too many people knew to find me there. Instead, I kept to the shadow of Mount Oetaea until I came to the Asopos River in a gorge between the mountains of Oetaea and Kallidromon. When the river branched, I followed the new stream further into the mountains – the ground beginning its incline where it met a rarely-used dirt path.

When I was searching for a suitable training area recently, I had found the pass on the mountain. Returning to Trachis that evening, I had questioned Agrias on its existence, but it was Melina who spoke knowledge of it. She told us that many winters ago travelers and merchants used the track when making their journey north from central and southern Greece. These days though, they remained on the road along the Malian Gulf or took a straighter path between the mountains of Parnassus and Kallidromon, as Alexis and I had when we travelled to Epidaurus. The mountain path was too difficult for the merchants' heavily-laden mules or oxen to traverse. I had not been very far along the walkway, but Melina said it wound around to Alpeni at Pylae on the gulf – or at least it used to. I wondered if there was also still a path to the west that met the main road near Mount Parnassos.

I trampled along, attempting to keep out the thoughts which threatened to overwhelm me. I ducked beneath low-hanging branches of the oak trees lining the track, still more slapping me in the face. The sun was almost fully behind the mountains when I reached the furthest part of the path I had been along. I had not brought a torch with me so I stopped, sitting beneath one of the large oaks.

The thoughts I had managed to keep at bay during my travel, sprung to mind too easily, their weight a crushing force at my chest as I attempted to draw breath against their severity. *My father lied to me about my mother. He knew what she was, what I could become. And he kept it from me.* My fingers pressed into the dirt beside me. *How could I have trusted him so blindly? How could I have simply allowed him to turn from conversations about her so easily? Why did I never press him to know more about her family and his?* I knew the answer: I had never wondered about them because he had never made them appear important. He made himself important. Only him. He made me believe he was sacrificing a normal life for himself so I could be safe as we travelled from town to town, aiding those who required it or asked it of us. But it was never about me. It was always about him. About keeping me from Dianthe and my mother's kin. I had often wondered if he was afraid they would take me from him because they did not approve of his relationship with my mother. Now I knew that to be the truth, only not the true reason why.

What else had he lied to me about? How many of the stories he told me about Theseus or Heracles were pure fabrications? Perhaps Heracles did not turn the spring at Thermopylae hot. Perhaps it was the Dyras River which saw his poison washed off. Or perhaps it was as Thaddeus believed; that Heracles had died across the Gulf at Euboea. Or maybe it was as Cleomenes' healer, Macrobio, had said – that he was in Thessaly, and it was only his final resting place which saw him at Mount Kallidromon.

I picked up a handful of small pebbles and pulled green acorns from the oak's branches above my head. Sighting a tree with a thick trunk on the opposite side of the path, I lined it up and threw one of the nuts in my hand. I missed by quite a distance. Growling at the attempt, I threw another and another. Same result each time. Finally, I stood, turning sideways to the tree and narrowing my eyes, focusing only on the dark bark. I drew my arm back and loosed the acorn. It hit with an echoing crack, no doubt having split the nut's skin. I cheered myself, the triumph at finally hitting the stupid tree turning into a flood of hot tears.

It had been my father who taught me to focus on a distant target, who had taught me to find the center with deadly accuracy. I allowed my tears to fall, sliding back to the base of the oak tree and wrapping my arms around my drawn-up legs. Hiccupping breaths accompanied my sobs, but I did not attempt to quiet them until much later, when the pain at his betrayal had once again been replaced by anger.

"What else did you lie to me about? How can I ever trust you again?" I yelled into the darkened tree line.

"With time and further conversations with your father, I am certain you shall forgive him and learn that what he did was for the best. For you both," Nasrin's voice was soft, but still it startled me. She stepped out onto the path, a blazing torch casting shadows and light across her face. I had once again been so consumed by my own thoughts that I failed to notice the approaching light.

I scrambled to my feet, stumbling slightly as I swiped at my eyes. "I have no words to speak with you," I insisted.

"But I have some to share with you," she said, pinning me with a hard stare. My jaw clenched but I did not drop my gaze, having no intention of being the first to do so.

"How long have you known about who – what – my mother truly was?" I demanded.

"Wine?" she offered, ignoring my question and holding up an amphora and two cups. Without waiting for an answer, she set the torch into the vee of two branches and poured each of us a skyphos.

"How long?" I pressed, belatedly wondering how she had found me.

"He was scared," Nasrin replied, once again refusing to answer my question. "He regrets what he has kept from you."

I opened my mouth, prepared to unleash an angry tirade, but halted at the glare she gave me. I had never seen Nasrin look as serious, or as fierce, as she did at that moment. Since her arrival in Trachis, Nasrin had become akin to a mother figure to me. Melina too, to some extent. Both treated me as their own child, offering guidance or someone to enjoy womanly pursuits at the agora or in the queen's sewing room with. I had gone from no mother figures, to having two within the space of a few moons. Just as the daughter Alexis grew inside her belly would have. Tonight however, I wished it was as it was before with none considering me their daughter. I closed my mouth again and took the skyphos of wine she offered.

"Parents do not always tell their children everything," Nasrin continued before taking a swallow from her cup. "They cannot, as much for their own sake, as for that of their children. Your father did the best he could in a situation he never imagined himself, or you, in."

"You have known for some time about my mother, about what she was, about what I am." This time I did not pose it as a question to her, but rather a statement.

"I do not know everything, I am certain, but your father and I have spoken of much since reuniting in Konitsa. He did not want any secrets between us. He had kept many from me when I last travelled with you, though I had shared all of mine with him."

"He appears apt at keeping much to himself," I murmured.

"Can you blame him? How do you think you would have reacted had he told you what your mother was? What there was a chance you were? He would not do it to you. He wanted it no more for you than your mother did. When I saw him again in Konitsa, he had lost much of the fear he once held that Zita's family would find you both. He spoke with pride to Irina, Theron and myself of the woman you had become. Of the warrior and loyal person you were. He spoke to us of the love you had found here in Trachis and how he believed he need not fear interference from your mother's family any longer. There was no sign you possessed any of her traits." I did not speak as Nasrin took a moment to gather her breath from the speech.

"As I am certain you are aware, Theron and Irina have known your father for many winters. They also knew your mother and they asked Leandros many questions about his time since last they were together. He answered them all, filling in the story for me as he spoke. He and I did not finish our conversations about you until after ..." She faltered. I drew a breath, understanding she was about to say *until after Ava's death*. "Until after we left Konitsa on our way back here. But I know that instead of burdening you with his own fears, he put away his pain and his anger at Zita's family and he loved you without question. He ensured you had everything you needed, everything he could provide. Never once did he consider leaving you, you must know that." I only grunted a reply, though I knew deep down that much at least was true.

"There was much I kept from my own daughter. We had always been close, but there were truths I never shared with her. I did not believe she needed to know of them. Indeed I still do not believe if I had my time again, that I would tell her all the reasons which saw us leave Pārsa and come to Greece."

"Pārsa?" I frowned.

"Apologies, you know Pārsa as Persia. Your father is the only one who knows the entire story."

"Do you plan on telling me or are you just going to hide behind half-made statements and believe that I shall not press you for answers either?" I asked, my frown deepening.

Nasrin took a deep breath before she replied. "If you wish to hear my truths, then I shall tell them to you."

I did not reply right away, surprised she would actually make the offer. "I shall listen," I told her, some of my anger dissipating as curiosity bloomed.

Though Nasrin and I had grown closer since her return to Trachis with my father, I realized I knew very little of her past, and clearly what I had learned when she and Ava travelled with us four winters ago was far from the entire story.

Nasrin nodded and swallowed audibly, settling herself beneath one of the oaks and offering me a place beside her. I remained a little way from her, wanting to see her face as she spoke but I sat down, taking another drink from my cup as she did the same. "You know I was born in Babylon, though it was not merely to a noble family as I would have had you and Ava believe," she said. "My father, Nidintu-Bel, was the son of Nabonidus, regent of Babylon. My grandfather had not been in Babylon for many winters and so it was my uncle, Belshazzar, who ruled over our city in his absence. I also had three aunts, two of whom were wives of Persian men, and Bel-shalti-nanna, who was the high priestess of our moon-god, Sin. My mother was there also, though I do not remember her as she died before my third winter.

"The same winter that my mother died, my grandfather returned to Babylon. He wished to assist Uncle Belshazzar in devising a strategy against Cyrus, King of Pārsa. It had been reported that the king intended to march upon us and take Babylon for himself. Cyrus' men came, his chief governor, Gubaru, entering the city without a fight and demolishing our outer walls."

"Why did your people not defend themselves?" I asked.

"A great festival was being held and those who should have, did not notice the Persians divert the Euphrates River into a canal and enter through the dry channels."

"Oh," I said, uncertain what else to add.

"Belshazzar was killed and grandfather fled to Borsippa, leaving the rest of us to fend for ourselves. When Cyrus then turned to Borsippa, my grandfather surrendered, agreeing to renounce his claim to ownership of Babylon. Cyrus accepted and allowed my grandfather to go to Carmania, where I presume he still lives – if he has not passed into the next life. Half a moon later, Cyrus returned to Babylon and proclaimed peace. He spoke with all rulers of the former Chaldean empire and spoke of fulfilling the will of Marduk."

"Who was Marduk, and why did a king of Persia need to fulfil his will?" I interrupted.

"Marduk is the Babylonian god akin to the Greek god Zeus – chief god of all. He is known by fifty names and holds the power of thunder and lightning bolts. He conquered the monster of chaos named Tiamat to become God of Earth and God of the Sky. We Babylonians believe we owe our existence, and the existence of nature itself, to Marduk. Without him we would not be. Our destiny is in his hands."

"Oh," I said again, briefly wishing Alexis could hear Nasrin's tale – she would love learning of the gods from across the waters.

"In this manner, Cyrus believed himself to be doing as Marduk wished and set about re-affirming our standing with many other nations, ordering exiled deities my grandfather had banished to be returned to the city and displayed for all to see. And, most importantly for many in the city, he decreed that the Jews be allowed return to their homes in Judea, to the south-west of Babylon, near Egypt if that was their wish.

"When he spoke with my father and the others who had once held positions of power in Babylon, he gave them a choice; to either accept that Babylon would now answer to Pārsa and remain as nobles in the city or find themselves banished to the desert where certain death awaited them. There was no choice for my father – with the recent death of my mother, he knew he must remain in Babylon and care for me. He also feared the same fate would await him if he attempted to take the throne from Cyrus, though it rightfully belonged to him.

"He no longer held a royal title, neither of us did, but we were comfortable and our home was grand. I was educated in the art of archery and horseback riding, as other noble children were. In addition, I was taught matters of coin and negotiation, for my mother had left me a stretch of land with a home on it and I was expected to take care of and accept coin in exchange for another family to live there.

"We remained in comfort and safety until my twelfth winter. Cyrus returned to Pāsārgād not long after he was in Babylon, but for the entire three moons of every winter thereafter, he and his nobles returned, overseeing their administration from our city. Travel to and from the mountain location of the capital was almost impossible during the rains, so Pāsārgād was only used in the summer and spring. It was during one of those particular winters that I met Darius, the man who is now King of Persia, and my life was completely changed."

17

"The nobles of Pāsārgād had been in Babylon for a number of weeks and many of them spent time at our markets, partaking of much wine which always led to disagreements and fights. I was also there, my tutor teaching me to barter a better price for the items we needed for our home – whether it be food, clothing or wine.

"We had almost finished our lesson when I noticed a young man of perhaps twenty winters following us; pausing at the stall beside and pretending to inspect the merchandise he found as he watched us from the corner of his eye. He was attractive enough I suppose, but appeared self-important, buying items without attempting to bargain for them, and then passing them off to surprised young women he passed. He followed us for half a candlemark before I finally confronted him. He did not confirm, nor deny, that he had been doing so, smiling arrogantly and telling me we would meet again soon.

"I did not see him again for another two weeks, and had all but forgotten him, until he arrived at our home and asked to speak with my father. I was sent to the back room to prepare food for our guest, but hid instead, listening to each word spoken. I expected to hear words of a proposal, and I wondered if my father would deny him as I was already promised to another, or if the young man came from a higher standing Persian family, and therefore offered far more coin which my father would not refuse."

"The young man was Darius?" I guessed.

Nasrin nodded. "He was but a noble's son at the time. Not yet old enough to enter Cyrus' army, yet wishing for all the glory he believed it would bring. There was something about him which made me uneasy, though I could not have said what it was at that moment."

"Did he ask to wed you?"

"No. He said he had observed me in the market and believed I would make an excellent slave as I was skilled in the act of barter."

"A slave?" I echoed.

Nasrin nodded again. "In those days, the royal Persian families had no slaves, but the nobles had enough for them both."

"What did your father do?"

"He denied him. Told him I was worth far more to him than the amount Darius would pay to have me as a slave. As you may imagine, Darius was furious, he was not used to being denied anything; such was the standing of his family name. He attempted not to show it and returned the following day, attempting to persuade my father with offers of further coin and riches, land, status, whatever he desired. My father would not be swayed and Darius left again.

"When Darius returned a third time, his polite request, his friendly manner had disappeared and he threatened my father and our family. He said he had the ear of King Cyrus, and if my father did not gift him with me, he would see to it that the king learned of a treasonous attempt at murder. Darius promised he would ensure my father and the rest of our family were killed, our home burnt to the ground before he swooped in and *saved* me. Ensuring he got me without having to part with any of the coin he had spoken of."

"Did Darius somehow know you were once royalty? Is it why he suggested purchasing you as a slave rather than as a wife?"

"He did not know of my lineage then. He just wanted what he wanted, and he was rarely denied anything."

"What happened ? Did your father still tell him no?"

"He did, and it was this final denial which set Darius and I on the course to be inextricably linked forever. Three days went by and we neither saw, nor heard from, Darius. My father believed the young man must have found wise council and been encouraged to accept his answer. But … I later learned that Darius had used the time to learn my daily activities and movements. When he had all the information he required, he returned to our house, finding me alone there preparing the evening meal for my father and the guests he would entertain that night. He was silent as he entered, surprising me and placing a dagger at my throat, urging me to keep quiet as he had his way with me. When he was done, I could barely move. My clothing was bloodied and torn, my skin scraped and bleeding. As he turned to leave, Darius promised that no husband would want me now and that my father should have taken the generous offer he extended. He laughed and returned his dagger to its holder, threatening to return because he could."

"Nasrin," I whispered, thoughts of Kuria's damaged body filling my head. "I am so sorry."

She only nodded in reply and continued. "My best friend, BehnAm, whom I had known for many winters, had been invited to my father's banquet with his own father. It was he who found me after Darius was gone. He aided me to clean up and dispose of the evidence of what had happened, vowing to find the one who had so defiled me and kill him. I begged him to leave Darius alone. I did not want BehnAm in danger and made him swear that we would never speak of it again. I felt such shame and I would not bring the same down onto my father or our family by allowing anyone else to know what had happened. Besides, if Darius was as influential as he claimed, who would believe me and take any action against him?"

"Did Darius return as he promised?" I asked quietly, rising from the ground and resettling myself beside Nasrin, reaching for her hand and squeezing it gently when she put it in mine.

"No. BehnAm told me his father had recalled him to Pāsārgād, and he left immediately. I cannot tell you how relieved I was to learn of it, though there was yet more I had to endure by his hand, however indirectly it may appear." Nasrin paused again.

"If it is too painful to speak of, you do not have to," I told her, recalling all too well how difficult it had been to speak of my own shame with Alexis.

"It is not that. It was all such a long time ago. I cannot say I have fully made my peace with everything that happened, but I know one day Darius shall pay for what he did to me."

"What happened after Darius left?" I asked after a few moments.

"I learned I was with child. There was no mistaking whose it was, for I had laid with no other. BehnAm insisted I finally tell my father what had happened with Darius, but still I refused to do so. BehnAm broke his word to me and told Arakha – my future husband and a man I trusted as much as BehnAm. The three of us had spent much time together in the winters since Cyrus had come to Babylon. Arakha served my uncle in the army before his death and provided protection for my father afterwards. Arakha was older than BehnAm and I by almost five winters, but he too had no siblings and the three of us grew close quickly, my father naming him as my future husband the winter before.

"Arakha was just as incensed at what Darius had done as BehnAm and he too vowed to go to Persia and kill him. I told him he could not as the shame which would be cast upon all of us would ensure Darius truly won. We would not have been able to show ourselves in Babylon, and where could we go with such a knowledge following us? He agreed to keep my secret and we planned to get rid of the baby when it arrived.

"But before it did, my father learned of its existence. He was furious, demanding I tell him who I had laid with. I refused to speak the name and he threatened to turn me from our home. My father believed the good marriage he had intended for me was now in jeopardy and he called me many hurtful names until BehnAm told the lie which has haunted me for many winters." Nasrin paused and I settled an arm around her shoulders, waiting for her to go on. "BehnAm claimed responsibility for my condition, though he told my father he had raped me; that I did not lie willingly with him as he suspected I may have. BehnAm said he was jealous my father had named Arakha as my intended, rather than himself and that he took me against my will as punishment for it. I wanted to deny his words, but BehnAm demanded my silence, allowing my father to hand down his punishment: death."

"Nasrin, I am so sorry," I whispered.

"I attempted to stop the execution, threatening to tell my father the truth, however unwilling I was to do so, to save BehnAm's life. He would not allow me and told Arakha and I that it was best for all concerned if he took the blame and we continued on in our lives together. Reluctantly we allowed him to die with the honor he wanted, though it was only the two of us who knew of his honorable sacrifice. Arakha spoke with my father, telling him he would still have me, despite what had happened.

"We were wed barely a week later so to all outside our home, it would appear that our wedding night was a success, and I carried the child of our union. When my daughter was born, we did not give her away as we originally planned, but kept her, promising to teach her to be as kind and unselfish as BehnAm had been. We kept her in his memory, and in defiance for what Darius had done to us. Arakha and I could not have been happier to welcome her into our home."

"The daughter ... that was Ava?"

"Yes."

"She never knew Darius was her father."

"No. Not even when we found ourselves in his palace nine winters later."

"How did that come to pass?"

"Cyrus died the same winter Arakha and I were wed. His son, Cambyses the Second, succeeded him without incident, though there had been rumor that Darius may attempt to claim the throne for himself. Cambyses ruled for eight winters before he too died and a man claiming to be his brother took the throne. Darius, who was by then high in the ranks of the Persian army, serving as Cambyses' royal spearman, did not believe the man was who he said he was and worked tirelessly to prove it. Darius eventually killed the imposter and took the throne and title King of Persia for himself.

"When we learned Darius had been officially named as King, Arakha said he could not keep silent any longer. He told my father the truth of what had happened to me by Darius and how BehnAm had died needlessly. My father was almost as enraged at the news as he had been when he learned I was pregnant and he vowed that, king or not, Darius would be made to pay for what he had done.

"My father re-named himself Nebuchadnezzar the Third and took back his rightful title of King of Babylon. He put to death those who had been loyal to Cambyses and Cyrus during their reigns and ensured any of Darius' followers in Babylon were also killed. My father had hoped to face Darius personally in the ensuing battle, but he did not – Darius sent his man Zopyrus instead.

"Zopyrus claimed he was glad Darius sent him, as he did not wish to call him King any more than we did. It was a lie but there were too many who had believed him, and he enacted the downfall of my father's rebellion, retaking Babylon for Darius and Persia."

"What happened to your father?" I asked, though I could already guess the answer.

"Zopyrus killed him before he returned to Persia. Arakha felt responsible for my father's death. He had been the one to speak the truth of Darius' treatment of me, and he had also been one of the first to believe Zopyrus' story about wanting to defect from Darius' army. He swore he would make Darius pay."

"I cannot imagine it ended well for him," I murmured.

"No."

"He sounds a good man."

"He was a wonderful husband, friend and lover, and we had many happy times together. There were of course hard times, such as the deaths of two of our children but overall we were happy together."

18

"You had more children than just Ava?" I asked, having never considered the possibility.

"Yes. The winter after Ava was born, I birthed a son named Aspamitres. Over the next four winters I birthed a son and a daughter, though neither saw their first moon before they passed. When Arakha decided to rebel once again against Persia, Aspamitres was not in Babylon and I was pregnant again.

"We sent word to the friend Aspamitres travelled with, asking him to continue onto Ur, where my aunt was the head priestess, rather than returning home. Arakha wanted me to take Ava and go as well before the Persians arrived, but I would not, determined not to leave his side, just as he had never left mine all those winters, despite the knowledge that there was little I would be able to do in a battle in my current condition.

"Arakha reluctantly allowed us to remain with him in the palace that had once belonged to my uncle and grandfather and named himself as a son of my father. He gave himself the title of Nebuchadnezzar the Fourth and incited another rebellion from the people of Babylon."

"Darius finally came to Babylon, determined to put down the rebellion once and for all. When he found me there and learned the man calling himself Nebuchadnezzar was my husband, he ordered his men to capture Arakha's chief followers. Then, he gained entry to the palace and killed Arakha without hesitation and without honor – sending him to Ereshkigal in the Underworld as he slept.

"Darius took Ava and me from the palace, saying he would not be denied me this time, though I would return with him to Pāsārgād not as a slave, but as his wife to produce strong sons for his line. It was three winters before Ava and I saw Aspamitres again."

"He allowed you to take Ava with you?" I asked, surprised.

"Yes," Nasrin nodded.

"Did he question if Ava was his, given her age?"

"He did, but I insisted she was Arakha's daughter. Thankfully she had not inherited her father's eye color so he could not be certain. I told Darius he had not spoiled me at all. My husband loved me and our children proved our devotion and love to one another.

"Darius was angry, though he hid it well behind his arrogance. I believe he only allowed Ava to return with him to Persia as he harbored doubt about my answer as to the truth of who her father was. He could not bring himself to kill her if she was of his flesh."

"Ah," I nodded.

"I was terrified of how he would treat me but found that I suffered less from his hand, than that of his favorite wife and queen – Atossa."

"You spoke of being with child when Arakha raised his rebellion. Did you birth that child in Persia?"

"Yes. Ava and I had been there less than a moon when I birthed a daughter named Andia. I named her as soon as she was pulled from my body, mouth open and screaming for all to hear, but I did not get to hold her. She was taken from me, Darius intended to have her killed, for now that I was his wife, he could not have me mothering children to other men."

"Did he kill her?" I asked carefully.

"I can only imagine it to be so, if she survived past her first moon. My previous two children had not so I cannot be certain she had the strength to do so," Nasrin replied with a sad shrug. "I never heard her spoken of again – not even by the woman who had taken her away, and she was one of the chief midwives in the palace so she was there often."

"May I ask what suffering you endured at the hand of Darius' queen?"

"Anything you can imagine. She marked my face, my body, caused *accidents* so Darius could not lie with me. She was determined to produce a son who would be named as successor upon Darius' death, her jealousy at my arrival barely veiled, even in Darius' presence."

"Could you not speak to him about it? Ask him to protect you?"

"Why would I have done that? I wanted nothing to do with him. I was almost glad Atossa hated me so much, though at times I wondered if I would see another day in the palace. Every night Darius was kept from my bedchamber was a blessing."

"I see," I murmured with a slow nod.

"It did not keep him from me all the time, but with my wounds he showed far more care than the first time he had me in Babylon. Besides, had it not been for my constant injuries, I would never have been able to spend so much time with Democedes – Darius' chief physician, and the man who aided me in my escape from Pāsārgād."

"I recall you spoke of his assistance in fleeing Persia," I nodded.

Nasrin smiled, as though remembering the man she spoke of, and I allowed her the reverie before she spoke again. "Darius had told me he intended to gift Ava to Democedes as incentive for him to remain in Pāsārgād. You see, Democedes too, was not originally from Persia, but taken as a spoil of war when the Persians defeated Polycrates at Samos. Democedes wished to return to his home in Croton but Darius claimed he was far too valuable to lose; having healed both the king and queen on a number of occasions, as well as the excellent care he took of me.

"Democedes had no interest in accepting the gift – Ava was a mere child at eight winters old and he held a fondness for her only akin to that of a father. When Atossa learned I carried a child inside, and this time there was no doubt it belonged to Darius, she increased her attacks against me. She was also pregnant and determined it would be her child named as Darius' successor, not mine. She caused me great harm and when I birthed Darius' son, he was not alive. Soon after, she birthed their son Xerxes, her plan perfectly executed with her husband none the wiser.

"Democedes of course knew what had occurred, and we began to conspire to be rid of our Persian master. After a number of moons, he was able to get Darius to agree to send him to Greece to explore the option of war against the west. Unfortunately, Darius had by then put another child in my belly. This time though, Democedes and I were able to keep the knowledge from all those in the palace and when my son Artabanus arrived, Democedes arranged for him to be sent to Verkâna – or as the Greeks call it, Hyrcania – with a woman who traded with the palace.

"As soon as Artabanus was safe, Democedes performed a procedure on my stomach, which nearly killed me, but he assured me it would prevent me from ever carrying another child for the king. He was due to set sail for Greece the following week, taking his future wife, Ava, with him. They left with the company of men and ships Darius had allowed and it was many weeks before we heard any news from them.

"When word was received, it was not happy for Darius. His men reported that Democedes has escaped from them, taking Ava with him and returning to his home in Croton. I waited another few days, until finally a messenger arrived from Democedes telling me Ava was safe and well in Miletus where I could meet her and leave, just as he had.

"I was overjoyed our plan had succeeded, needing only to create my own story before leaving to ensure Darius never came looking for me. I feigned lamentation at hearing of my daughter's disappearance and the inability of Darius' men to secure her and Democedes and return her to me in Pāsārgād. I appeared to grow more and more despondent until finally almost a moon after Democedes' message had arrived, it was reported to palace officials that I slipped out during the night.

"Democedes had a number of friends in the palace who were only too willing to lie for the two of us, and they told Darius I had trekked up the mountain to the north-west, slipping and falling as they watched."

"Did Darius or Atossa ask for proof of your death – a body or some other token?"

"I have no doubt they would have, and we made provision for it; Democedes' friends were given the story that wolves had claimed the broken pieces left behind before they could rescue them from their fearsome mouths. I can only presume the explanation was accepted, for I heard no rumor that Darius sought me."

"So you came to Greece after that? What about the sons you had sent to safety? They were not with you when Father and I met you in Hermione."

"No," Nasrin replied with a shake of her head. "After I collected Ava from Miletus we did go to Ur where Aspamitres was still with my aunt. I am certain he would have come to Greece with us, had he not overheard Bel-shalti-nanna and me conversing about the terrible things that had happened to me in Persia. Aspamitres never appeared more akin to his father and grandfather than he did at that moment – insisting Darius and Atossa pay for what they had done; from the killing of his father and siblings to their treatment of me.

"He was bent on revenge, and though he spoke words of agreement when I told him there was nothing to be done and we were better to just leave, he snuck away during the night. He warned the couple who had taken Artabanus for me that Darius had learned he was his son and intended to find them and kill them for their disloyalty. By the time Ava and I reached Verkâna, they were long gone. I had no idea where to begin looking for them, nor for Artabanus, who had also disappeared. I did not feel it was safe to remain in Persia and in the end, I had no choice but to go ahead with my original plans, putting the last of my affairs in order before Ava and I returned to Miletus and the boat that would take us to a new life in Greece."

"You ... you made a difficult choice to leave your sons behind in Persia."

"Yes. I had hoped that once we were reunited, I could put behind me the past of having to send my children away to remain safe from those who would do them harm." She gave a humorless laugh. "One was the prince of Babylon, the other the prince of Persia, though neither are likely to ever be called the same. Indeed, they may never grow past their childhood, such is the reckless and unpredictable nature of revenge. If Aspamitres faces Darius or convinces Artabanus to before he is ready or has the skills to carry out the harm he intends, well … perhaps I have already lost my boys to careless actions."

"You do not mourn them?" I asked, noting that no tears fell across her cheeks as she spoke of the possible deaths of her children.

"I mourned them the day I left Persia, and many days both before and after. I cannot change their fate any more than I can change my own. I wish they would join me here in Greece, that I could look upon their faces and see the young men they are becoming, but I do not hold out hope it shall be so, and after so many winters, how could they know where to look for me, or how to find me? Aspamitres especially has never even seen my face. I choose instead to believe that they remain in Persia, biding their time and learning all they must before they face Darius." Nasrin paused and I found no words to fill the silence that ensued. "So, that is my story and now perhaps you understand that parents do not – indeed cannot – always speak of what has come before, of who their kin are, for fear of the child rejecting themselves or fearing themselves. Perhaps if Ava knew her father was Darius, she would have believed there existed evil or malice inside her, just as he possessed."

"Or perhaps it is yet another compelling case of parental selfishness. Perhaps if Ava had learnt her father was Darius, she would have chosen to remain in Persia to get to know him and you would have had to leave without her," I countered, though my words had lost some of their earlier sting.

"Just because one particular parent is not there, it does not mean that they could have enriched the child's life if it were so. Of course, it depends on circumstance, but in this case, I do not believe it to be so. Nor do I believe your father thought it worth the risk to allow you to know of the creatures your mother called kin." I opened my mouth to argue, but Nasrin continued before I could. "Your father and I did the best we could under the circumstances we found ourselves in. We were gifted children who did not come to us in quite the way we imagined, but we kept you safe, loved and cared for you the best we knew how." Nasrin stood, picking up the amphora and torch once again. "If you cannot understand that to be the case, then perhaps you ought to think on it some more. You shall soon find yourself with one who calls you their parent and there shall be decisions you have to make to keep her safe, of that I am certain. It is the world in which we live that sees it so. Do not judge Leandros too harshly. He believed he was doing the right thing for you, for you both, by not speaking of it. Speak with him now. Hear his side of the tale, you owe him that much at least." I found myself without a reply once more, though Nasrin did not appear to want one. "Allow us to return to the palace together, unless you wish to make your way back alone?"

I hesitated. I was far from ready to speak with my father about anything and would have been content with my own thoughts, but I was not certain I could find my way back in the dark. I drained my wine and gave Nasrin a nod. "I shall walk with you," I replied.

Nasrin gave her own nod and we began to make our way back along the path and down the mountain towards Trachis.

When Nasrin and I arrived back at the palace, she did not press me to join her or speak with my father. She simply took my hand in hers and squeezed gently. "Think on what I said. Find a way to forgive him and then learn all he has to tell you of your mother's family." I said nothing, only nodded in reply.

I dismissed the two soldiers waiting and pushed open the door to our apartment, Alexis rising from the bed and wrapping her arms around my waist, careful not to injure herself on my cuirass when I entered.

"Thank the gods," she murmured. "Where have you been? I was worried."

"I am sorry," I replied, placing a kiss on the top of her head.

She drew back, placing a hand on the hinge at my side and I nodded. With practiced efficiency, Alexis took off my armor and placed it over the chair.

"Talk to me," she said, pulling me towards the bed. "What happened? Why did you attack your father?"

I sat beside her, keeping her hand between mine as I exhaled a long breath. "My grandmother is here. She has told me much about my past. Many things my father has kept from me."

"Leandros' mother is here? When did she arrive? Why have you not introduced us, did he not know she was coming?"

"It is not his mother. It is Zita's."

"Oh."

"I ... I have met with her a number of times late at night these past weeks."

"Oh, thank the gods," Alexis exhaled, her chin dropping to touch her chest with obvious relief.

I frowned, lifting her chin so our eyes met. "You are relieved I have been meeting with her?"

"I ... er," Alexis stammered, her cheeks heating beneath my stare. "I knew you had been going *somewhere* at night. I have often woken and found you gone. I thought ..."

"What?"

"It feels so foolish now to say it ... Hesper warned I might have irrational thoughts whilst our child grew inside me and I ... well I feared ...

as I have not given you the attention you deserve of late that y–"

"Alexis," I scolded. "How could you even consider it? After all we have been through? Yes! I crave to hold you and love you as I did before you were with child, but I would never go to another for that. I want no one else."

"I know, I know. I am sorry. It is why I never said anything. Hesper assured me it would not be true, Thaddeus as well. But Moeris avoided my questions when I asked him why he found himself outside our door when you were gone. His reluctance to give me answers fueled my doubt."

"So that is why Thaddeus came looking for me," I murmured, closing my eyes briefly. "I am sorry I gave you a reason to think I would be with someone else. I have not known how to tell you about Dianthe or what she spoke of. I do not want to keep things from you, especially something as big as this."

"Dianthe. Your grandmother. Share her words with me now."

I nodded and told Alexis everything from the moment I first met Dianthe at the agora, when Thaddeus and I were collecting the wine for my father's banquet, to the argument I had with my father earlier and to Nasrin's confessions on Mount Kallidromon.

"Are you certain what Dianthe told you is true?" Alexis asked when I was finished.

"What reason does she have to lie to me? She has provided enough proof, and my father's reaction speaks louder than anything else. He was furious the truth had come to light after so many winters. I caught him in his lies."

"Perhaps. Though perhaps there is more at work here. She gave you an explanation as to why they have not come to you before, but can you be certain she speaks without hidden reasons of her own?"

I shrugged. "Perhaps I am unable to tell anymore who speaks true and who does not. If you met her you may find the truth or lies easier. Would you do that?"

"I am not certain it is a good idea. Your father would not be pleased you are meeting her again."

"It is none of his business if I choose to meet Dianthe again. I want the truth, and the only way to get that is to see her again." Alexis nodded slowly, weighing up my words. "Of course … if you are with me, you can ask Dianthe about her past, learn more about the places she has been, what the lands beyond those you know consist of, how the people there dress or speak …"

Alexis shook her head, but she was grinning. "You seek to entice me by using my weakness for knowledge? Who is the devious one now, *Princess*?"

She loaded the final word and I smiled, raising an eyebrow. "Did it work?"

"Yes," she replied. "You know I could not resist such an opportunity."
"Good," I grinned, placing a kiss on her lips.

19

"You are well?" I asked Gnosidicus when he opened the door.

"I am," he replied, stepping aside to allow me to enter. "The men you sent have treated me with dignity and friendship, and for that I thank you."

"Of course," I said, inclining my head. The men he spoke of were waiting outside, the two having alternated between inside and outside duty for the past moon. "They have not caused your wife and daughter too much trouble feeding them?"

"Not at all, I believe my family enjoy cooking for more than just me," he grinned.

"Good. I have not seen Antigonos since we last spoke but Agrias has banned him from the council meeting tomorrow and I intend to visit him tonight."

"You are delivering news of his banishment?"

"No, he is already aware of it, though I would have loved to be the one to tell him," I grinned."

"I am glad you are to see him – his wives may have suffered his anger since he was told. I have not been called to his home for almost a moon, or received reports his family are unwell, or attended by another, but would you ask to see them for yourself while you are there?"

"I shall. The women are the reason I want to go see him. Is there anything else you need? Herbs? Wine?"

"No, I have all I need here, and the soldiers accompany me to the agora when the need arises."

"Good," I nodded again. "I shall see you tomorrow." Gnosidicus opened the door for me again, the older of the two soldiers entering when I stepped out. "Sleep well," I told him, turning from the muted light of his torches and making my way to the opposite end of town.

The door was answered by a young woman I knew was one of Antigonos' wives. "May I come in?" I asked. She nodded in reply, calling to the other women when I entered.

"You have news of Antigonos?" one of them asked.

I frowned and shook my head. "Why would I have news? Your husband is not here with you?"

"No, he left two days ago. He did not say where he was going, but he has not returned," the same woman replied.

I growled, yanking open the door again and stepping out onto the street. "Brygos!" I yelled. The young man appeared from the shadows of a home across the road, crossing quickly to me. "Antigonos has gone."

"What? When? I have been here for the past week, just as you asked. I swear, I have nev–"

I held my hand up. "Two days ago. You did not realize you had not seen him going to the agora or visiting friends for *two* days?"

"Skylar, I am sor–"

"Do not be sorry. Just go back to the barracks. I shall decide what to do with you later." Brygos dropped his gaze, his feet dragging as he returned to the palace.

I turned back to Antigonos' wives clustered in the doorway. I stalked over to them. "I need a torch." The youngest wife fetched one and handed it over quickly. I spun on my heel, taking a step forward before facing the women again. "Are all of you well? Do you need the healer?" They shook their heads, appearing frightened with the suggestion. "Do not be afraid to seek Gnosidicus if you need him. I do not believe your husband shall return. Not yet at least," I muttered the last words.

They nodded and hurriedly closed the door before opening it again a moment later and sending three out in the direction of Gnosidicus'. I waved to the remaining women and set off. If Antigonos had left town, I believed he would go back to Epirus and when I had proof of that, I would advise Agrias. I did not expect Antigonos to return unless Andreas or the Molossian army was by his side.

I hurried to the last of the houses on the north end of town, all but one lit by torches in the windows. I slowed and drew my sword from its sheath, approaching the darkened one. The roof had caved in on one end, the rest barely held aloft on the charcoaled wooden beams. I ran a finger over the wood, the ash blackening my hands, still warm as though the fire had only recently burnt out. I rounded the house, smelling the death before I saw it.

He was strung up from the tree overhanging his yard, half his body burned beyond recognition, the other sliced with shallow, but painful cuts. I wrapped one arm around his legs, my other slicing through the rope noose and freeing him. I sent a quick prayer to the gods asking Charon still accept him as I lay him down and went to the closest house.

I knocked, noting movement inside and a cry of fear before it went silent ago. I gripped my sword tighter and barged inside, finding a man and his wife huddled together by their hearth, eyes wide as they took in my armor and weapon. "When did Antigonos burn the house next door?" I demanded.

"T-two days ago," the man stammered.

"And you did not respect your neighbor enough to cut him down from his own tree?"

They shook their heads. "We did not dare."

"Is he still here? Did he leave a man to watch over you?"

"He could be, we do not know but ..." the woman pointed to a second room. I indicated they lead the way. Two children slept in a bed, the words *remember him* smeared in blood on the wall above.

I left the house and proceeded to the next – finding an elderly man and his wife just as scared and the words *be afraid* on their wall. The third house was the same; a man, wife and their three children too frightened to go outside in case Antigonos was still there. *Tell no one* was written on their wall and Antigonos had threatened to do to them what he did to their neighbor if they said anything.

"Is you loyalty to your King not higher than your fear of the man? I growled.

"Please, we want no trouble ... our children."

"Give your friend a proper burial. He deserves that from you at least," I said, sheathing my sword and stalking back to the palace.

20
Temple of Anthela

"Quiet, please," Agrias commanded, rising from his throne. The murmuring died down, those gathered in the room giving their full attention to the king. I sat in Alexis' throne on one side of Agrias, with Moeris on his other in Melina's usual place.

"I call beginning to our autumn assembly," Agrias announced. "We welcome new faces and old friends. As you see, seated beside me are the joint Generals of our army – Skylar and Moeris – the highest ranked officers we have. From this time forth they shall occupy these positions at our assemblies and I shall turn to them, along with Thaddeus, when making decisions put before me of a capital nature.

"For any matters which you, the council, are expected to reach decision, you may also call on them for guidance. I trust both implicitly to give considered counsel on any matter and encourage you to speak with them whenever the need arises or in my absence. Now, I ask the council representatives to give their report of our town since last we met and bring forth any pressing business for decision. Who wishes to speak first?" Agrias re-seated himself between Moeris and me and Stavros stepped forward assuredly, holding the king's eyes without hesitation as he bowed. "Stavros, good. Proceed," Agrias nodded.

"Gratitude, my King. I am pleased to report that this day, as with so many before, we bring no one before you for treasonous behavior. There are no capital, nor non-capital offences which need addressing. All is well within our town."

None that you know of anyway, I thought. Stavros began to weave his way through the gathered crowd, placing his hand on the shoulders of men he passed, or clasping arms with them as he continued to speak. "Our King spoke of our generals of the army: Skylar and Moeris. Under their tutorage these past six moons, our soldiers have grown strong and disciplined. Where before we had boys pretending to be men, now we have boys who think as men, armed as warriors. As soldiers. As a force to be reckoned with.

"Their training continues day by day, and those who sought to cause harm and discord amongst our people have fallen under the spell of our leaders and no longer harbor such thoughts beneath their chests." His gaze fell on Sander and Kleitos, standing in the front row of the soldiers. Neither boy looked away.

I smiled to myself; for I had told them that what had gone before could not be erased, but they must acknowledge their part in it and face whatever was spoken about it with stoicism and the knowledge they toiled hard to make amends.

"It is no secret to any in this room that there were murmurs of dissent when Skylar first claimed Princess Alexis from Melanthios," Stavros continued, circling the room. "But with what she has achieved with our people, as well as our soldiers, and how she holds account of herself every day, the feelings no longer exist with any who call Trachis home. We wish to take this opportunity to welcome her officially into our council." Stavros bowed to me, his grin wide when he inclined his head to the floor. I nodded in return when he straightened, searching a number of other faces in the crowd; satisfied they agreed with him.

A second man stepped forward as Stavros moved back to his original position. He was shorter and rounder than Stavros, but I knew him far better than the previous speaker; it was Ophelos, Alexis' grandfather.

"We remained at home this past summer and with that decision, we have not seen losses to our land or our standing amongst our enemies or allies. We encountered our usual summer, facing neither extreme heat nor cold winds, though the storms provided much to see with Zeus' lightning bolts and his great rumblings flashing across the sky. Our few crop plantings were plentiful enough and merchants were able to bring the rest of what we required.

"Our merchants also report good trade conditions within our agora and saw a slight increase in trade. After speaking with our new arrivals, we believe this was due to travelers from Thessaly heading south for the Isthmian Games in Corinth just after our last assembly in Mounichion. There was also greater interest in their wares as people travelled to Olympia for the Olympic Games three moons ago." Ophelos gave a nod to Agrias to indicate he was finished before returning to stand between two other merchants.

"Thank you, Ophelos, Stavros. We are in an enviable position given our juncture to the north and south lands for trade, but we must not fall to complacency. We must continue to build our city, our soldiers and our reputation. With the arrival of Skylar and Leandros, and our new alliance with the Spartans, we are making great strides in this area.

"Of course, with greater infamy and alliances with such a powerful king, we shall come under scrutiny from many who want what we call ours. But we shall be prepared and shall not fall victim to their attacks. We shall not bury sons or fathers unnecessarily and we shall not make alliances with barbarians such as we have in the past. Moeris?" Agrias indicated the named man.

Moeris replied with a nod, standing as he addressed the crowd. "We lost many good men in the fight with the Epirotes and Illyrians, but we sent many to the Underworld in return. We have since learnt that the Illyrians did not intend to make us their enemy. They have asked our forgiveness for their part in the battle. To atone for their error in joining with Melanthios, they declared war against the Molossian tribe of his family. It appears they were successful in wiping out at least half of them, the rest surrendering, or in hiding."

"We do not yet have all the details of the attack," Agrias continued as a murmur swept the room. "Though I know Andreas, father to Melanthios, and the man my daughter once called husband, lives. He intends to come here by the new moon." The men looked worriedly at each other, the noise level rising as they questioned one another as to Andreas' intent – just as I had before Alexis and I left for Epidaurus. "Please, do not be alarmed, he brings no army with him. He wishes only to see where his sons were killed so he may mourn them properly." Agrias and I had only shared the news of Antigonos' return to Andreas with Moeris. We had decided to keep it from the small council until we knew what the two of them intended. "His impending arrival does bring up a matter I wish to discuss with you all. Once Andreas has departed again and Alexis has birthed our new princess, I shall take my family to Aigai. I wish to introduce her, along with Skylar and Leandros, to my brother and his family."

"Shall you return in time for the summer campaign?" Stavros asked.

"I would expect so, though at this stage I do not know if we shall need to go to war. It perhaps depends more on our allies rather than our enemies, for all appears quiet at the moment."

"Very good," Stavros replied with a bow.

"If we do not need to speak of upcoming campaigning, perhaps we could discuss some new buildings?" Epiktetos asked.

"Of course," Agrias approved. "Buildings to house what exactly?"

"A proper metal workshop and a building where we can produce coins," Epiktetos replied.

The king raised his eyebrows and turned in his throne to face me, a grin across his face. "These suggestions have originated from your mouth, I suspect?"

"They have," I nodded. "Would you allow me to speak of them; to give my reasons?" Agrias dipped his chin in reply and I stood, addressing the room. "If we are to excel in our warfare and put fear into those who would seek to oppose us, we must produce our own weapons, our own armor. If we are forced to wait until the spring assembly to receive replacements, how do we adjust to alterations or new items before the summer campaigning season?

"Furthermore, now that we are allied with the Spartans, why should we not produce coins of our own? Why should *our* name not be known throughout central Greece, Attica and the Peloponnese as a town of means and worth?"

"Would we not become greater targets if we began such actions? As King Agrias notes, we are in a unique position with the Pass to the north and south. If we make our strength known, would others not wish to take what we have built here for their own?" a voice in the crowd asked.

"Perhaps, but at least if they came, we would be prepared and protected," I replied.

"You speak of new buildings, and they are easy enough to construct, but who shall make the weapons or coins? We have no one with the ability to craft such items," Stavros said.

"Actually, we do," my father replied before I had the chance. He emerged from the throng to stand before the assembly.

My father and I had not spoken since I confronted him at the banquet and, had the assembly not been held, I would have ensured it continued. Unfortunately, I knew I would have to acknowledge him and speak alongside him to convince the council and Agrias the workshops should be built – it had been our idea after all – and no matter what had transpired between us since, I knew it was still an important step for Trachis.

Father met my eyes, and I nodded curtly, encouraging him to continue. He turned and faced the assembly as he spoke. "A number of winters ago, Skylar and I found ourselves at Thorikos, near Athens. We spent time with the metalworkers, learning how to produce bronze for weapons and the delicate art of coin making from their Celators. The processes can be time consuming and skill is certainly involved, but if we could seek out other talented metalworkers and encourage them to come to Trachis, we could have our first batch of swords and shields ready for the summer campaigning season. I am certain we could convince them to remain a little longer and share their skills with those who were interested, thereby equipping our town with the trade."

"And the coins? Would you also seek to find Celators to come to Trachis?" Agrias asked.

"Initially, yes," father replied. "If we could not encourage Celators from Athens to travel this far north, we could seek assistance from our neighbors – the Boeotians. They too produce their own coin and are quite skilled." He moved closer, passing a coin made in Thebes to Agrias.

"I am certain Cleomenes would also have no hesitation in sparing a Celator or metalworker from Sparta to aid us," I added, not missing the tightening of my father's jaw at the mention of the city he had never allowed us to enter.

"Indeed," Agrias murmured, turning the coin in his fingers.

I knew the Boeotian design of coin our king now held; it was known as a stater, cast in silver and minted at Thebes. The obverse side held a shield representing the Boeotian League, and the reverse a sunken shape which resembled a ship's sail. When my father and I had first been in Corinth for the Isthmian Games, I had seen similar silver staters with a flying Pegasus on one side and the same sunken shape divided into four distinct parts on the other.

"If it would be acceptable to you, King Agrias, I would ask to oversee construction of the buildings and the initial weapon and coin production. If no one else can be found, I believe I have the skills to produce what we want," Father said.

He found and held my gaze; the king still inspecting the coin in his hand. I had to admit, he had played it well. If Agrias allowed him the running of the workshops, I could not insist on him and Nasrin leaving Trachis as I had demanded, Agrias would want them to remain.

"I too have an offer," Ophelos entered the conversation. "I have spoken at length with Leandros and finding land to house these new buildings is not necessary."

Agrias finally raised his eyes to the two men who stood side by side. "How so?" he asked.

"There are two rooms at the front of my own home which are in need of repair. I had intended to have them seen to this winter, though I believe with slight alteration to my original plans, they would lend themselves easily to a metalworking area. Without the need for a totally new construct, we could begin creating the weapons and coins sooner rather than later."

"What additions would you need to include?" Agrias asked.

"A bloomery furnace, an anvil and the necessary tools and molds."

"Was your intention to make the items from silver or bronze?" Agrias asked, addressing my father.

"Silver for the coins and bronze for the armor."

"And where are we to source that from?"

"The mines in Thorikos are deep and plentiful with the silver ore we require. I shall travel there myself to mine it."

"You have knowledge of how to do so?" Agrias asked, his eyebrows rising on his forehead.

"Yes."

"Did you learn it also from your time in Thorikos?"

My father hesitated before answering. "The process was not unfamiliar to me prior to then." He appeared uncomfortable and I wondered at his reluctance to speak of it. I did not have to wait long to find out. "As you know, King Agrias, I once called Thrace my home." There were a few murmurings at his words, but Father continued, his eyes on Agrias rather than anyone else. "The tribe I belonged to – the Bessoi – lived on Mount Rhodope. We had warriors who protected the priests and priestesses of our tribe, and warriors who protected our women and children. Some of those latter warriors were also expected to mine gold and silver from the hills which held their ore. I was one such warrior and spent much time in the dark with only the echoing sound of breaking rock to accompany me."

"I see," Agrias nodded. "Then it appears we indeed have the knowledge we need to begin."

"We do, though we shall need to set up trade with the miners at Chalcis in Euboea across the Malian Gulf."

"Why?" Agrias asked.

"It would be more cost effective for us to produce our own bronze for the armor, rather than purchasing it directly from a source. We shall need copper from the Euboeans to mix with tin for such a creation. It is here though that I require further knowledge – I do not know who provides the tin we shall need.

"I shall send word to my brother, I believe he sources tin for his own use from across the sea in the west," Agrias said with a nod.

"Thank you," Father replied.

"I see no reason to deny this request and it appears we have the knowledge required to carry it out, so I shall put it before the council to make their decision. Are there further questions before we vote?" No one spoke up so Agrias requested the yay and nay votes. There was no one who opposed the idea. Agrias nodded again and addressed my father. "I shall speak further to you and Ophelos after the meeting. We shall inspect the rooms in question and make note of what you require to begin."

"Perhaps giving our young men tasks such as you speak of would prevent some of them from making foolish decisions about their futures," Ophelos said, his gaze finding Sander and Kleitos again.

"A worthy task indeed," Kleitos replied with a nod, not afraid to meet the eyes of the man he injured.

"Is that all the business we have?" Agrias asked.

"It is," Stavros acknowledged.

"Good, then I wish to ask Leandros to step forward."

My father was surprised at the request but did as asked. This was the part of the assembly I had least been looking forward to. In what I knew was an attempt to heal the rift between Father and I, Agrias had spoken of my assistance today. I did not want to participate, but eventually agreed; Agrias and Alexis both keeping at me in their own ways until I relented.

"Men of the council and assembly, I present to you this man, Leandros, who I name as philos – a friend of the king for life." A number of voices cut over the king's words. Agrias held his hand up for quiet, continuing when the murmurings died down. "I understand Leandros has never held the title of noble or aristocrat, nor Macedonian; indeed, he spoke this very day of being a warrior in his native tribe of Thrace. But he has shown his commitment to us and to me in particular without hesitation or falsehood and I know it shall continue to be so for the rest of his days.

"I do not require your approval in this matter, though I ask for your acceptance. Many of you shall not be surprised at my choice and have welcomed Leandros into your homes and hearts – speaking words to me that it is as if he has always lived amongst us. I profess to feel the same."

"I did not expect to receive such an honor," Father whispered, dropping to one knee and bowing his head before Agrias. "Thank you, my friend."

"It is my pleasure," Agrias replied.

The king stood, approaching my father and offering his arm. My father took it and pulled himself to his feet. Agrias turned back to me and nodded. I retrieved an item from the table beside the thrones and joined them.

"Leandros, your daughter is now my daughter and though you hold high place in our family, I wish for you to hold high place amongst all our people. We present to you this himation in the royal purple color I favor. From now on you shall be treated with respect and loyalty, as a royal, a nobleman, an aristocrat, a warrior. You shall never fall from my favor, nor I from yours."

"The bond we have formed shall never be broken, though death shall one day divide us. I shall go to the Underworld with loyalty and respect for you and your people on my lips," the gathered men said, a response echoed a moment later by my father.

"They are your people now as well," Agrias said with a grin.

"Indeed," my father replied, returning the king's smile.

I lay the material over my father's shoulders, pinning it in place. I embraced him stiffly as he did the same. "I have not forgiven you," I said into his ear. "I shall not commence speaking with you once we are done here. I did it only because Agrias asked it of me."

"Understood," he murmured. "Though I hope you change your mind soon enough. There are words to be spoken between us that should not wait much longer."

I only grunted as reply and released him. Agrias too hugged my father, though their embrace was filled with more warmth than ours had been.

When Agrias released my father, he addressed the assembly again. "Before I call our meeting to an end, I wish to acknowledge those senior council members attending the assembly in Delphi as our delegates at the Great Amphictyonic League. Epiktetos, Stavros and Ophelos attend on our behalf, though given the construction to take place at Ophelos', I believe two men shall be enough this autumn. Are you agreeable to the same?"

"We are, King Agrias," Epiktetos nodded.

"We shall leave in a few days," Stavros agreed.

"Very good. Now come, allow us to welcome our newest friend and share wine and stories of a fanciful nature."

21

Though I called for her, almost a moon passed before I saw my grandmother again. Alexis had spoken of little else when she and I were alone – her curious nature outweighing her fear at meeting the *creature* Dianthe was. She asked me how Dianthe had appeared, how much I resembled her or my mother. I had few answers for her, but I told her what I could.

My father and I were also still estranged, me ignoring his attempts at conversation and apology just as I had told him I would at the assembly. Thankfully, the construction of the metalworking area at Ophelos' house, coupled with his journey to Thorikos and back, had taken much of his attention and we saw little of each other. Nasrin also allowed me space, the two of them moving out of the palace and into the spare rooms at Ophelos and Aspasia's house soon after the meeting of the small council.

As I returned from the barracks one morning Dianthe finally appeared, suggesting she meet me and my princess at the Temple of Anthela. I immediately agreed, hurrying back to our apartment to fetch Alexis.

A candlemark later, we arrived, Dianthe seated casually on the bench outside, her face covered just as it had been the first time I saw her at the agora. We had ridden Skotos and I once again left him beneath a tree away from the temple itself when he began to stamp at the ground.

I made the introductions and though Alexis offered her arm, Dianthe did not take it. I shrugged when Alexis looked to me; perhaps she was not familiar with the gesture. Alexis did not appear offended and laced her hands together around her belly instead. "Please, do not fear you must remain covered, Skylar has spoken to me of what you are. Of who you are to her. I am not afraid to see you," Alexis said.

"As you wish," Dianthe nodded, reaching up with her clawed fingers to remove her hood.

Alexis drew a quick breath but did not turn from Dianthe when she revealed herself. "It is a pleasure to meet you," Alexis smiled.

"And you," Dianthe replied, inclining her head once again.

"I have so many questions, if you would permit them."

I grinned. I should not have been surprised at my lover's forthrightness, though I had expected her to wait a *little* bit longer before launching into her interrogation.

"Of course," Dianthe said, unperturbed by Alexis' words. She smiled, revealing the pointed teeth and Alexis once again showed her composure by not reacting to her more … unusual features. "Perhaps first though, you would permit me to make welcome your child, my great-granddaughter."

Alexis looked to me, a flicker of apprehension crossing her face and I wondered if she was also recalling my father's fear that they would have taken me from him if they had known of me. I worked to keep the frown from my face and nodded.

"O-of course," Alexis stammered.

"How far along are you now?" Dianthe asked.

"Four moons," Alexis replied, her hands remaining beneath the swell of her stomach.

"You appear quite large already," Dianthe noted as she stepped forward.

"My friend Hesper agrees," Alexis said. "It appears our child has grown quickly almost from the time we returned to Trachis from the Heraion."

"Perhaps she carries two children for us, just as your mother did," I offered, taking one of Alexis' hands in my own.

Dianthe considered it. "Perhaps," she finally agreed. "I shall easily be able to tell if I place hands on her. May I?" Again, Alexis' gaze flicked to mine, but it was she who nodded her approval this time. Dianthe smiled and reached out, laying her hands atop the roundness. She was still for a long moment, then drew her hands back quickly, as though stung.

"What is it?" I asked. I could not tell if it was surprise or fear on her face but suddenly Dianthe did not appear comfortable.

"Her heart beats strong," she murmured.

"What is it?" I asked again.

"I-I must leave, we shall meet again another day," she said, backing up.

"No, wait," I pleaded, following and reaching for Dianthe's arm. She kept it from me, her gaze on Alexis' belly and briefly finding mine before she disappeared before us. "No!" I shouted, turning in a circle. "Stay! Tell us what you felt."

"Skylar?" Alexis asked, her voice wavering as she spoke.

"Come, we must find Gnosidicus," I said, taking her hand and leading her back to Skotos. With Alexis safely atop my steed, I drove him quickly towards Trachis, riding directly to Gnosidicus' home rather than waiting for him to come to the palace. Alexis had said nothing as we travelled, and I too had many questions I did not want to voice yet.

Thankfully, Gnosidicus was home and after helping Alexis to the ground, I told him I was worried about the baby, leaving out what, or rather who, had caused my concern.

He settled Alexis onto a bed in the room he often saw patients from and asked me to remove her chiton. He handed me a length of material to cover her chest as I gathered her chiton below her stomach. Gnosidicus may have attended countless births and was intimately familiar with the female and male bodies but his first thoughts were still to his princess' modesty.

When she was covered again, he approached. "You are feeling unwell?" he asked, placing his hands on her stomach in a similar fashion to Dianthe.

"No, I feel quite well. The sickness I endured early on has passed."

"She is large for her moons, is she not?" I asked. "Could she be carrying two children for us?"

Gnosidicus nodded. "It is most probable, unless you can think of another explanation?" I paused, frowning. "You are aware it was Hera who gifted us with this child but what we did not tell you was that she took something not only from Thaddeus, but from me as well. The child inside Alexis shares blood with all three of us."

"Ah, so there is your explanation," Gnosidicus grinned. "Given your height and that of your father and his Thracian people, your child shall simply be tall, as you are."

"Can you be certain?" I pressed. "Can you assure us that she is well and that Alexis carries only one child?"

Gnosidicus continued to slide his hands to all sides of the roundness, concentrating as he felt for whatever he sought. "There," he eventually said, pointing to a slight quiver at the top of Alexis' stomach. "Your daughter moves within, she is strong. I feel only one child and though you are larger than others in your condition, I believe it is more to do with the mixture of her creation than anything else. Do not fear."

"Thank you," Alexis whispered, allowing an audible sigh to escape her lips. She reached for my hand, gripping it strongly as our eyes met and pulling me close. "Perhaps Dianthe was just overcome by emotion, having lost her own daughter," she whispered.

I nodded, unconvinced it was the real reason, but having no other explanation for her strange behavior.

"Another five moons shall see your daughter arrive, and all these questions shall be answered. I am certain it is just your Thracian blood that runs through her and makes her larger than expected," Gnosidicus assured us. I only nodded, keeping further thoughts of doubt to myself.

22

"Master I tell you, Skylar is not your Chosen One; it is the child her wife carries for them. I am certain of it."

"How? How can you be certain? You have insisted for winters it is Skylar I have waited for. Implored me to keep watch over her and heal her when she was close to death last winter. What now causes you to speak otherwise?"

"Because I have felt her power. Do you not see how it could be so – given that it was you who orchestrated the gift of a child? Gave Alexis the desire to want it? You convinced your mother to place a part of Skylar within Alexis. You believed it would bind them even closer and assist you when you appeared to her ... but now it appears it has done much more than that. You have *created* your Chosen One." The volume of Dianthe's voice increased the more she spoke, her excitement obvious.

The idea was appealing, the God of War could not deny that, but was it true? Had he truly succeeding at bringing forth his Chosen One? Could he finally have what he wanted?

"She is growing more quickly than any mortal child, she must be close to seven moons now, not the four they expect. It has to be my presence in Trachis which is responsible for it. She is one of us. She grows fast, as a full Ker child does," Dianthe continued.

Ares stroked the short bristles of his goatee, considering her words. He would not rush blindly ahead. He would keep to his plan. He must be certain before making any decisions on the child. "Skylar must be tested just as all others before her have been. The line defaulted to Skylar after Zita died so she must be given the opportunity to prove herself."

"But, Master," Dianthe began.

"No. I have given you my answer. We shall discuss matters again after Skylar's test is complete." With those final words, Ares disappeared and Dianthe was left alone in his palace.

She did not understand why he insisted on continuing with Skylar. She had felt the child's power. She had no doubt of the destiny it carried with it. True, she had believed it would be Skylar who brought about the prophecy. She had believed it right up until the moment she had touched Alexis. Then she knew just how wrong she had been.

"You speak eagerly of this new Chosen One," a voice echoed through the halls but Dianthe knew exactly who it belonged to.

"Eavesdropping again, Canace?" she replied. "I imagine that without reason or invitation to Ares' side, you must lurk in the shadows, awaiting a gleam of information. How sad that must be for you."

Canace sneered as she fluttered down from her hiding position, her rage flying to the surface as it always did when her aunt taunted her on the subject of her inferior line. "It is a travesty that it is your treacherous daughter who spawned the one the master believes is the Chosen One. The power should have been mine the night Zita was killed."

"And yet it was not. You missed her child. You killed the wrong man. You allowed yourself to be fooled so easily."

It was an old argument between the two of them, one that had begun when they learned Leandros was alive, and that he and Zita had had a daughter. Both remained passionate about bringing up the truths of times passed whenever possible, which only fueled their hatred and rivalry towards one another.

"You never wanted the line for yourself. Never wanted what our Master sought from you. You even attempted to help Zita escape our kin and when she was discovered, you were too cowardly to even finish the line as you so desperately wanted. That task was left to your mother and me."

"Which you failed at. You further bore a male child as testament that you would never possess what Ares needed."

"Tell me, Aunt, why now you are so determined to see the Chosen One discovered? If you had your wish all those winters ago, there would never have been another born in your line."

"I was young then, I did not understand why it was important I continue the line and ensure Ares' Chosen One was brought into our care. Now I do. Now I know I was chosen to bear the line, as my mother was before me and my daughter was after me. Ares has forgiven me for past mistakes and I know the responsibility I carry for him now. I shall see it through to its end."

"So you say, though allow us to hope those you hold in such high esteem to aid you in this task remain able to do so without … tragedy befalling them."

Dianthe stalked towards Canace, their faces almost touching when she spoke again. "Do not threaten my granddaughter or her family, or you shall learn how far I am prepared to go to see my responsibility through this time."

Canace merely laughed as she stepped back, pushing off into the air again. "You know I rarely make threats, Dianthe. I make promises instead."

"You shall not succeed in bringing harm to them," Dianthe warned, though she recalled all too well how Canace had once promised to end Zita's life. Canace laughed again and disappeared.

23

I stood on the edge of the Melas River with the seven new recruits to the army of Trachis whose induction I had overseen last spring. There had been spirited debate about allowing Sander and Kleitos to be inducted with the others, given that they were four winters short of the required joining age. I had spoken vehemently for their inclusion, understanding just how much could change in even one winter. I was not prepared to have them languish or find further trouble to get mixed up in when there was a suitable alternative available. Eventually they had been allowed join, though I had to take responsibility for any missteps they made. So far, they had made none, and I could not be prouder of them.

"Welcome to your new training arena. Unlike in Sparta, I would prefer to aid you in the areas you need improvement in, rather than call you out on them in front of the other men. Eventually I expect all the soldiers to complete this course four times a week, but for now, Moeris and I have agreed that it is just for you to build up the strength and endurance you shall need should you find yourself in battle," I told them.

In the frustrating week since the strange meeting with Dianthe, I had spent more time between the Melas and Dyras Rivers than almost anywhere else. The physicality and mental strength needed to train in the area ensured that when I returned to Alexis and the palace each evening, I could set her own fears and questions to rest and assure her all was well with our child. I did not necessarily believe it to be true myself, but I would not add to her worries by speaking my thoughts on the matter.

"I do not wish to lose any of you because you were not prepared before you faced an enemy. I hope not to have you in harm's way until you have developed the skills you require to keep yourself alive, but I cannot guarantee it shall be so. So you must take this seriously. What I teach you here, what Moeris teaches you and, perhaps most importantly, what you can learn from older soldiers can prepare you for battle. We shall run drills and practice formations but, depending on who your enemy is and where you face them, it can never truly mirror battle conditions, much as we wish it could.

"War is messy, it is not uniformed and enemies do not always fight fair. They shall not wait until you have finished battling one of their kin, as we do when we spar each morning. They shall take advantage of your distraction and cut you down or launch their spears to find your leg or arm, allowing their comrade to finish you off; unless of course they aim for your chest or neck."

I heard the intake of breaths from the young men. They understood that this was no play arena. Good. "The skills you learn from me shall put you in good stead to fight and remain standing for many candlemarks. Your bodies shall develop muscle to help you hold off larger opponents, and when you are ready, Moeris and I shall identify your strengths and work individually with you to develop them.

"I do not stand here and pretend it shall be easy. There are days you shall hate me for the number of times I make you repeat a particular action. But know that I do it only to ensure you are the best you can be, not as punishment."

"We trust you," Kleitos said, the others nodding in agreement.

"Good. Allow me to explain the course and demonstrate each obstacle, then it shall be your turn. I shall remain at each station until all of you are done and help or answer any questions you have." They all nodded again and I returned it before going on. "First, we must swim across the Melas. You have all indicated you are proficient swimmers, so that should not pose a problem to you."

"Are we to disrobe first?" Sander asked.

"No, and you shall complete the rest of the course in your wet clothes. Battles and wars are not always fought in bright sunshine. You must be comfortable with the extra weight of a wet tunic and armor should you find yourself fighting in the rain. Once across the river, pick up one of the objects there and carry it the sixty-five feet to the third task."

"What are they?" Kleitos asked. "They appear to be cauldrons but there are legs attached."

"Correct," I nodded. "They are an old-style cauldron but their handles caught my eye and I knew they would be perfect for what I had planned. So far, I only have three, though I have more coming."

"Those handles, they are not simply to aid in lifting them, are they?" he added.

I grinned. "No. Once you reach that tree, you shall tie one end of the rope to the handles, throw the other over the lowest branch and hoist the cauldron up to touch the branch."

"Sounds easy enough," one of the other boys said with a shrug.

I lifted an eyebrow, still grinning. "We shall see. Now, near the hoist, are a number of log piles and burning fires. You must draw your sword before you reach the first log pile, jump it and continue on towards the fire pit. Do not allow the flames to touch your legs as you leap over the top. This particular challenge is to teach you how high you must jump to avoid the swinging weapons of enemies you have cut down, but who still have strength enough to wield their weapons."

The boys nodded, though I could tell they did not believe it to be particularly hard. They would soon learn it was; especially if the light breeze which stirred the leaves nearby picked up.

"Once you have cleared those obstacles take one of the practice shields on the ground and face your fellow soldiers. The six of you who are not completing the challenge shall line up, three per side, several feet apart in the open area. You must run between them, fending off the attacks with sword or shield without falling. Make no mistake; if you stumble in battle, you die.

"The last challenge shall see you attempt to lodge a spear into the target I have chosen. It is set at a distance of forty-five feet from where you launch it from. If your spear misses the target altogether, two rocks chosen *for* you not *by* you shall be added to the cauldron on your next run. If you hit the target, but it fails to remain lodged in the trunk, one rock shall be added to the cauldron. Again, you shall not be the chooser."

The boys looked to one another, no doubt hoping the rocks of the area were small, or that they showed proficiency with the spears.

"The course is to be completed as many times as possible in half a candlemark. I would advise you to work slowly through each task to avoid injuring yourself. Speed shall come when you are more familiar with the movements, I do not expect you to complete it many times in the beginning. Ready?" The young men nodded. "Good, then allow us to begin."

Ensuring my xiphos was all the way into its sheath at my thigh, I entered the cold water of the river. It was not far to the other side, and my head and shoulders were above the waterline as I waded across. It would not be so for the recruits who accompanied me. I pulled myself out onto the opposite bank, Kleitos and Sander leading the others across. I offered my hand to each boy when they arrived, lifting them easily from the water.

We crossed to the second task and I picked up the cauldron, which I had filled half way with small rocks. It was not particularly heavy – though I had many winters of training on the boys – but the legs at the base made it awkward, digging into my thighs as I walked. I carried it to the tree and worked quickly to tie one end to the handles. When it was secure, I threw the other end over the branch and began to lift it off the ground. As the boys had suspected, the task was simple enough, but what I had failed to tell them was that the rope had been lathered with olive oil, making it slippery to handle. They were quick to pick up the addition when my hands slid up and down the rope as I attempted to get the cauldron all the way to the branch.

"An interesting twist," Kleitos grinned.

I returned his smile as the cauldron finally reached the top. "I thought so," I replied; the olive oil on my hands would make the rest of the course more challenging.

I allowed the rope to slip slowly back through my palms, the cauldron landing on the ground with a soft thump. I untied it and led the boys to the log and fire section. Unsheathing my sword, and gripping it tightly against the oil, I jumped each of the piles and flames, picking up one of the shields beyond as the boys joined me.

"The wind alters the height of the flames," Kleitos noted.

"And therein lies the challenge – the height can change between one run and the next and as you tire, your jumps shall not be as high." He nodded, though it was more to himself, as he considered the fires behind us. "Stand as I explained and draw your weapons," I directed.

Each recruit took his position, four on one side and three on the other. I tightened my hold on my sword and began to run between them. They went fairly easy, basically only offering their swords to meet mine as I passed them.

I shook my head and returned to the starting position. "Again," I told them. "You cannot simply stand there and allow the man running between you to get past. What if you were standing guard at the palace? Would you allow your enemy to brush past you with no more than a passing glance?"

"No," the boys replied, their heads slightly hung.

"Then show me how you would defend your home. You want to get past my defenses. You want to draw blood. You want to stop me reaching the end. Swords up."

I ran through again and this time their intent was true. They spread themselves further apart so they had room to swing their weapons. I grinned, meeting each sword strongly with my own or the shield on my other arm. "Good," I nodded. "That is how I want you to behave every time you reach this section. Do not forget what you fight for. *Who* you fight for. Your friends, your family, those in your town. Many of you have younger brothers or sisters, allow their faces to be the ones you see before battle. Fight as though their very lives depend on it because if war finds us that is exactly how it would be."

"Though he is only six winters old, my brother, Lysistratos, would probably attempt to fight beside me if there was a war," Kleitos laughed.

I grinned and nodded along with him and the others. "I do not doubt it," I agreed. Not only was Lysistratos the same age as Nikomachos, but he was just as determined to carry a sword. "He shall make a fine soldier one day, just as you are becoming," I told Kleitos.

"Thank you," he mumbled.

"Come, I have the final task to show you before it is your turn."

I led them to the spears and picked one, weighting it in my hand. Focusing on the tree I had chosen, marked with several tiles at its base, I planted my feet. I hoped I could hit the mark – I could only imagine the good-natured ribbing I would endure at the hands of the recruits if I did not. Until it came to their turn of course. I drew the long wood back behind my shoulder and loosed it, finding the bark with a satisfying thud.

They cheered and clapped my effort and I gave a quick bow, grinning back at them when I straightened. "So, now you have seen what to do, are you ready to begin?" I asked. They nodded enthusiastically in return and we walked back to the river, the seven of them crossing over using the stone bridge just down from where we had swum across. I remained on the other side, close enough to give aid if required, as they stroked back, and pleased to note that the first across – Sander – helped the others out as I had done earlier.

24

The boys had done better than I expected for their first half-candlemark training session, though I suspected it had more to do with not wanting to be the first to admit defeat, than true strength and skill. They would be sore in the morning, and though they begged for one last run, I did not allow it; mostly because I wanted them to be able to return again in two days' time.

"You have done well with them, the youngest two especially, given their behavior so recently." I jumped and drew my sword from its sheath, facing the newcomer.

He grinned and held his hands up to indicate he was no threat. "Apologies if I startled you, Skylar. Do not be afraid. I mean you no harm."

"How do you know my name?" I asked, taking a step closer so the tip of my sword pressed against the exposed skin of his chest.

"I know far more than just your name," he said, still smiling. "But I believe the question is, do you know who *I* am?"

I tilted my head, regarding him. He was handsome, muscular, his features strong and somewhat familiar. He was as tall as me, his clothing in leather; pants as dark as raven's feathers and a black and red sleeveless vest. His boots were also possibly leather, and though I had never seen a pair, I imagined they were similar to the fawnskin embades my father had worn when he lived in Thrace. His chin and mouth were surrounded by short hairs in the same color as his pants, as was the shoulder length hair tumbling from his head. A light breeze blew up but not one strand moved out of place.

Dark eyes momentarily flashed the same red as Dianthe's when I returned my gaze to his and instantly I knew. "Ares," I whispered.

"Skylar? What is it?" Sander asked. I glanced behind me; the seven recruits approaching, swords drawn as they searched for what I saw.

"They cannot see me. Only you can," Ares said, folding his hands behind his back.

"Why?"

"It is what I want for our first meeting," he shrugged.

"Who are you talking to?" Kleitos added.

I drew a long breath, lowering my sword slightly and turning back to the boys. "No one. I … I thought I heard something. You are excused from training in the barracks tomorrow – rest and soak your tired bodies in the baths. I expect you back here at first light the day after."

A few of them groaned but nodded and replaced their weapons at their thighs as they ambled back over the bridge towards the town. Kleitos hung back, obviously wanting further words. "What is it?" I asked.

"You did not ask for my help in creating this area."

"No. I wanted it to be a surprise. You have shown promise in devising strategies for battles but there is still more you must learn," I said, placing my hand on his shoulder as I continued. "A good leader requires the ability to see the larger picture and act accordingly, but a good soldier requires core strength and endurance. I want to teach you to have both."

"Oh," he mumbled.

"Go. Rest up. You did well today." He nodded and turned, jogging to catch up to his friends.

When they were out of sight, I addressed Ares again. "So, you are Ares, God of War. Leader of the Keres."

"I am and Dianthe tells me you are my Chosen One."

"Apparently."

Ares grinned. "I come bearing a gift. You had none of the gifts a bride deserved, and yet you were one as well, no matter that you played the part of the groom," he said, bringing one hand from behind his back and holding it out to me.

I replaced my sword and took the length of leather from Ares, holding it up so the amulet on its end caught the light. "It belonged to your mother."

The black gem was half the length and width of my first finger. Two thin pieces of silvery-red iron wound their way from top to bottom, holding it inside. The soft leather was looped through a second section of iron at the top.

Ares took it again and placed it over my head. With hands on my shoulders, he turned me, tightening the leather at the nape of my neck when I held my hair aside.

"This amulet has passed through every generation of your family since its creation. I understand your grandmother has spoken to you of your mother and the proud line of Keres you belong to. Allow me now to speak of the amulet itself. It is the catalyst to the powers you have inside you. Just as Zita, Dianthe, Rizpah and all the others before them were given it before their tests, so I gift it to you."

"What does it do?" I asked as Ares returned to stand before me.

"It enhances your natural talents and provides you with so many more through the four elements in holds inside. I can guide you in calling forth those elements, though first you must know what it is made from." I nodded, holding his eyes as he spoke. "The dark gem is jet; a powerful and ancient stone which many healers are afraid to speak of, and almost never possess themselves. The iron around it is hematite; a protective element."

"I always believed iron was silver but this has a reddish tinge to it," I marveled, holding the amulet out from my chest to inspect it again.

"True. Hematite is actually the principle ore of iron, an oxide. In its powered state, it turns a blood red color; which is how it received its name. For that reason, hematite has always been associated with me; with war. There is power in hematite and once you accept its power, it shall travel through your blood and make you unstoppable and insatiable in your desire to fight for those you love, those you have sworn to protect."

"You crafted the amulet then? For your Chosen line?"

"No," he smiled, shaking his head. "Many winters ago, my Keres spent time in the presence of the Valkyrie in the north lands. It was that friendship which saw the amulet created. The Valkyrie spoke of crafting a powerful item that would link a specific line of the Keres and me if I provided them with a drop of my blood. With the mixture of our blood, it ensured the amulet was sacred to me and to the one specific line of Ker. They told us a magnificent warrior would be born to that line and she would alter the world as we have known it with her courage and talents."

"Me."

"I cannot be certain of course until you have used the amulet, but it appears you are what the Valkyrie spoke of – different to all others in the line. Half-mortal, though if that helps or hinders your abilities we are yet to discover."

"Perhaps it strengthens my link between the mortal and immortal worlds. Perhaps that is the change you speak of that I am to make in this life."

"Perhaps," Ares agreed. "There were those who suspected your mother was with child; it was no secret she wished to leave the life she had always known, but I did not believe she ever truly would. For the longest time there was no indication she had birthed a child. I could not feel you and I dismissed the rumors of it when they reached me."

"And yet I was alive."

"Yes. Tell me, for I am curious; you appear to accept the title of Chosen One readily, to welcome it without question, though you have only just learnt of it."

"Why should I not when my father was so determined to keep it secret from me?" I shrugged. "I do not believe he would have ever spoken of it, had Dianthe not approached me last moon."

"I could not agree more. He must have believed we did not know of you, for if we did, he would have expected us to come for you sooner," Ares mused.

"Dianthe says you did not approach because you felt I was not ready. That you alone always decide when a Ker is ready to be tested. You believe it to be so now?"

He smiled again. "Yes. Now you have all you never knew you needed or wanted." I frowned and Ares' smile grew. "You have a lover – a partner – who has accepted everything in your past and still wants to be with you, who loves you without hesitation. You have a child that grows inside her because you faced and overcame your past and your fears. You have found people you care about more than just for a short time; people you would remain with and do all in your power to protect for the rest of your days. The king and queen mean more to you than any of the townspeople you have ever come across before. Thaddeus, Hesper and their children hold special place in your heart, you do not wish any harm to come to them."

"You speak true," I agreed. "But I could have used your assistance, or the amulet's, in many battles before."

"Perhaps. But you had less to lose then. Now you have everything to lose; happiness, family, friends. Only *now* can you harness the power meant for you and use it to keep those you love safer than any others. Only now can you become a Ker, just as your mother was before you."

"Are you are saying I am going to change? Am I to have taloned fingers and red eyes?"

"I cannot say for certain," Ares replied, lifting a shoulder. "But your wings lie beneath your skin, begging to be released. You have felt them wanting to emerge this past moon, have you not?"

I frowned but realized the constant itch at my shoulder blades had been the sign. I reached a hand to my right shoulder, a slight tingle greeting my fingers when they met skin. "Dianthe spoke of the Keres drawing strength from feeding on mortal's blood. Is *that* something I shall want once I have my wings or use the amulet?"

"Again, I cannot say, though perhaps you shall have many differences to the other Keres in the line. It would not surprise me to find it is so. At this time, the depth of the qualities and talents you possess are as much a mystery to me as they are to you. But if you would allow me to remain at your side and guide you in the use of the amulet, we can learn of them together. You can achieve so much more than you ever dreamed of."

I swallowed loudly, unable to deny the seduction of his words and promises. Perhaps if I held such power, I could make right the wrongs that had befallen Nasrin and bring her sons to Greece so they did not have to live with their hatred any longer. Perhaps I could end Andreas' interest in Trachis as well. If I could command the elements, I could ensure Andreas or any in his tribe never gave thought to coming here again.

Ares' voice pulled me from my thoughts. "Allow me to assist you as I have since you first arrived in Trachis. Together we can achieve so much."

"Dianthe says you healed me when I was injured. I owe you m–."

He waved away my words. "I could not allow you to die. How could we have known what you could become, what you could overcome, if you had met Hades in his realm?" I frowned as he went on. "Your travels to Epidaurus at the suggestion of your healer was not coincidental, neither was your time in Corinth. It was *I* who ensured those closest to you spoke the words. It was I who asked my mother to gift you and Alexis with a child. You were not certain you wanted it, but I could see into your heart and when given another way, I knew you would agree."

"You ...?"

He took my hand and I quieted. "*You* are the one I have waited for, Skylar. You hold the power the Valkyrie spoke of so long ago. When Dianthe convinced me of it, I knew I must assist you in readying yourself for my arrival in whatever manner I could, and that included ensuring you and the princess created a child together."

"Oh," I whispered, uncertain what else to add.

"Perhaps I have spoken of enough today. You need to process it all. I shall leave you to your thoughts but know that you only need call my name and I shall appear to you."

I nodded as reply, knowing he spoke true; I did not even know where to begin with it all.

"Think carefully on the power you could wield and what could be achieved if you allow me to assist you with the gifts you have. Though I speak of you protecting those closest to you, you can of course harness the amulet's power at any time and aid those who cannot aid themselves, just as you have always sought to do with nothing but your sword and your determination." I swallowed. Ares placed a hand on my shoulder and I met his gaze. "I shall allow you time to consider all I have said. But I hope it is not long before we can meet again and that you shall favor me with the answer I seek."

"For now I have only one question," I said, finally finding my voice.

"Of course."

"My ... my father. He kept knowledge of you to himself. He feared you or Dianthe would find us and take me away. Should I worry you shall kill him now for keeping us apart for so long?"

"No. What would be the point? We are together now so he did not succeed, at least not forever. Besides, the honor and decision would belong to you if you felt that was what he deserved." He tapped me on the chest. "You shall know in your heart what punishment to inflict and I hold no doubt you shall act as you see fit." I nodded at the truth in Ares' words again, anger at my father's betrayal firing my blood. "I shall see you again soon, Skylar." Ares gave a final nod before a flash of light replaced his image. I turned my head from it and when I looked back, he was gone.

25

I did not need time to consider Ares' proposal, though I took Alexis' advice and waited, a week having passed since he appeared to me. I had spoken to her of our meeting when I returned from the training area that afternoon; showing her the amulet he had given me and telling her where it had come from, and to whom it had once belonged.

I was in no doubt I wanted his help. I wanted to know what the amulet would enable me to do, what I was capable of if I truly was the Chosen One. The thought of controlling fire, water, wind or earth was appealing. The defenses I could give Trachis if it were so, how safe I could keep all of us when we travelled to Aigai to see Agrias' brother and family.

What punishment I could administer to Father for his hurtful lies. The thought popped unbidden into my head and I clenched my jaw. I had not forgiven him, nor had my anger dulled at his secrecy. But there was something … something I could not name that told me I could not – should not – use the amulet on him. Perhaps it was because it had once belonged to my mother. Perhaps there was a part of her that lived on inside of it that prevented me from raising it against him, even though I considered it.

Since I had begun training the recruits in my arena, my father and I had barely seen one another, and the times we were forced to be near, he kept his distance. I was careful not to allow him to see the amulet. I did not want to answer his questions, or for him to think I wore it so he would attempt to talk to me. I had no doubt he would recognize it. My mother must have been wearing it when they met. Perhaps even the night she died. I had so many questions about it, about her. Finally, perhaps, I had found people who had known her and were not afraid to speak of her with me, who would share all they could with me and answer me anything I asked without censor or secrets.

Never before had I wanted to know about my mother as deeply as I had this past moon. At the abaton in Epidaurus I had recalled that by the time I met Nasrin I was long since past the age of wanting a mother or mother figure. Now though, I found myself desperate to know Zita. To know her thoughts, to understand why she did not want the power of the Chosen One for herself. How she could want to leave the Keres. Did she fall in love with my father only because he was not one of them?

The itching at my shoulder blades had increased as the days went on and I found it increasingly distracting as I trained in my bronze armor. I scratched at the skin but my wings – if I indeed possessed them – remained hidden beneath. They too, were obviously waiting for the right moment to emerge.

With Alexis' hand in mine, we returned from visiting Skotos and Calla at the stables and I rubbed at the infuriating spot again. As we passed through the walkway, voices floated out of the banquet hall. I frowned. Agrias had not mentioned he was expecting to entertain guests today. I slowed my pace, Alexis immediately falling into step.

Hesper and a number of slaves made their way beneath the veranda from the kitchen to the hall, their hands full with platters of food and amphorae of wine as they rushed inside. As we drew level with the door, Alexis sucked in a deep breath, and pulled me back out of sight.

"What is it?" I asked, my voice immediately dropping as my arm wrapped protectively around her waist.

"Andreas," she managed, the color draining from her face.

She sagged against me and I wrapped my other arm around her, holding her up. "Basileios' father? Agrias did not tell me he was arriving today," I whispered.

"Perhaps he did not know."

"Impossible. He was due almost a week ago. The scouts have been on constant alert."

I peered in through the doorway. Andreas and Agrias stood eye to eye and there could be no mistake that the Molossian tribesman was the father of Basileios, Melanthios, Marcario, Cleon and Xylon; each son had inherited a feature of his father. From the length and color of his hair, to the same eyes, nose or chin to the menacing sneer I had encountered so often from Melanthios. It was strange to see each within the one body and I wondered just how similar his thoughts were to Melanthios and the younger boys; Basileios being the lone son who shared none of their lust for battle and greed.

"Shall we not share the food my women have brought for us? You must be famished from your journey," Agrias said.

"Cut the pleasantries. Where is your daughter and the common whore you have permitted to wed her?" Andreas snarled.

Alexis drew a sharp breath. My jaw and hands clenched at his words, but I remained silent, her fingers sliding between mine. "Skylar," she whispered.

"Shh," I soothed, pressing my lips to her head. "Just wait." So, the news of our joining had reached him. I had hoped his attention would be kept closer to home over the summer with the battle against the Illyrians, but I was not surprised he had learned of it; his inside man, Antigonos, obviously the bearer of the news.

"Neither Alexis or Skylar are here. They journeyed to Aigai to visit my brother. I am certain you recall meeting him. He remains King of Macedonia." The threat was barely veiled, though neither Andreas, nor I missed the king's undertone. "I do not expect them to return for many moons. A winter perhaps," Agrias continued.

"You shall recall them both. Immediately."

"Why?" Agrias asked, feigning nonchalance as he picked up a fig and popped it into his mouth.

"Do you believe I am stupid, Agrias? Do you think I would not find out this … *girl* had made claim to your daughter? I know she is the one who killed my sons."

"If Skylar accidently fought or felled any of your sons in battle then you cannot find fault with her for doing so. She picked up weapons to aid me, my town, against men I was surprised to suddenly call enemies."

"I have heard of her reputation; her and her father. If you were so surprised to find yourself under threat, then why were they here?"

"A coincidence, nothing more. They were passing through on their way to Thrace where Leandros hails from; he is a member of the Bessoi tribe," Agrias paused, allowing Andreas to take in the information. The look on his face suggested he was aware of the Thracian tribe's reputation for fierceness and independence. "Skylar was injured fighting for the life of your son, Basileios. She did not know who he or Alexis were, yet she defended them without hesitation."

"He was still killed," Andreas countered, shoveling a handful of figs into his mouth.

"True, and I share your loss. Basileios was a good man, a good husband to my daughter."

"He was weak. A disappointment. I was ashamed to call him son. He could not bear me an heir though I provided him with a decent wife. I know he planned to leave me, to leave Epirus. I know he intended to defect to Trachis and that you aided him. I also know it was Melanthios who killed him that day you speak of."

"Oh?" Agrias said and I saw his sudden discomfort.

A warmth at my chest drew my attention to the amulet I wore. I looked down, an orange glow visible beneath my cuirass. I released Alexis, placing my finger to my mouth when she attempted to protest. I drew my sword, weighting it in my hand as Agrias caught my eye. He shook his head, the motion barely imperceptible and I waited, wondering what else Andreas knew. If he moved against Agrias I would not hesitate to show myself. I would deal with him just as I had his sons if I had to. Or perhaps it would be the amulet which aided me, in the short time I had had it, it had never glowed before. It would be a fitting way to test my capabilities.

"It is no secret that Melanthios harbored feelings for his brother's wife. Ever since she arrived in Epirus, he wanted her for himself. I told him to bide his time. I knew Basileios was not akin to the rest of us. He had never had the stomach for the killing. I knew there would come a time when Melanthios could have what he wanted, and I helped him when the opportunity arose."

"You did not hesitate to have your own son killed?" Agrias asked, taking another fig.

"No, though had I known I would lose all my sons in this place, perhaps I would have accompanied them when they came."

"You have not come to merely see the place they lost their lives, have you?"

"No. I have come to claim what is rightfully mine."

I tightened my grip on the sword in my hand.

"Rightfully yours? What do you mean?" Agrias asked, hand poised on its way to his mouth.

"Your daughter. She belongs to me. To us."

Alexis collapsed against the wall and I barely got an arm under her in time.

"How so? Your sons have all perished, there is no one to claim her. I am free to wed her to anyone I choose, and I have done so."

"That is where you are wrong. I am here to claim her. I am the last living male kin of Basileios. She belongs to me. The so called 'wedding' you speak of means nothing. Two women cannot be joined as such."

"And why not?"

"Because they cannot create a child. Your line cannot continue. When I return with her to Epirus, I shall ensure she gives a son to the Molossian tribe."

Alexis' breathing was shallow.

"Then you have not heard, Alexis is with child. She and Skylar are to be parents this spring."

"Impossible. The child must belong to one of my sons. If not Basileios, then Melanthios, he had time with her when the Illyrians descended on your town."

Agrias shook his head. "Melanthios never lay with her and even if he had, she would be further along."

My eyes drifted to Alexis and just for a moment jealousy and fear flooded through me – Gnosidicus had confirmed she was large for her moons. Was it possible the child belonged to Melanthios? I shook the thoughts from mind, annoyed with myself for even considering it. Hera's actions in Pera Chora, the tests Deacon had performed at Epidaurus and Ares' own admission of his involvement told us otherwise. The child which grew inside Alexis was mine. Ours.

"I do not believe you. You have made a grave mistake by allowing your daughter to be wed to someone who has no status. She is a *woman*. Unimportant for anything other than birthing children for our lines."

"Then you have also not heard that Skylar has allied us with the Spartans. King Cleomenes himself was present at their betrothal. He is a close friend to her and he would not take kindly to hearing you speak of her in such a manner."

"I do not care what the King of Sparta *thinks*. He is not here to defend her name, and I would dispatch of him just as any other enemy I faced. I have not forgotten his interference in Stratos when he thwarted my men. Perhaps when I leave here, I shall pay him a visit. Slit his throat in his sleep then drag his body out into the street and tie him to a column for the birds to pick at until his precious people find him."

The amulet glowed brighter. I moved out of sight of the banquet hall and took it from beneath my cuirass. It was warm between my fingers, the heat travelling through my hand and up my arm. Andreas' sword was at his side, but his shield lay against the wall outside the room. His back was to us, and it would be easy to catch him unawares and kill him before he had a chance to even draw his weapon. I inhaled deeply, putting the amulet back beneath the bronze. Not yet. Not when I did not know how to use it. What if I wounded Agrias rather than Andreas? I needed to speak to Ares. I needed him to teach me how to wield the weapon he had gifted me.

"You cannot deny that it is my right to claim your daughter as my own. Have her return to Trachis immediately, or you shall find yourself meeting Hades before moon's end."

"I shall not. I am satisfied in the partner I have chosen for my daughter. Our ties are severed. You cannot have her."

"Do not test my patience, King."

"I have no intention of doing so, Andreas. You shall do what you believe is best, just as I have done. Now, if you shall excuse me, I have matters to attend."

"We are not done here."

"For now, we are. Feel free to remain and finish your food. One of my soldiers shall see you to your lodgings. Oh, and just so you know, our soldiers are far better trained and equipped since your last visit, so you may want to consider whether your own men are skilled and healthy enough to face us, given your recent battle with the Illyrians."

"Come," I whispered to Alexis, taking her hand. I led her back to our apartment, the amulet dark again at my chest. "Remain here. Keep the door locked," I told her.

"Where are you going?"

"To find Ares. I cannot allow Andreas to threaten your family. I need to know what I can do with the amulet."

"I saw its light. What does it mean?"

"I do not know but I have to find out."

She nodded, pushing up onto her toes to kiss me. "Be safe. Do not allow Andreas to see you."

"He does not know what I look like," I reminded her.

"No, but how many other women warriors are there here?"

"Good point," I conceded. "I shall be careful and return as soon as I can."

26

I took Skotos and rode the narrow path between the palace and the base of Mount Oetaea. When I reached the Melas River, I stopped, slipping between the tree line and dismounting before I spoke Ares' name, the god appearing almost immediately.

"The amulet was glowing. Is that what it did for my mother before she used it?" I asked.

"What were you doing at the time?"

"Andreas is here. He is the father of the man Alexis was once betrothed to. He has come to claim her now all his sons are dead."

"You were angry?"

"Among other things, yes."

"What else?"

"Fearful. Protective. Alexis was with me. I wanted to use the amulet but as I do not know how, I held back. I did not want to risk harming her or her father." Ares only nodded. "Teach me how to use it. What is it capable of? You spoke of me being able to use the four elements. Dianthe told me they were fire, water, wind and earth. How can I do that? Can I choose which one I want to call on first or is there a specific order?"

Ares grinned and held up his hand. "For every Ker in the line, the element of fire has always been the first to be harnessed. Your mother was the lone exception when she brought forth the water element. I do not know what yours shall be but allow us to see which you are favored with."

I took the leather from my neck, the swinging gem catching the light of the sun and reflecting it off the trees. Ares stood behind me, his fingers working to loosen the hinge at my side.

"What are you doing?" I jumped, spinning to face him as I slapped his hands away.

"If your wings emerge when you use the amulet, you do not want to damage your cuirass, do you?"

"Oh. No," I replied, allowing him to resume the task before I set the bronze aside on the ground.

Ares nodded and, with his hands on my shoulders, he turned me to face the largest of the trees nearby. It was the one I had taken my frustration out on the day Alexis had refused to accept my gift of perfume; the bark still bearing traces of my attack.

"Wrap your fingers around the amulet, hold it so as much of your palm touches it as possible. Focus your mind. Your thoughts shall become one with the amulet. It understands your wants, your desires, your fears. It feeds off them to carry out whatever you would ask of it. You need speak no words out loud for it to be so."

Ares' voice was soft, seductive almost at my ear. The feelings of fear and restlessness which had consumed me since I saw Andreas at the palace cooled with his voice. A deep calm washed over me as I stared at the tree ahead. I trusted Ares and the amulet completely.

"Direct the amulet to the tree. Send it up in flames," he continued.

I nodded, settling my gaze on one of the deep cuts and raising my arm. I narrowed my eyes so the tree was foremost in my vision, conjuring up burning forests and flames in my mind. The amulet remained dark in my hand. There was not even the slightest glow. I squeezed my eyes shut, thinking of the flames heating cauldrons of water, the flames of the forge in Thorikos when I had heated the silver for the coins. I opened my eyes. The amulet remained static in my hand. Had I imagined the change of color back at the palace? No. Alexis had seen it as well.

I frowned. "What is wrong? I am concentrating just as you said," I growled, dropping my arm to my side.

"You must *want* to call forth the power, it must be topmost in your mind," Ares replied.

"It is," I snapped.

"Remain calm. Attempt it again," he soothed. I took a deep breath, that calmness washing over me once again.

I spread my legs to shoulder width apart and brought my hand up. I exhaled slowly and closed my eyes. I imagined Melanthios tied to the tree, flames licking across his skin as they engulfed the bark of the trunk and scorched its leaves. My hand began to warm. I gasped, opening my eyes.

The amulet was glowing, yellow at first, but darkening quickly to a deep orange, the heat intensifying with the color. My shoulders prickled beneath my tunic but I did not reach to touch them. I grinned.

"Good," Ares said, and I heard the smile in his voice. "Keep concentrating. Envisage what you wish for and make it so." Nearing hooves broke my concentration and I turned. "I shall remain hidden, unless you wish me to appear," Ares murmured, gone in a flash of light before I could even acknowledge his words.

Thaddeus appeared on the path, running alongside his horse, Darko. Alexis rode atop the animal and two bags were strapped across Darko's rump. I lifted a brow. The amulet continued to glow and I closed my hand to conceal it, the skin of my shoulder blades itching feverishly. "What are you doing here?" I asked, crossing to Thaddeus and Alexis, scratching absently at the left side of my back.

"Agrias asked me to find you. Andreas has arrived," Thaddeus replied.

"I told him we already knew," Alexis added, allowing me to assist her from the horse. "Father has requested we leave Trachis so Andreas does not accidently discover us, or discover me at least."

"And go where? I shall not leave your parents to face Andreas alone. He does not appear to have brought his men with him, but who is to say they do not follow, as Melanthios had his men do when he came?"

"Skylar, you should consider the request. You have your child to think of now as well," Thaddeus counselled.

"I *am* thinking of her and we are not leaving. Ares and I have a plan."

"Ares, the … the God of War?" he stammered.

I only nodded in reply. "I shall explain when I return. Wait for me at our apartment and find the king and queen."

"And your father, shall I fetch him also?" Thaddeus asked carefully.

"No."

Thaddeus nodded and took Darko to stand beside a flat rock, offering Alexis his hand as she climbed back up.

Ares' voice was suddenly at my ear, but he did not materialize beside me. "Return to the palace with your family. I believe I have a way for you to harness your powers, but it shall take a little time to organize."

"You are not going to share your thoughts with me?" I murmured.

"Not yet. When the times comes, you shall know. I shall guide you through it, just as we have begun today."

"The Molossians carry shields with Zeus' standing eagle on them – does the King of the Gods lend support to them? Would he stop me if I used the amulet against Andreas?" I asked, the thought suddenly occurring to me.

"If he cared intimately about their fates, I doubt he would have allowed you to kill Andreas' sons and remain in this world," Ares replied.

I nodded, hearing the truth in his words. "Wait," I said to Thaddeus, crossing to them and halting Alexis' progress onto Darko. "I *shall* come with you now. Alexis can ride with me."

"Of course," Thaddeus nodded, waiting until we were settled atop Skotos before turning Darko and starting off down the mountain path.

I was far from satisfied with what I had achieved with the amulet so far, but I did not doubt Ares' words; he would ensure I could protect those I loved from harm and dispose of the ones who threatened them.

*

We had returned to the city without incident. Hesper met us at the stables and told us Andreas had retired to his room, she then fetched Agrias and Melina and brought them to Alexis, Thaddeus and me. I had already spoken of Ares, what the amulet could do, and how he would teach me to use it, but kept words of Dianthe and what she had told me of the Keres to myself; that was not important for now. I hoped.

"Are you certain you can use this amulet … this weapon?" Agrias asked.

"Yes. With Ares' guidance I possess something that can keep us safe from any attack Andreas attempts. You need to meet with Andreas again and tell him you have sent for Alexis and me."

"No. I was adamant I would not request the two of you return."

"I understand. But we must not bring down another war on Trachis. If Andreas believes you are cooperating with him then there is a chance I can deal with him before he expects such a fight. How long would it take for us to get here if you truly were to send a messenger to Aigai?"

"Given Alexis' condition, half-a-moon perhaps."

"Then we shall leave the palace until that time, or until I have gained enough knowledge to use the amulet against Andreas."

"I thought you did not want to leave," Alexis said, moving closer and taking my hand.

"I do not, but it is too dangerous to remain here where Andreas is. The risk of discovery is too great."

"Where do you intend to go?" Thaddeus asked.

"We shall not be far. In town somewhere," I replied.

"Andreas has shown an interest in the metalworking hut, so you cannot go to Ophelos and Aspasia's home," he noted.

"I have no intention of being so close to my father," I muttered.

"Perhaps we could trouble Gnosidicus for a room," Alexis suggested, squeezing my hand.

"Yes," I agreed with a nod. "I am certain the healer would have us. Agrias, we must remain vigilant with our scouts. Speak with Moeris and have him place a number of men at the Melas, Dyras and Spercheios rivers. If Andreas has already sent for his warriors, we want to have as much time to prepare for them as possible."

"Should you not go to your father; include him in your plans? He is as skilled as you when it comes to making plans for battle," Agrias suggested.

"No," I replied. This was my battle now and I would deal with it as I saw fit.

Agrias exhaled loudly. "It saddens me to see the two of you at such odds. I wish you would reconsider your position and speak with him. But if you are determined to keep away then I shall tell him of Andreas' arrival," he said, holding his hand up when I began to protest. "As Thaddeus notes, Andreas has an interest in the metalworking area, so he may meet his people there rather than anywhere else. Your father may see or hear something before we do."

"If Andreas is smart, he shall not call his men to come all at once as Melanthios did. Perhaps he shall place them within the town in small groups, or individually even," I mused. "A small number of men travelling together would not arouse suspicion with our scouts, especially if their weapons were hidden."

"You believe they would be dressed as merchants?" Melina asked.

"Perhaps. They would be hidden in plain sight, it is the perfect cover. Ensure Moeris has extra soldiers patrolling the streets," I ordered, meeting Thaddeus' eyes. "Anyone they do not recognize should be questioned further. I have no doubt Andreas is cunning, he would not have remained as feared all these winters were it not so. But we shall be ready for him."

"You shall keep our loved ones safe, as you always do," Hesper agreed with a tight grin.

"Always," I nodded, addressing Thaddeus again. "Tell Moeris to look out for Antigonos also, with Andreas being here, I would not be surprised to find he is as well."

"I shall tell him," he nodded.

27

Shouting and cries of fear drew my attention and I was out of my chair before Alexis or Gnosidicus could react. "Remain here," I commanded, crossing to the high window which faced the street. Women ran past the healer's house, grasping their children's hands and pulling them along behind. Two of our soldiers quickly followed, shepherding a number of elderly citizens and slaves along the road and back to their own homes.

The door shook loudly as someone pounded on it from the other side. "It is me," came Thaddeus' voice. I opened it quickly, remaining hidden behind the wood until he was inside.

"What is it?"

"An army," he panted, attempting to regain his breath.

"Andreas' men?"

He shook his head. "No. They do not carry his shields. They march from the north and the south, their ships anchored in the Malian Gulf, past the mouths of the Spercheios and the hot springs. We have perhaps a candlemark before they converge and reach the town."

"What designs are on their weapons?"

"A bird holding a flaming torch."

"Andreas' tribe carries shields with standing eagles, so they cannot be his men," I agreed. "Who are they loyal to? Are you able to tell what kind of bird?"

"A vulture perhaps? I have never seen them before, they are not a familiar enemy."

I nodded to myself, already planning the attack. Perhaps this was Ares' doing? Though if this was his test, certainly he would have warned me of it so I could ensure Alexis was safe. I reached for my cuirass, pulling it over my head as I spoke again. "Andreas would expect us back any day now, so it is time he knew I have arrived. Take Gnosidicus and Alexis back to the palace, ensure they are safe, along with your own family and Agrias and Melina. Take Nasrin as well."

"Of course," he nodded.

The familiar weight of my weapons and a specific purpose was a comfort; Alexis and I had spent almost half a moon cooped up in Gnosidicus' house with nothing to do but wait for the time to pass. The healer had entertained us with stories and we swapped knowledge on different herbs we had used to treat injuries, but even Alexis was craving the feel of the sun on her face and a walk through the agora.

"What are you going to do?" Alexis asked, halting my movements with a hand on my arm.

"I shall go to their leader and speak with him. If he is not willing to come to terms then I shall kill him and the rest of his men to protect you and our families," I replied, placing a quick kiss on her lips. I fastened my belt and slid my sword into the sheath at my thigh. I took my shield and opened the door again, ensuring the street was safe for my lover and the old healer to travel through before I allowed them past me.

"Be safe," Thaddeus said, offering me his arm.

"And you," I nodded as I took it.

"We shall see you again soon," Gnosidicus added as he made his way outside.

"You shall."

"Do not take any unnecessary risks. We need you," Alexis whispered. With her hand on her rounded belly, she kissed me again, her tongue finding mine. The familiar whisper of desire skated along my spine and I wrapped my arm around her waist, pulling her closer as I deepened our kiss.

"Not as much as I need the two of you," I murmured when we parted. "I love you. Go with Thaddeus and be safe." She nodded in reply and followed the men out the door.

I took a deep breath and squared my shoulders, closing the wood with a satisfying thud behind me. The streets were mostly empty, frightened faces peering out of the doors of houses I passed, whimpering children being told to quiet by their mothers. I trailed Thaddeus, Gnosidicus and Alexis for two blocks before turning into a side street, hoping to catch a glimpse of the approaching army closer to the water.

Hesper had visited us every couple of days while we had been at Gnosidicus', bringing news from Thaddeus and the king. There had been a few new faces in town but all appeared to have legitimate business or were simply passing through, gone again the next day in most cases. I had told Hesper not to take the same streets each time she came and to stop in at a number of merchant stalls or other homes before and after she reached us. Andreas knew she was Alexis' closest friend and if he was watching her, I did not want him to discover us, or capture and torture Hesper until she gave us up.

The agora was deserted, goods left on many of the tables, too cumbersome to flee quickly with as the merchants abandoned their posts. The amulet pressed into my breastbone as I jogged along but so far it remained cool and dark.

I had seen Andreas only once during our confinement in town. One night, whilst Gnosidicus and Alexis slumbered, I left the healer's house, attempting to call forth the fire element Ares had spoken of. I wanted to remove the Molossian threat so we could return to the palace sooner rather than later. Nothing had happened, I was unable to convince the amulet to change color; not even when I saw Andreas standing on the northern balcony, his hands wrapped around a slave girl's neck as he drove himself inside her.

I had returned to the town cursing Ares' name, and threatening to discard the amulet if he did not appear. I implored him to come and help me as I wanted. As he had promised to. But even if he was incensed at the disrespect I showed him, he remained hidden. When I got back to Gnosidicus', I found the old man awake and waiting. He chastised me, giving his word he would not speak of it with Alexis, if I gave mine that I would not leave again. I did so but only because I felt as though I must wait for the right time – the way Ares had waited for me.

I turned another corner and almost crashed into my father. "Skylar, thank the gods I have found you. The palace has been breached," he said, his words tumbling from his mouth.

"How is that possible? Thaddeus said the armies were at least a candlemark away," I replied, noting he too wore his armor.

"I cannot explain, I can only report as Moeris reported it to me; he asked me to join the fight. Please, can we put our quarrel behind us? For now at least?"

If the army had already arrived, then remaining at the metalwork hut or out of the fight was not an option for my father – even I knew that – but I was not ready to forgive him. "What about the army marching from the north?" I asked instead.

"There is no army at the north; they are all at the palace."

"Gods, Alexis," I murmured. "Come, Thaddeus took Alexis and Gnosidicus back there. I told him to find Nasrin as well."

"She is with them. We must hurry."

I only nodded in reply, turning back towards the palace, my father a step behind as we ran through the empty streets, jumping smashed amphorae as we went. Though we were far from making amends, I could not deny I was glad to have him at my side for the fight. I feared for Alexis and what we would find when we reached our home, but I knew we could face it together, just as we always had.

By the time we reached the outskirts of the town, the huge army came into view. Metal swords and shields met with force, the sound of which could be heard from where we were. Our men and theirs battled and felled one another all along the east balcony and through the imposing portico and entrance; line after line waiting for their chance to test their skill against the enemy.

Father and I drew our weapons, racing into the fray and slicing and discarding a large number of enemy soldiers before they realized they were under attack from behind. Cutting a path through, I reached the entrance, taking a bow and arrow from the loose grip of one of our dead soldiers and lighting it from a nearby torch. I fired it into the crowd, finding an unguarded neck with deadly accuracy. I picked up the quiver of arrows and continued in the same manner until they were all gone, by which time my father had joined me.

"Am I glad to see the two of you," Moeris said, skidding to a halt beside us. "I cannot explain how they arrived so fast, but we are surrounded – there are hundreds of them along the northern balcony and between the palace and the stables," he reported, without needing to be asked.

"Did you see Thaddeus?" I asked, gripping his arm tightly.

"Skylar!" the named man's voice cut through the sounds of the battle and I turned, my stomach clenching when I saw the blood leaking from the cut on his head and dripping off his chin.

"Where is she?" I asked, rushing to his side.

"He took her."

"Who?" I asked.

"The soldier. It was as if he knew exactly where to find us."

"Where were you?" my father asked. I did not care for the answer, wanting only to find Alexis. It was Melanthios all over again, Thaddeus again the one who had allowed her to be taken.

We fought our way inside the portico, soldiers streaming in behind. The four of us drove them back, managing to get the doors shut and locked against them. I searched the blood-spattered crowd for my lover. She was nowhere to be seen.

"The kitchen. I believed the women and children would be safe there. Agrias agreed," Thaddeus replied as though there had been no interruption between Father's question and his answer.

"Where are the king and queen, and your family and Nasrin now? Are they hurt?" Moeris asked.

"They were not harmed. They remain hidden in the kitchen. But ... they took no one else, Skylar. It was as if the soldiers had been sent to find Alexis specifically. To take her and leave everyone else untouched. They only hit me because I refused to release my grip on her," Thaddeus said. "It does not make sense."

"No," I murmured. The sounds of battle suddenly fell silent and I frowned, my father catching my eye and noting the same.

"What ...?" he began. I ran to the doors, pushing the locking device up and throwing it aside before yanking them open.

28

The soldiers were still there – friend and foe alike. The enemy soldiers were now gathered between the balcony and the town itself, whereas our men were huddled on the plain to the north, their weapons gone, defeated in stance. Andreas was among them, as cowed as the rest. I frowned, not having expected to see him there.

There must have been a thousand men between us and Trachis, perhaps more. They stood so close together that it was impossible to tell the exact number, the colored plumes on their helmets the only way to distinguish one from the other in a sea of black leather. They held no shields. No swords. No javelins or axes. And they were silent. Completely silent.

A single figure emerged from the plain beneath the northern balcony. He was tall, muscular. He held no shield, but the long blade of his sword sat across the throat of my lover as he walked her to the front of the waiting army. The amulet warmed beneath my cuirass, a faint orange glow visible in the corner of my eye.

Moeris broke from our group, heading directly for the soldier and Alexis. "No!" I yelled, throwing my arm out to stop him. He shook me off and kept running, raising his sword as he neared. I took a step forward.

"Wait," my father cautioned, putting his hand on my shoulder and holding me in place. "Look. The soldier does not believe Moeris can harm him." Father removed his hand and I remained where I was, watching. I gripped my own weapon even tighter, heart pounding as I prayed Moeris' reckless run did not cause the death of my wife and child.

Moeris slashed and attacked, but his sword bounced off some invisible shield. The soldier raised no defense of his own but neither did he draw the metal across Alexis' neck in retaliation.

I considered my earlier thought about the army belonging to Ares. With the soldier's calm demeanor, and the unseen but obvious shield, I was almost certain of it. But why had Ares placed Alexis in danger? And how had my father known she would be safe even when Moeris attacked? What had he seen that I had not? Or was it simply because he had witnessed it before?

Alexis' eyes locked with mine and I saw her fear. She was calling to me, but I could not hear her. My shoulder blades itched savagely and I squirmed in my tunic. The soldier encouraged Alexis forward roughly and she stumbled, his sword drawing a slither of blood from her neck. I took another step towards them. My father did not attempt to stop me. He halted them when they reached the head of the gathered army. Still silent. Still motionless.

A faint shimmer in front of Alexis caught my eye, but I had no time to question anyone on it before a much brighter light flashed beside me. Tearing my eyes from Alexis, I found Ares and my grandmother standing beside me.

"Thrax," my father growled, at my side once again.

"Thrax?" I repeated.

Ares grinned and nodded. "It is what I am known as to the Thracians. You still recall much of the old ways, even after all these winters, old man."

"Some things are hard to forget. Especially when you are involved," my father spat. "You have returned to his side?" he added, addressing Dianthe.

"I came to see the error of my ways," she replied, just as frostily.

"Realigning with your master was the only error you made. I believed if ever we met again you would aid me in hiding your granddaughter from the rest of your kin."

"Why would I do that when she holds such power? Without her, Ares can never have what he wants."

"You once wished that what he wanted would never come to pass."

"Those days are long past."

"If you had spoken of the child growing inside Zita, we could have aided in her birth. Zita did not have to die," Ares said, a smug grin gracing his lips.

"She died because of you," my father shot back.

"You should not have kept Skylar from us. How do you think she felt having to constantly move? She never had the chance to make friends, to know a real family. You denied her those things. You should have left her for us the night Zita died instead of running as a coward. She could have had everything she ever wanted with us. She could have known her power sooner."

"Stop it! You speak as though I am not here, and do you not see the army before us?" I interrupted, the bronze of my cuirass growing hotter by the moment. "They are yours?" I asked, catching Ares' gaze and nodding towards the gathered army.

He nodded. "Your test."

"Tell them to release Alexis."

"That is for you to do," he replied.

"How can I be certain she is not harmed?" I frowned, the prickling at my shoulders increasing with the heat of my cuirass.

"Trust me. Trust the amulet."

"The amulet?" my father repeated, his mouth dropping open as I turned to look at him. "You have the amulet?"

I put my sword back in its sheath and drew the amulet from my cuirass to show him, allowing its growing light to replace the oncoming dusk. With its removal, my armor began to cool, the heat instead flowing as if liquid up and down my arms, filling me with a calm and certainty. I took the leather from my neck, enfolding the jet and hematite in my palm as I faced the army once again.

"When did you …? Skylar, do not do this. Please. Do not attempt to use the amulet. No good can come of it," Father implored.

An intoxicating confidence flooded my veins and I stood up straighter, allowing it to find every part of me. "Quiet. I am done listening to you. To your lies. It is time I found out who I truly am. A truth which should have been shared long ago." I could use the amulet, of that I was certain. There was no need to fear I would hurt Alexis when I did – the amulet would protect her as well as I ever had. Better perhaps. It knew my thoughts, my desires. It knew I loved her and that I would do whatever I must to protect her. She would be safe.

"Please," Father said again.

Ares silenced him; sweeping him aside in a gust of wind. "Your daughter is a powerful Ker whether you like it or not. She has decided to embrace what I have offered her. You have no say in the matter any longer."

Nasrin, Agrias and Melina had arrived, though I did not know when or where from. They rushed to Father's side and aided him to his feet. I turned my gaze from them. They were unimportant. Alexis. The amulet. The soldiers before me were what I must focus on. I exhaled a deep breath, the ways in which I would bring about the deaths of the army before me playing in my mind.

Ares approached, speaking quietly, his hands on my shoulders. "When you dispense with these soldiers, everyone shall know of your power. No one shall attempt to bring harm to Alexis or your child ever again. The three of you shall know true protection and you can become one with your

Ker family."

"I am ready," I told him, no doubt clouding my words or my ability.

"Then save your princess from the clutches of a man who would not hesitate to take her to his bed and kill the child within her so he could place one of his own inside."

My breath caught in my throat as Ares' words cut through me. Fear, pain, anger, pure rage, swirled through my heart and heated my stomach. I would kill him. I would kill them all. I would prove to Dianthe and Ares that I was who they had waited for. I was their Chosen One. I would embrace my destiny and my family line. I would be all my mother could not be; all those who had come before her could not be.

The itching sensation high up on my back intensified, laced now with sharp bursts of pain either side of my spine. I clenched my jaw against it as the amulet grew brighter, the orange now mirroring the sun when it reached the highest point in the sky. Blowing out the deep breath I had been holding, I lowered my chin to my chest, squeezing my eyes shut against the stabbing sensations at my back. It was akin to the sword thrust of the Molossian tribesman who had bested me when I first arrived in the Spercheios Valley, only this time it felt as if he was using two swords.

I dropped to my haunches, the amulet continuing to heat and fill me with calm assuredness. I was not afraid of the pain. I understood my wings needed to break free. I must have them before I could destroy the army. Before I could save Alexis and our daughter. I drove my fist into the ground, panting as I waited. Over the sound of my own breathing there was nothing. No one spoke. No one cleared their throat. No soldier's armor clanged, no weapon found another. No sound until the screech of a bird broke the silence overhead, and with it the amulet's orange light brightened between my fingers and the agony at my back reached its peak.

My tunic ripped, a metallic ping following almost immediately as my wings broke through my skin and everything above, two perfectly round pieces of bronze landing beside me as the pain diminished as quickly as it had arrived.

I stood and turned my head, finding long, black poles, pointed at each end, extending from my back. As thick as javelins, and just as smooth and deadly when I ran my hand along one of the shafts. Long tendrils of black silk dropped from them. No, not silk; feathers. Wide, soft feathers. I stroked the nearest ones, surprised that though they appeared fragile and slightly damp with newness, they were strong. Arrows would not be able to penetrate them if they were suddenly loosed in my direction.

Ares was at my side again, removing the hinge pin; my cuirass falling to the ground in pieces. He circled me but did not place hands on me again. "My Chosen One," he grinned. "Take your revenge on the men who would claim your Princess as their own. Show your father the power you possess.

Show him that he did not succeed in keeping this from you, though he attempted to for so many winters. You belong to us just as much as him and with my guidance, you shall become known throughout Greece, and perhaps beyond. You shall never fear anyone again." I nodded in reply, a smile finding its way to my lips.

I wanted to invoke fear into the hearts of those who would consider taking what was mine, what was ours. Never again would Andreas – or anyone else – come to claim Alexis. She was mine. Andreas would not leave Trachis alive, I would ensure it was so. I searched the gathered crowd around me, Moeris and the soldiers of Trachis stood, entrapped in another slightly shimmering cage. Mouths open and disbelief written across their faces. Andreas' reaction was the same, though his had a reasonable dose of fear as well. Good.

My father pounded his fist, his cries of anger lost behind another transparent wall of Ares' making. I realized it was not the first time I had seen those shimmering walls; I had found myself behind one at Aphrodite's temple in Corinth. Had it been Ares who helped Aphrodite and prevented me from going anywhere other than into the room with Alexis? I would ask him later.

Turning my attention from my father, my gaze fell upon my broken cuirass. I barely gave it a glance, though I knew I would never again wear it. Without thought of doing so, I raised my arm, exposing the amulet to the enemy soldiers. Alexis' eyes widened. "Skylar?" she murmured, the wall no longer between us.

"And now you die," I grinned.

I held the amulet up higher, the hematite searing the tips of my fingers, its impression bound to leave a permanent reminder on my skin. The smell of blood streaking down Alexis' neck inflamed my senses as much as her perfume ever had and I knew it was time to end it.

I closed my eyes for a moment, gathering thought of what I wanted from the amulet. I did not need Ares' guidance. I did not need his words or my father's lies. I did not need to know of my history from Dianthe or the proud line I belonged to. I could feel it. I knew it all. I was who they had waited for. My name would be known throughout Greece. Throughout Macedonia and Thrace. Throughout Persia. I would have what I wanted and no one could stop me – not even the gods.

I opened my eyes again, finding the pair hidden behind the soldier's helmet across from me. I took a step forward, rebalancing my weight to accommodate my new wings and sent up my wish. A long finger of fire flew from the amulet's core. With tight swirls of red, yellow and orange, it streaked forward, headed directly for the soldier who held Alexis. A mere moment later, it connected with the plume on top of his helmet, setting it alight before engulfing his entire body in bright flame. The heat radiating from his burning skin and clothing caused the rest of the army to take a step back. He released Alexis, his hands going to his head as screams of agony filled the air.

Alexis stumbled, scrambling away from the writhing fireball until she was back at my side. The army stood in bewilderment, as I did, mesmerized by the sight of their leader on fire. He ran around and around, grabbing at his head and arms until finally he fell to the ground, dead. The flames disappeared, leaving only a pile of blackened bones. Absently I reached out my hand and steadied Alexis, my other still holding the amulet, now trained on the rest of the soldiers. None of them moved any further than the one step they had already taken. They appeared too stunned to decide if I was a threat to them now that Alexis had been released.

I caught her eye. She did not appear scared of me exactly. Apprehensive perhaps, but curious, as she reached out to touch the feathers of my wings. "They are soft," she murmured.

I nodded and held my arm up. She hesitated only a moment before wrapping her own around my waist and hiding her face from the burnt man before us. I settled it around her shoulder, a new wave of calm command coursing through my blood. For Alexis and our daughter to be truly safe, I must destroy the rest of the army. To send that message to everyone gathered.

My grin was almost a snarl as a bird called out above me again. I concentrated on drawing forth the heat and power of the adrenaline flowing through my body. My heartbeat was loud in my ears and chest. My wings responded when I flexed them; extending out either side of me instead of hanging at my back.

Ares' soldiers finally found voice and weapons, looking to one another as they produced swords and shields apparently out of nowhere. They raised them, but before any could give a command to charge, I gave my own order to the amulet. A massive fireball shot from the amulet, consuming each and every soldier who held Ares' shield. They ran about, clutching uselessly at their bodies, just as their leader had. Human fireballs. The stench of cooking flesh permeating the air around me, filling me with a sense of triumph.

When the last of my enemies were dead, their bodies no more than charred remains, Alexis raised her head, her eyes flitting over the scene before resting on mine. "You killed them," she whispered, her voice filled with awe.

"For you," I nodded. "I would kill anyone who attempted to take you from me."

"As you always have."

"Yes."

Alexis dropped her eyes, following the caress of her finger as she drew it along my collarbone, my body instantly responding. I placed a finger beneath her chin, raising her face until our gaze met once again. My breathing grew shallow as the black center of her eyes increased. I could see the power of the amulet had drawn her in. I could feel it in her touch. The battle lust I had always experienced was nothing compared to what I felt now. Desire and an insatiable hunger for her ran rampant beneath my skin. I wanted to feel her body against mine, to run my hands across her naked flesh as I brought her to the pinnacle of pleasure. My needs were reflected on her face.

I swallowed loudly as her fingers untied my sheath and belt, dropping both to the ground before drawing the fibula from my shoulder. She aided my tunic to join them, exposing me to those who remained outside the palace, her eyes hungrily tracing every rise and curve as I had done to her body so many times.

Alexis wet her lips with the tip of her tongue. I could wait no longer. I would not wait any longer. I must have her. I pulled her against me, finding her lips with unerring accuracy. She drove her hands into my hair, her mouth possessing mine with the same ferocity that I took hers. I slid my hand to Alexis' thigh, drawing her chiton into my hand, a puff of breath expelling from her mouth when I found the hot, soft skin of her leg. I slid my fingers higher, drawn to the warm center, her hands tightening in my hair.

The amulet was still in my hand, though my grip was loose on it. It had lost none of its color, nor its heat, and I could feel its hold over us both. I wished Alexis and I were alone but I had no intention of taking her anywhere, close as we were to satisfying one another's desire. Besides, it would not be the first time I had had an audience for such actions.

The amulet knew what I wanted. A wall of fire sprung up around Alexis and me, hiding us from the view of our families and the soldiers of Trachis as effectively as it hid them from us. Without sound or sight of anyone else, I could almost believe we were the only ones there. Completely alone. Able to enjoy one another without interruption or needing explanation.

I broke our kiss. My heart beat furiously in my chest as I stripped Alexis of her chiton and trailed one finger between her breasts and over the round, firm stomach where our child grew. She opened her thighs as my hand slipped lower, finding her slick beneath my touch.

"Skylar," she sighed, arching her back and inviting me inside. "Gods how I love it when you touch me." I was taken back to the first time we had been together, at the hot springs, my thighs moistening as I recalled my words to her that day. *"I want to touch you ... everywhere,"* I had told her. *"Please,"* she had begged in return. *"Show me how you feel."*

Show me how you feel. The words reverberated inside my mind, as though she was speaking them to me now, not eight moons ago. *Show me,* she insisted, and I noted the high color in my lover's cheeks.

She untangled her hand from my hair, gliding it down to my forearm, holding my hand in place as she moved on me. "Love me," she murmured, her eyelids fluttering shut.

"For you I would do anything, my Princess," I replied, just as I had that day. Without breaking the sweet contact that was turning my blood to liquid fire, I circled Alexis, pressing my front against her back as I kept up the movements.

Alexis pushed back into me and I gasped at the sudden pressure against my own sensitive flesh. I swept aside her hair, bringing my teeth down onto her neck and biting as I slipped inside her.

"Skylar …" she cried, a combination of wanting and ecstasy. She reached back and fisted her hand in my hair again, ensuring my teeth remained hard against her flesh as I gave her what she wanted. What we both wanted. Needed.

29

I sat on the soft grass, attempting to catch my breath again after the intensity of my release. The wall of flames spluttered out and disappeared as I opened my hand. The amulet was still in my palm, but the jet had returned to its darkened state, rather than the brilliant orange it had been. A torch had been dug into the ground nearby, lighting the area around me and I wondered how long Alexis and I had been inside the fire, sating our desire for one another.

Alexis. I grinned, recalling the guttural noises she made as I drew the last spasms from her body. Ever since I had known her, I had wanted her. I would have given anything to call her mine long before I did. If I had had the amulet, perhaps I would have. How many others could I have had, or saved, if my father had never kept the truth from me? Would Kuria still be alive? What would I have done to Stamatis when he attempted to send me from their room?

The curve of Alexis' spine faced me as she knelt on hands and knees; her breath just as elusive to her as mine was to me. I trailed my finger down her back, wondering again at the softness of her skin. She jumped, scrambling away from my touch. I raised an eyebrow but allowed her to gather her chiton and press it to her chest, as she stood. "Oh gods. What have we done?"

"Do not pretend it was not everything you wanted," I smirked, standing as I felt my wings retract beneath my skin.

"You ... I ... no. No!" she shouted, holding her hand up when I took a

159

step forward.

I shrugged, re-settling the amulet around my neck and reaching for my tunic. "Come find me when you want to feel alive again, sweetheart."

She took another step backwards, wrapping the material around her body without breaking eye contact. "I shall never want that again."

I laughed.

"How quickly you forget the way your body reacts when I touch you."

"It was a mistake," she insisted, moving even further away.

I held my hands up and gave her another shrug. "We shall see. I look forward to seeing you back in our apartment. I am certain you shall not deny either of us of the pleasures that await."

"I never want to see you again. I hate you." Ares approached Alexis. "Take me away from her. Do not allow her to find me," she pleaded with him.

"Of course," he said quietly, offering her his hand.

"Skylar! Alexis!" my father shouted. I turned, watching as he ran towards us, waving his arms almost comically.

"We shall see you again soon, Granddaughter," Dianthe said.

"Indeed," I nodded, pulling my tunic over my head and pinning the fibula at my shoulder.

"No, Alexis, do not leave. You must not leave, not with him," Father insisted. Agrias and Melina approached apprehensively, their eyes on me rather than their daughter. The invisible wall no longer held Andreas or the soldiers and though they barely moved, I heard their hushed tones and saw the furtive glances they cast in my direction.

Before my father could make his case with Alexis, she took Ares' hand and they disappeared, along with Dianthe. I shielded my eyes from the light and when I looked up again, they were gone and Father was crossing to me.

"Skylar, you must go after them. You must find Alexis."

"It is of no concern to me where she goes," I replied, belting my sword around my waist. I did not care about Alexis' reaction, or her words. She had learned I truly was part Ker and she could not handle such a truth. I was always powerful and strong, but when my wings emerged, it became clear I was not just of this world. No mortal could handle the parts of me which came from Ares, and the Keres. Perhaps I was destined for someone more akin to me – a goddess perhaps – though which of them would lie with me if I proposed such a tryst? Alexis could still be a fun diversion, though in her condition there was much I could not do with her, and I had needs to be met and satisfied. "Good riddance to her I say." I did not need her. I had the amulet. I would have whatever – and whoever – I wanted.

"She is your lover. Your wife. Your heart's deepest des–," my father continued.

"She is nothing but a princess I took to bed," I interjected. "I am the

Chosen One; I could have as many princesses, or indeed queens as I wanted. And I shall when next given the opportunity." My gaze found Melina's and I smirked. "Perhaps Queen Melina would wish to place hands on me again." My father attempted to slap me, but I deflected the blow, pushing him backwards hard enough that he stumbled and fell to the ground. "Do not raise your hand to me, old man," I warned. "Now that I can wield the power of the amulet you would be wise not to incur my wrath any more than you already have."

"You are not yourself."

"I am more myself than I have ever been," I assured him. "With Ares' help I have begun to learn who I truly am and the power which was always meant for me."

"He lies to you."

"As you did? What truths does Ares keep from me that could *ever* compare to all the ones you kept from me?"

"What has he shared with you? Has he spoken to you of the night your mother died? Has he told you who created that amulet and for what reason?"

"He has told me all I need to know for the moment."

"Then you lie to yourself if you believe you can trust everything he tells you."

"I need him no more than I need you. My powers outstrip even his godly ones, though I shall remain in his confidence until I have learned all I need to about how to call forth all four elements."

"That would be a mistake."

Before I could make response, Andreas approached Agrias, grabbing his arm and turning the king to face him. "So, this is how she was able to claim Alexis for herself. With magic. What truly happened to my sons here, Agrias? Was it she who killed them? They displayed wounds earned in battle, but were they mere fabrications to make it appear so? Did she use that ... that ... *gem* on them?"

I crossed to Andreas in three strides, dropping my face so it was level with his. "Your sons got what they deserved. They cast fear amongst their enemies, yet they bled as any other soldier. They were weak, their bodies only blood and bone. I reached inside Melanthios and felt the life draining from him until he breathed his last breath and I did not show him mercy or end his suffering. I ensured he felt *every* last squeeze of his insides until I ran his own blade across his throat." Andreas drew his sword as I drew mine.

"Stay your hand, Skylar," my father warned.

"This does not concern you. It is between Andreas and me, as it was always meant to be."

"Please, Skylar, help us to find Alexis. Do not allow her to remain with Ares," Melina pleaded.

"She shall not be far. Do not worry," I replied, spinning my sword around my hand as I addressed Andreas again. "When Agrias told me you were coming, I knew it could not be just to see where your children died. I knew you must have another reason. You want to claim Alexis for yourself." Andreas nodded, taking a step to his left as he raised his sword. "You cannot have her," I told him.

"She does not appear to want for you any longer, and you speak words of not needing her. So why do you care who has her?" Andreas asked, swinging his sword in my direction.

I fended off the attack, laughing. "She may say the words now, but you underestimate the pleasures I have given her. She shall not remain far from my bed for long." I thrust my sword at his leg, but he evaded it with a block of his own. "You cannot know how many times I wished you had been here when your sons were. I would have killed you just as quickly as I killed them."

"Enough!" Father yelled, wrapping his arms around my chest and pinning mine to my sides. Thaddeus disarmed Andreas, holding him in place with the point of his sword under his chin. I struggled in my father's grip but could not break free.

"Release me," I demanded.

"Not until you take control of yourself. Re-sheathe your sword and return to the palace with us. We must find Alexis."

"You do not need me for such a task. I have no interest in speaking to her again, at least not with words such as you suggest." I laughed until I began to choke; bile rising in my throat. Tremors gripped my body.

"Skylar?" Father asked, alarmed. He loosened his grip and turned me to face him. My head throbbed and a wave of sickness washed over me. I sagged into his arms, my sword dropping from my hand before he gathered me up and held me to his chest.

30

I opened my eyes, the familiar ceiling of the apartment I shared with Alexis greeting me in the muted light from the high window. I attempted to sit up, the light blanket covering me slipping to the ground and revealing the thick length of rope which restrained me.

"Leandros, she wakes," Thaddeus' voice cut through the silence.

My father slumbered in a chair near the door, waking at Thaddeus' words and the hand on his shoulder.

"Release me," I demanded when father stood.

"I shall leave you," Thaddeus said. He nodded to my father, but kept his eyes from mine, closing the door quietly behind himself.

"Untie this rope and allow me free movement."

My father crossed to the bed, pausing to gather the blanket from the ground and place it back over my body. "No. It is well time you heard what I had to say."

"Where is my amulet?"

"Out of your reach for the moment, thank the gods."

"Where is it?" I asked again, teeth gritted as I strained against the bindings.

"Your mother never wanted you to have to make the choice to use it or not."

"It has been you who has kept its existence from me all these winters, not she," I countered, attempting to call to the amulet with my mind.

"And what do you know of the amulet?"

"I know it was made for Ares by the Keres and the Valkyrie," I replied, frustrated the amulet did not appear in my hand as I wanted. "Today's display against his army was only the beginning, the first of the four elements I shall be able to wield to take down enemies. Ares shall teach me to call forth each at will."

Father sighed and sat on the bed beside me. "You speak true of the amulet's origins. The Keres and Valkyrie united to create it for Ares, but did he speak of the reason the two clans were together in the first place?"

"It is of little consequence, for it was done long go."

"Perhaps then he has not shared with you the nature of the Keres. They are bloodthirsty creatures wh–"

"Who watch over their chargers and feed on their blood when they die the violent death they are fated for before escorting them to Hades in the Underworld, yes I know."

"Who were once banished by Ares for disobeying his orders and inciting fights between friends, lovers and strangers alike," my father amended, his jaw clenched as he spoke. "They caused anyone who found themselves beside another to be overcome with a kind of battle lust. They lost all sense of who that person was to them and took to them with a ferocity not seen outside the battlefields.

"Their banishment saw them spend time with the Valkyrie, and a deep wish to earn back their Master's favor. They asked the Valkyrie to aid them in creating something powerful – something to befit the God of War and put them back in his good graces."

"And so it came to be," I said. "They were allowed return to Ares' side to await the birth of his Chosen One. To wait for *me*."

"Do you know what Ares intends for his Chosen One?"

"He shall help me call forth all the elements so I can keep those I choose safe and destroy those who would oppose me."

"Hmph. If only that was the truth."

"Oh? And what is it *you* believe he wants to aid me in achieving?"

"Ares wants to challenge his father, Zeus, as ruler of the gods. He could never attempt it alone; too many of the other Gods would stand beside Zeus and defeat him. But if there is one who truly can command all four of the elements, well … you have seen its power."

"And I have barely begun to learn of them," I grinned.

"Is that really what you want to be part of? Would you allow yourself to be used in such a manner? To be someone else's puppet? If Ares succeeds in his wish to rule over the mortal and immortal realms, the world we know would never be the same. We would be subject to constant war, death and destruction. No beauty would exist for he would turn friends to enemies, allies to foes."

"Why then did he banish his Keres for doing the same so many winters ago?"

"I cannot say, perhaps he did not wish to draw the attention of his father yet. He has planned to overthrow him for as long as any can remember. Just as Zeus overcame his own father, so Ares seeks to do the same.

"You must not fall for his charms, his words, for they are false. To see you behave as you did when you harnessed the fire element frightened me. His influence over you is already great, and I implore you to turn from it. You have always been strong. Use your strength now to shake yourself from his spell."

"And if that is not what I want?"

"It must be. You cannot allow him to defeat Zeus. No good can come of it. For us or the immortals."

"I am sorry Father, but I am not my mother. I intend to continue the tradition she never wanted."

He inhaled sharply. "Was it Dianthe or Ares who told you she did not want the responsibility?"

"My grandmother."

"Did Dianthe also tell you that she aided your mother and me to leave Thrace?"

"If she did, it was only because she also once harbored the wish to deny the destiny of her line with her actions."

"Yes. Perhaps it is time I told you what happened in Thrace when your mother and I decided to leave."

"I have no wish to hear your stories, Father. They are always spoken without complete truth." I attempted once again to free myself from the ropes, my struggling in vain; they held fast. "Perhaps if my mother was here, she would confirm what you say, but she is not and that is your fault. Had the two of you spoken of my existence with Dianthe, *she* could have ensured I was born without causing mother's death," I continued, slamming my head back against the bed, defeated and exhausted from the attempt at escape.

Father drew another deep breath, standing and pacing across the room before he spoke again. "You wish for truth, Skylar? Then I shall give it to you. All of it. I shall tell you of my life from the moment your mother and I decided to leave Thrace until the night you were born. I am certain you have not been given the whole story from Ares, or your grandmother."

"If you believe you can speak without lies, then I shall listen," I snapped, realizing I had no choice until either the amulet came to me, or my father released me.

"My tribe of the Bessoi called the area nearest Mount Rhodope home. That is where our Priestesses lived. When your mother, Theron, Irina and I decided to leave Thrace, it was Dianthe who assisted us in inciting the fight with the Dentheletae so we could escape. Back then she supported Zita in her wish to leave the Keres and be with me." He shook his head, continuing to pace across the tiles as he spoke. "Unfortunately, in the ensuing battle, I was injured so badly I believed I would see Hades in the Underworld before I ever had the chance to leave Thrace. Your mother should have allowed me to die, just as I had been fated to do, but instead she swooped down and, in the guise of feeding from me, healed me instead. She picked me up and we disappeared from Thrace in a manner I am not quite certain I can explain. One moment I was lying on the ground, close to death, the next my arms and legs felt as though they were being pulled into the dirt beneath me, but I was travelling up towards the sky. Within moments I was plunged into darkness, wind burning my eyes until I could keep them open no longer and I fell into unconsciousness."

"You are not the only one to have travelled in such a manner."

"You?" Father asked, pausing in his pacing. "When?"

"When Alexis and I were receiving help from the gods," was all I offered.

"I see," he murmured, continuing a long moment later. "When I woke, Zita told me we were at Konitsa in eastern Epirus, and Theron, Irina and their children were with us. My friends had fought and killed the Molossian warriors of Konitsa whilst I recovered, Zita watching over me and the children. We knew we would be safe there; travelers kept clear of the mountains the Molossians called home because of their fierce reputations, as I told you previously; they still do."

"Did Dianthe know where you were?"

"No, we never saw her again."

"Was Zita's absence not questioned? I cannot imagine Ares was pleased. Was Dianthe punished for her daughter's actions?"

"I do not know how Dianthe was treated afterwards, though Ares' allowance of Zita's death tells you exactly how he felt about her defection." I shrugged, knowing it was Ares' only choice for such a betrayal. "Zita was forced to speak of what she was with us – how else could she explain how we arrived in Konitsa? I was surprised at first, though it explained the unusual red of her eyes, and how she had remained safe and yet been able to see every fight I had ever been in.

"Theron and Irina had, at first, a difficult time with the knowledge, though they soon accepted it. It was only because of Zita that they could be together with their children as they wanted."

I made no comment, considering his story. It sounded as though he had accepted Zita and her differences to him just as readily as Alexis had first accepted me when I arrived in Trachis. Perhaps our destiny was as my parents' was; to live without one another after sharing part of our lives – and the creation of a child – together.

"We remained in Konitsa for a number of moons. Until your mother told me you grew within her belly," Father continued. "She said we could not remain in the north, that her family may feel the life growing inside her and come for us. Neither of us wanted anything to happen to Theron and Irina if they did, so I agreed to leave with her.

"Zita could not take us away using the same method she had before, she was certain her family would feel her if she did. Leaving Thrace in that manner had only been possible because of the battle. We travelled south on foot instead, through Thessaly and Boeotia, moving from town to town every half-moon or more. As I told Agrias, I discarded the clothing and weapons that told of my true heritage and Zita removed the thick beard on my face so that I appeared more as the southern Greeks did. Your mother needed blood to sustain her, and you. She chose to drink only from animals, hoping it would help us remain undiscovered, and that their blood would suppress the powers of the Ker."

"What of the amulet? Did she still have it? Or did she leave it behind?"

"She had it. She told me of it and of her line as we travelled. She told me what Ares wanted to use the Chosen One for. She called it her curse and said she did not want that life for our child. When I learned of what had been foretold, I agreed with her, and vowed to keep it from you when you were born."

"It should never have been your decision, or hers. If there was ever the chance I was the one Ares had waited for, you should have told me," I growled, my anger gloriously heating my blood.

"So you could embrace it as quickly as you have now? You believe I would have wanted to take that risk?" he asked, his eyes narrowing.

"It was not your decision," I repeated.

He paused in his steps, folding his hands behind his back and staring out of the high window. "Regardless of your thoughts on the matter, we remained hidden from Zita's family. We travelled further south into the Peloponnese region, until Zita found it too difficult to continue. We found lodgings with a man named Sotiris and a moon later, you were born, and your mother was killed by the Keres."

"You lie," I insisted.

Father turned from his position at the window, shaking his head. "No. You asked for the truth, and that is it. You were barely half-a-candlemark old when your mother felt the presence of her family and knew they were coming for us. She did not know if they felt you, but she would not allow you to be found there. She sent us away before they arrived."

"You ha–"

"Just listen," he growled. I fell silent, knowing that though I may not want to hear what he had to say, that finally, it would be the truth. "I took you, wrapped in a blanket, from the house. Zita told me I must keep you safe, that we must move constantly so her kin never found you. I reached the olive groves near the house before the Keres arrived, flames trailing them as they descended. I watched, hidden between the trees, as they dragged your mother and Sotiris from the house, setting it on fire. I could not hear what was said, but Zita's wings suddenly extended and she pounced on Sotiris, killing him. I can only imagine the Keres believed him to be me and that Zita did it to protect us.

"With that act, I thought the Keres would forgive her but they turned on her, biting and tearing into her flesh, her screams filling the air as they attacked. You slept in my arms, but I could not bear to have you wake and hear her, so I fled through the grove, not stopping until I reached Sparta early the next morning." He breathed out loudly, his eyes meeting mine again. "I could not save her, could not go to her because I knew I must protect you. It was what she had wanted and I had to keep my promise to her."

I had no response. Images of my mother's limbs torn from her body merged with those of Kuria's torn and bloodied skin. I squeezed my eyes shut as my chest tightened. I felt her. Her pain. The sharp points of her kin's fangs as they sank into her skin. Her love for me and the wish that I live safely, away from the Keres. Hot tears pricked the back of my eyes.

A war raged inside; my thoughts bouncing back and forth between the love my mother had felt for me, and the anger at what she and my father had vowed to keep from me.

I exhaled loudly, hot anger flowing over me once again. I would not allow her wishes to fill me. I was the Chosen One. I had to fulfil my destiny.

She died to save me, she loved me more than her own self.

That was a long time ago and even her mother now believed she was wrong to want to flee, to end the line so Ares' Chosen One was never born. I would not do that.

"She saved us by staying, by killing Sotiris. I did not tell you who she was or who you may become because I gave her my word I would not," my father said, his voice quiet.

I swallowed, the tightness in my chest abating as I opened my eyes. He was lying. They were alone when I was born, the Keres knew nothing of me. If they had, my mother would still be alive. "Your words mean nothing to me. You would say anything to turn me against my family. You lie so as not to feel responsible for her death."

"You may not believe me. You may prefer Ares or Dianthe's version of how your mother left us. But ask them about that night. You shall soon learn they keep much from you. Perhaps then you shall speak to me and we can find a way together to deny Ares of what he wants. To deny him of you."

"Release me and then get out."

"I have no intention of going anywhere."

"He may remain, but he shall not join our conversation," Ares' voice filled the room, the God of War appearing a moment later.

My father opened his mouth to respond but Ares flicked his hand and Father flew backwards, unconscious when he hit the wall. Ares crossed to his prone form and took the amulet from beneath his chiton.

"Do not allow this to be taken from you again," he warned, my bindings disappearing as he neared.

"I shall not," I promised, rubbing at my wrists as I sat up. My head spun with the sudden movement and I pressed one hand to my forehead, holding the other out for the amulet. Ares knelt on the bed behind me instead, settling it around my neck.

"Father spoke of my mother's death. The night she died," I told him, my head clearing and leaving only a dull ache for me to contend with.

"Are you ready to come to Olympos? We have much work to do to prepare you for the use of the other three elements," Ares said, ignoring my statement.

"Olympos?" I repeated, the story my father told me suddenly unimportant.

"Yes. You need to recover from this first time. Away from the other mortals, I can ensure you and the amulet are not separated while you regain your strength."

"A wise idea," I agreed.

"My palace awaits, as do your kin. They are eager to meet you, Chosen One."

"I am ready," I said.

"Good."

Ares wrapped his arm around my waist and helped me to my feet, handing me my sword and holding me steady as I belted it around my hips.

"My cuirass."

"You do not need it. The amulet shall provide whatever protection you require. Besides, the last time I saw it, it was split in two." He grinned and took my hand. My legs took on the familiar pull as I was taken from the room and plunged into darkness. I attempted to keep my eyes open but lasted no more than a few seconds before succumbing.

31

I woke to a comfortable bed in a strange room with marble walls as dark as the jet of the amulet, and a ceiling so high I could not tell where it began. Torches burned low around the room, reflected against the shining floor and walls. I immediately checked for the necklace, relieved to find it at my throat where Ares had placed it. I was still dressed in my tunic, my arms and legs unbound when I shifted to take in the rest of the room.

"About time you woke."

I rolled onto my back, taking in the lounging figure. With a flushed complexion and dark, unkempt hair akin to my grandmother's, it was her eyes which drew my attention. They were so black they could have been made from the same marble as the walls around us. Her scant, leather clothing matched those eyes. She trailed her hand down my arm, fingers twining with mine when they met.

"And you are?" I asked.

"Eris; your reward," she grinned. "My friend Ares was impressed with your display with the amulet. Given your previous lover wants nothing to do with you, he suggested you and I may enjoy meeting."

"A generous offer."

"And not one you are unfamiliar with – you have always sought release after battle. I can only imagine after the power that flowed through you from the amulet, you have a need greater than you have ever known before."

"True," I replied, the battle lust lingering. A familiar heat stirred in my stomach as she released my fingers and slid hers to my thigh, slipping them beneath my tunic.

"I am not arrogant enough to believe that I shall be enough, given what runs beneath your skin, so I have asked Peitho to join us. Peitho," Eris called. The naked, full-figured form of a second goddess appeared, her long blond hair remaining behind her shoulders and affording me full view of her body.

I considered what I knew of the two women; Dianthe had spoken of receiving the Keres from Eris. I had never heard her paired with another – god or mortal – but certainly we shared the bloodlust and pleasures battle and death afforded us. Peitho, I knew, was the Goddess of Seduction and a close companion to Aphrodite, often aiding lovers within Aphrodite's temples, as well as elsewhere. I grinned, pleased I held Ares' favor in such a manner, and that he understood what I would want.

Peitho approached the bed, climbing up to stretch out on my opposite side to Eris. "The God of War speaks highly of you, and of what you shall become," she said, taking my hand to place at her breast. "Allow me to give you what you need in this moment and send you on your way well satisfied and ready to overcome any challenge Ares sets before you." With her hand covering mine, she drew it down her body, allowing me to feel the heat between her legs and complete my own journey of her most intimate place. I pushed through her, my breath catching at the sensation and my thighs tightening. The beat of arousal filled my being and I pressed inside.

"Remain faithful to Alexis, even here in this place when others are offered." The voice was loud and I jumped, but the two goddesses did not appear to hear it. It took me moment to realize it was Hera's voice and I hesitated in my actions as I recalled the journey Alexis and I had taken at Corinth. The pain of believing Alexis had chosen another at the temple cut through me with the same fierceness it had that night and I squeezed my eyes shut against the memory. I took a deep breath, a familiar calm enveloping me once more and when I opened my eyes again, the sting of the memory was gone.

Eris raised my tunic, her lips at my shoulder as Peitho squeezed my hand between her thighs and lifted herself to lay above me. "Take from us what you want. What you need. Tell us how we can give you the satisfaction you desire," she whispered.

With Hera's words, the growing heat and craving in my blood cooled, remaining at a dull itch to be scratched rather than a necessity or impending certainty. I removed my hand from Peitho, offering her a grin when she frowned. "I want the two of you to put on a show for me. Show me how the Goddess of Chaos and the Goddess of Seduction come together in desire. Show me the power of two goddesses and perhaps then I shall decide if you are enough to give me what I need."

The two women looked at one another and I saw their confusion. Obviously, Ares had told them I would be a willing participant when they appeared to me. And I would have been, had Hera not put doubt in my mind. Though I may not care what Alexis believed she did or did not want now I possessed the power of the amulet, or how I had insisted that I would have queens or goddesses whenever I wanted, I could not deny that I still wanted Alexis in my bed. I could not give her up so easily. I would have her again before long. I craved to feel her beneath me and atop me, possessing me with her hands and mouth as only she could.

As Eris and Peitho took to one another with a similar gusto, it was not them I saw before me, but Alexis and me. Hands, mouths, words and murmurings as they climbed higher on their journey. I ripped off my tunic and touched myself as I had the night in the bathing area in Trachis. Just as I had then, it was Alexis I saw, Alexis I touched and who touched me in return. As Peitho drew the cries from Eris' lungs, so too did I join them, the spectacular green orbs looming large in my mind as I surrendered to her.

When next I woke, I was alone. Though I had found release recalling the princess I had called mine for so many moons, I still craved the true satisfaction only she could give me. Perhaps when I had proved I could wield another element, Ares would take me to her and I could have what I wanted. I pulled on my discarded tunic and found my sword leaning beside the doorframe. I settled it at my waist and headed towards the sound of voices.

"How much longer do you expect her to slumber?" my grandmother asked.

"I cannot say. The closer we have come to having the Chosen One within our midst, the longer the recovery has taken after the first use of the amulet," Ares replied.

"But I have told y–"

"I know what you believe, but until I have proof, I shall continue with her as planned."

"And what exactly *do* you have planned for me?" I asked, stepping into another darkly marbled room.

Ares turned, smiling as he approached, hands outstretched to take mine. I raised my own, slipping them into his waiting palms. "You received my gift?" he asked, squeezing gently.

"I did," I nodded.

"But you did not enjoy it?" he added with a slight frown.

"I enjoyed Eris and Peitho fine, but we have other matters to attend now."

He hesitated, his gaze remaining on mine before he gave a curt nod.

"You require no more rest?"

"No. I am ready for you to show me how to use the other three elements of the amulet."

He grinned again. "Good. But we cannot do so here; mortals are not supposed to come to Olympos unless Zeus is informed or brings them himself."

"Then where?" I asked.

"Perhaps the Inhospitable Sea. It is time you met your kin," Dianthe suggested. Ares glanced briefly in her direction, inclining his head before turning his attention back to me.

"An excellent suggestion. Ready?" Though I was not eager to be sent to sleep again so soon, I nodded, the pull beginning in my feet and working its way upward as we left Olympos.

*

I opened my eyes as my feet met solid ground. Dianthe, Ares and I stood at the top of a mountain, overlooking a small island, surrounded by deep, green sea. Rain poured down around us, but we remained dry; sheltered beneath a laurel tree.

"Welcome to the island of Aretias, home of the Keres, and to the mortal women warriors known as the Amazons," Ares announced proudly, releasing my hands so he could spread his arms wide.

I frowned. "I believed the Amazons lived on the island of Lemnos in the Aegean Sea."

"There is a tribe there also," Ares nodded. "The Amazons at Lemnos worship my weak, lamed brother – Hephaestus – he has one of his forges there. The women here are loyal to me."

"They have built a roofless, stone temple to the God of War, and are much fiercer than those at Lemnos," Dianthe added.

"I heard that the Argonauts encountered Amazon women on their first stop after leaving Iolkos, and a deadly flock of birds on their last before Colchis. They were here, at Aretias?" I asked.

"They were. Many believe the Amazon women and the island we call home to be two different locations, but it is not so," Dianthe replied. "It is said Zeus provided the Argonauts with favorable winds so they would not encounter the Amazons here, and whilst that may be the truth, we still attacked them on their way past to ensure they did not land. We had heard Heracles travelled with them and we did not wish to meet him again. The men beat their swords against their shields and we were reminded of the rattle Heracles once used against us. We flew high above them and thankfully, they did not shoot any arrows." Dianthe pointed to the shore opposite the island. "Natives of Kerasous are the only visitors to our rocky shores now, coming here to perform fertility rituals with the Amazon women. They do not seek to hunt us Keres, though we remain hidden in the flocks of cormorants and seagulls who also call this island home."

"We are further from Thrace than I expected," I noted. "When you spoke of living in the Inhospitable Sea, I imagined you would be close to the Thracian coastline."

"There are no islands closer which share an affinity with our master," Dianthe replied. "Though it does not take us long to reach Thrace if battle between tribes breaks out."

"I imagine not," I murmured.

"Speaking of battles breaking out, whilst you have been recovering, I have taken care of the Molossian problem for you," Ares said.

"The Molossian problem?" I frowned.

"Andreas. He no longer lays claim to Alexis. His people have agreed to sever the alliance with Agrias."

"He is truly their enemy now?"

"No. I have ensured they seek no lands so far south-east. Agrias shall live without fear of an Epirote invasion."

"How did you convince Andreas to relinquish his claim on Alexis, for I cannot imagine he did so willingly?"

"He finds himself with Hades," Ares shrugged. "Antigonos too for his words against you, and for returning to Andreas when he was found out."

"You killed them?" I yelled, my fists clenching as I paced, drops of rain finding my head and face.

"Of course. And once their bodies were returned to their tribe – by me – the remaining Molossians quickly agreed to leave behind any association with Trachis, lest they meet the same fate as their leader and his companion."

"You knew I wanted to be the one to kill Andreas, just as I ended the lives of his sons."

"I knew you had attempted it … and failed."

"You should have aided me. I called on you for help that night. Why did you not come to me?"

"I am not answerable to you," Ares replied.

"And yet you wish me to be to you?"

"Please, there is no need for cross words to be spoken with one another. We are all on the same side," Dianthe interrupted. "Allow us to put the past behind us and look to our future."

Ares blew out a deep breath and nodded. "We are. I apologize for denying you your revenge. For both men. I did not want you to worry about them or what was happening in Trachis. We have much more important things to turn our attention to."

"I wanted to be the one. I wanted him to suffer just as I made

Melanthios suffer," I muttered, still pacing beneath the thick foliage. "I wanted him to know that I had bested him and all the Molossian tribesman who would have called a princess their own. She chose me above them all."

"She did and it is with Alexis in mind that you must attempt to call forth the element of water."

"Why should I think of her? I do not care for her any more than she cares for me now."

"I do not believe that is entirely true," Ares countered.

"Oh, why not?" I asked, hands on hips as I paused my stomping.

"If you did not care for her, you would have used Eris for what I sent her to you for." I only shrugged in reply. "Perhaps I should have mentioned earlier that Alexis *may* speak words of hatred. For those not of the Ker line, the response to the amulet can be ... unpredictable. Or perhaps she simply does not love you as much as I believed."

"Or perhaps she is not worthy of standing beside me," I snapped. "She may be of royal blood, but she is not worldly, she has not seen what I have. She does not understand what actions are needed to ensure the safety of many. It is best she is not with us here. She would divert my attention and encourage softer repercussions for those who deserve far worse. There is only one use I would seek her for now."

"As you wish," Ares said, lowering his chin briefly.

A thought occurred to me. "When I have mastered the elements, can I gift them to another to use?"

"No. Only you can call on them and use them," Ares replied.

"Pity," I shrugged again. "She may have been of more use if she could use it." With the power running through Alexis, she could have destroyed anyone who had treated her with disdain in Epirus, or in Trachis. She could have felt that same calm and confidence I had. She could have known there was no doubt she would beat them. She would win.

When I had mastered each element, I would not just remain in Greece. I would travel to Persia and make Darius and Atossa pay for what they did to Nasrin. I would torture and maim them as they had her, drawing out their suffering to the very end. How satisfying it had been to feel Melanthios' life drain from him. I should have drawn it out even longer. I should have sliced him open from stomach to throat while he still breathed. If I could have my time again, I would ensure he suffered for much, much longer.

"You consider much, Granddaughter. Care to share your thoughts with us?" I shook my head. Perhaps Nasrin would feel cheated if she did not witness Darius' demise; as I had with Ares' actions against Andreas and Antigonos. Perhaps her sons would also be disappointed they never had the chance to avenge their mother's honor. I could of course take Nasrin with me ... We could find her sons and together see their revenge enacted. But ... no. That situation was best left to Aspamitres and Artabanus. I had more than enough enemies in Greece to take care of. Or on Olympos, if my father had spoken true.

I took the amulet from beneath my tunic and lifted it over my head. "Teach me all I need to know," I said.

Ares grinned and gave me a nod, offering his hand. I took it and he drew me closer. Standing behind me, he raised my arm, the amulet facing the sea as he spoke at my ear. "The water churns in the storm. Waves crash against the rocks on the beach, the spray reaching high into the air before returning to where it came. Concentrate on the waves. Make them rise even higher, crash even harder against the rock and sand. Feel the power of them, of yourself."

I closed my eyes, taking with me the images he spoke of. I could taste the salt on my tongue, the rising tempest against my skin. Wind slipped through my hair as fingers, neither cold nor warm. But the heat and insatiable desire did not claim my blood as it had back in Trachis. My palm did not warm. I opened my eyes again, the jet was still the same, dark blackness it had been. There was not even the hint of orange. No glow. No change of any kind. I frowned, squeezing it tighter in my hand, imploring it to see what I saw in my mind. To hear my desires without spoken word.

Nothing.

I dropped my arm, swiveling on my heel to face Ares. "Why does it not work? Why does it not bend to my will as it did before?"

Dianthe spoke before the God of War could. "It is as I said."

"No. Perhaps it is because there is no danger. There is no one she cares for here who needs her protection, her help. That was what illuminated it before." Ares narrowed his eyes. "You say you do not care for Alexis now, but when you called on the fire element that was the case, was it not?"

"You know it was," I replied. A shiver ran the length of my spine, and with it, a flicker in the calmness and assuredness gnawed at my insides. I gave no outward sign of the change I felt, but I was suddenly no longer as drawn to Ares, or the amulet, as I had been only moments before.

Ares stepped back, addressing my grandmother. "Perhaps we should see just how deep those feelings still run," he said.

"If you wish to, though I believe you have your answer," she answered with a shrug.

Before either of them could speak again, a young woman appeared beside us, shaking the water from her hair. "How I dislike Aretias in the autumn," she muttered before turning her attention to me.

The Ker circled, looking me up and down. She stood as tall as me, hair trailing down her back in thick knots. One taloned finger tapped her chin and her narrowed eyes were colored in the deepest red. Her gaze was far from welcoming when it settled on my face and I rested my hand on the hilt of my sword, meeting it without fear. "So, this is the one who would be your Chosen One?" she sneered.

"What are you doing here, Canace?" Dianthe asked.

"I wanted to see her for myself. There has been much talk about this … mortal being. She does not appear so special to me."

Heat flowed through me, but it was not from the amulet. My hand tightened against the handle of my sword. "Perhaps you should have been in Trachis earlier. Then you would know what I am capable of."

Canace's wings emerged from her back and she stepped towards me. "If you are one of us, then prove it. You carry a sword as weapon; there is no evidence you resemble us in any manner. Your eyes are treacherous blue. Your teeth and fingernails are short and blunt. Spread your wings and battle against me with the gifts of a Ker. Prove you are who my Aunt and Master say you are," she taunted.

With one hand I looped the amulet back over my head, the other drawing my sword. "I do not have to prove myself to you. I do not answer to you." My wings remained beneath my skin, there was no itching, no piercing sting, yet I was certain they would emerge before long. She set herself and waited. My blood fired and I lunged. She fended me off easily, her solid wings sending me stumbling.

"My son was born the winter before you, yet somehow you usurped his power."

"I took nothing from him. You bore a male child, not a female as the rest of your line always have. The power was never fated to come to you or your child, not even on my mother's death."

"And what do you know of your mother's death?" Canace asked, her talons slicing my arm as she swiped at me.

"Canace," Ares growled.

"If I was to believe my father's *latest* version, it would be that her kin killed her."

Canace smiled, exposing her sharpened fangs. "Finally, the mortal speaks truth with you," she laughed.

I paused in my next attack. I had warred within when he told me of that night, his words ringing true, even though I believed he would say anything to turn me against my mother's family. Lost in my thoughts, I was not prepared when Canace came at me again. She knocked me flat on my back, hands pinning me to the ground, just as the wild boar had near Corinth.

Her wings extended above us, blocking Ares and Dianthe from sight, though I could still hear my grandmother's voice demanding Canace release me. "Zita defied her family. She did not deserve to carry the line of the Chosen One. I was there that night. I ordered her to be found. Had your cowardly grandmother also been there, she would have known I was sending the wrong mortal man to his death."

Dianthe attempted to pull Canace from me, struggling against the stronger, young Ker. "I knew Zita would be killed. I felt her that night, just as my mother and Canace did," Dianthe said. "She must have fed on human blood to give her strength for your arrival. But for leaving us, there was no choice but to kill her. I knew if she was ever found, that would be her fate. She knew it too. That was why I was not there – I could not bear to watch my daughter die."

"No, it was grandmother Rizpah and I who were sent to do what you could not," Canace said, shaking Dianthe off and sliding a glance behind her before refocusing on me. "Had my aunt had the strength of character, I would have known to keep looking for your father. I would have found him and I would have found you. I would have killed you both and then the power of the Chosen One would have fallen to me, regardless of the *son* I had borne." She spat the word 'son' with such venom that I almost pitied the boy; he must have incurred so much of her displeasure and wrath all these winters. "I killed your mother and when the time comes, I shall kill you. The power shall be mine and there is nothing you can do to stop it."

"If only that were true," I panted. My fingers closed around the handle of my sword and I drove it between Canace's hip and ribs, pushing it up through her body until it pierced the skin above her breast.

"Skylar, no!" my grandmother cried. But it was too late. Canace's eyes widened in surprise, blood coating her lips as she choked to her death. My head pounded, pulse beating behind my eyes as I felt her last breath within me.

I pushed Canace from my chest and got to my feet, ripping my sword from her body. I wiped the blade across her wings, their length and width shrinking with each passing moment. I slid my weapon back into its sheath, scrubbing at Canace's blood on my cheek.

"Do not punish her, Master. She does not know the rules yet. She does not know we do no—"

I turned back to them, Ares held his hand up and my grandmother fell silent. His lips quirked in a smile but he shook his finger at me. "You certainly possess a quick temper and I cannot deny that that fire inside you excites me. However, Dianthe is right. It has long been forbidden for my Keres to kill one another, even when given provocation, just as it is forbidden for them to incite fights amongst others."

"I do not believe she is much of a loss, for now there shall be no question as to who holds the line of your Chosen One," I countered.

"There has been no question for quite some time," Ares agreed. "But we shall need *all* our Keres if we are going to safely birth the child Alexis carries, so I must ask you not to kill any more of your kin."

"The child? What has she got to do with anything?" I asked as a wave of nausea washed over me.

"She is my Chosen One," Ares replied simply.

"What are you talking about? *I* am your Chosen One."

"No. You are not. You cannot conjure the second element. You are just as all the others were – able only to use one element."

"No. I simply need more practice."

"Did you require practice when you destroyed that army? How quickly were you able to call forth all you needed then? You were angry when Canace spoke of killing your mother, I could sense it. You hated that she had overpowered you so easily. But you did not reach for the amulet. It did not react to your danger. You are not the one. You cannot use it again."

The throbbing in my head increased but I refused to allow it to consume me. "Test me again," I pleaded.

"We are done here," Ares said, turning from me as light engulfed him.

"No, please. Allow me another chance to prove myself."

The brightness paused in its intensity and Ares faced me again. "Fine. You wish for proof you are not the one we have waited for? Look here." He held out his hand and the image of Alexis being held by the soldier in Trachis appeared. "Call on the amulet, send forth those flames just as you did then."

I took the amulet from my neck, weighting it in my palm as I watched the scene before me. A spark of the fear and anger I had felt flared briefly in my chest, but the amulet remained dark. "Showing me that proves nothing," I said with a frown. "I dealt with those soldiers already. There is no threat."

"It would make no difference. You are not the one," Ares repeated.

I grabbed his arm as he turned to leave once again. "Test me again," I said through gritted teeth.

"And when I have proven you wrong, you shall not question my decision again," he growled.

I nodded in agreement, believing this time I would be able to make the water do what I asked of it. Ares disappeared, reappearing before I could even turn to my grandmother. He was not alone and pushed Alexis towards Dianthe.

"Why did you bring me here? You promised I would never have to see her again!" Alexis cried, fear plastered across her face as she huddled against Dianthe.

The amulet flared orange for a moment in my hand and Ares crossed his arms over his chest. "Well?" he asked.

I drew a deep breath, a gentle prickle announcing the presence of my wings. I waited for them to emerge. They did not. Dianthe took Alexis by the throat, lifting her off the ground. Alexis grabbed at the fingers at her neck, her feet kicking out as she struggled for breath.

"We are waiting," Dianthe rasped.

I repositioned my feet and held the amulet higher, silently asking the waves to rise until they were tall enough to reach us up on the mountain and crash over my grandmother, releasing Alexis in the process.

Nothing happened. The amulet remained cool and dark in my hand. Dianthe tightened her grip on Alexis. The amulet flared orange again but still my wings remained beneath my skin.

"Enough," Ares said. Dianthe released Alexis and she ran to Ares when he held his arms out to her.

"I just need a few more moments," I insisted. The pain in my head ebbed and flowed as though it was the very wave I attempted to control. Ares did not reply, removing Alexis from Aretias before returning alone.

"It is time for you to leave as well," he told me.

"And go where? Can I not remain here with my kin? Can I not learn of their ways? Perhaps with their influence I shall be able to use the amulet. Perhaps it is only tiredness which sees me unable to call on it today."

Ares took my hand and before I could say anything else, he pushed up into the air and I lost all sense of myself in the sudden darkness.

32

Dianthe and Ares watched as Skylar stumbled past the Temple of Anthela. "Are you certain this is where you want to leave her? Her disorientation is apparent, as it always is when the amulet's effects begin to wear off."

"She shall find her way back to the palace eventually. All of you found something familiar to cling to afterwards, she shall be no different. Besides, she can defend herself if the need arises."

"You are not concerned she shall be able to travel as we do? That she shall go back to Aretias to find you?"

"I see no reason to suspect it. If she could, it would already have happened. No, until it is time for the child to be born, she can do as she pleases." They watched a little longer before the God of War spoke again. "I had convinced myself it had to be her. That she was the one the Valkyrie spoke of. She showed such promise and embraced our ways without question. She sounded so certain she could use the amulet again after the first time."

"That is true. Had I not felt the power of the child myself, I could still have been convinced of it too, the effects of the amulet can linger, the belief can last for moons, or sometimes winters, though perhaps that has more to do with parental influence than the amulet."

"You speak of Canace."

"Yes. But it matters not. We know who the true Chosen One is now. All shall be as it was fated."

"Indeed," Ares nodded, turning his gaze back to the mortal and whispering, "This shall not be the last time we see one another, Skylar. When it is time for your child to be born, I shall come for you." His words were taken on the breeze and surrounded Skylar, embraced her. They kept her going though she did not know where she was headed.

33

I walked until the sun began its descent behind the mountains. There was something I needed to find. The thought gnawed at me. Compelled me to keep moving. If I found it, it would explain why I was in Anthela. I was missing something. Something important but I did not know what it was, or where I should go to find it. I just kept walking.

Without warning, the trees I had been travelling through ended and I found myself by a spring. I knelt down, cupping my hands and drinking long gulps of the heated water before standing again, my eyes taking in the rest of the area.

The stream snaked its way through heavy undergrowth away to the left. A tall waterfall dominated the other end, steam rising all along, dissipating the higher into the air it reached. A marble altar stood between the waterfall and the trees nearby and I crossed to it, taking in each of the carved pictures. There was no mistaking the central figure in each carving; Heracles. He carried a club and wore a lion skin over his head and down his back, as though it were a himation. I drew a deep breath and placed my palms on the smooth top. As my skin made contact, the confusion which had plagued me cleared and I fell backwards as though I had been slapped.

Dianthe. The Keres at Aretias. Ares telling me it was the child inside Alexis who would bear the title of Chosen One, not me. I remembered everything. I remembered how badly I wanted to be with Ares and my kin. The disappointment and anger when he told me I was not who he wanted.

I pushed myself to my feet. "I am the one. You are wrong. I am the one," I muttered into the stillness around me.

I did not expect an answer, and none came. I *had* to be the one Ares was waiting for. I was different to all the others in the line. I was half-mortal. How could it be the child? I paced back and forth between the altar of Heracles and the spring, careful not to touch its surface in case I found myself on my back again. The skin at my temples tightened and I rubbed at them to dissolve the gathering pain.

The amulet had glowed when I attempted to use it again. It had not obeyed my wishes until ... I paused in my steps. It had not changed color until Ares brought Alexis to the island. It reacted to the child's presence when she and Alexis were put in danger. And it was not the first time it had happened. When Dianthe met Alexis. When the army arrived in Trachis. It had only ever glowed when they were nearby. When Andreas wanted to take Alexis from me.

I took the amulet from my neck, holding it up, watching as it caught the final rays of sunlight. "My child holds the power now. It is time I returned to Trachis and took back what is mine." Hesitating, I placed my hands back on the marble surface. This time it did not cast me aside. I needed to eliminate the child. Only then would the amulet's power revert back to me. It must be the way. Canace had always believed it, so why should I doubt her words? Though we had only met once, she had never spoken lies.

I closed my eyes and sent up a prayer. "Aid me Heracles, greatest of heroes. Gift me with strength to call on the power I so desire and overcome those who would oppose me as you did on so many occasions."

"Skylar?" Thaddeus questioned tentatively.

My head whipped up. "What are you doing here?" I asked, placing the amulet back over my head as I settled my hand on the hilt of my sword.

"I came to find you. I have been worried. We all have."

"Hmph. Last I recall you aided my father in keeping me strapped to my bed against my will."

"That was a moon ago. Winter is almost upon us. Hesper shall soon birth our fourth child."

"What? Do not be absurd, it was only yesterday, perhaps the day before."

"No. You ... you called on the element of fire and destroyed that army weeks ago. Andreas disappeared soon after and we received word he had been killed. The Molossians have broken our alliance without repercussions. Agrias is at a loss as to what convinced them so. Was it you? Did you return after you disappeared from your room and murder him? Did you convince his tribe not to retaliate?"

"No," I replied, unwilling to inform him who had worked on my behalf.

Thaddeus approached, resting against the altar and regarding me. "You ask for Heracles' aid, but perhaps it is Athena you should call on instead."

"Why?"

"You recall the story of Heracles and the Stymphalian Birds?" I only nodded in reply, knowing so much more about them than when I shared the story with he and Cleomenes in the summer. "I was retelling it to a traveler a few days ago and he believes it was Athena who provided Heracles with the rattle, not Hephaestus. He told me Athena suckled Heracles when his mother left him for dead to avoid Hera's wrath. She has held a soft spot for him ever since; aiding him against the Thebans and with his twelfth labor. The goddess assists leaders who pray to her and possess good judgement and wisdom. If she believes victory can be theirs, she stands beside them as asked."

"There are always many versions of the stories we have grown with. We can never know what the real truth is, for we were not there. Perhaps it is time I sought what I want without the assistance of the gods."

"Does what you want include Alexis? The two of you ... after you used the ... amulet you ..."

I hesitated. To get what I wanted I knew I would need Thaddeus' help. "Of course," I lied. "Is she well? How is our child?"

He exhaled, loudly. "Thank the gods. Your father was afraid we had lost you to Ares. That both of you may be lost to the God of War's influence."

"You did not answer my question about the child," I interrupted.

"I am certain she is well but ... Alexis has not been in Trachis since the day of the battle with the army either."

"Do you have Darko?" I asked, looking around for his horse.

"Yes, he is in the trees."

"Good. We must return to Trachis as quickly as possible. I must gather the rest of my weapons." My father would know where Alexis had gone, I was certain of it – they had shared so many confidences since meeting. "I must find the princess and my child."

*

While Thaddeus went to tell Agrias and my father I had returned, I went to the room Alexis and I shared, changing into a clean tunic and finding my shield. I took a bag and packed an extra tunic, a length of rope and the small dagger which had once belonged to Antigonos as well. It would be strange without my cuirass, especially for what I intended, but mine was useless in its present state. Slipping my arm into the holds on my shield, I opened the door, knowing that the next time I found myself at the palace, it would be with the power of the Chosen One flowing through my veins.

My father and Thaddeus' voices reached me across the courtyard as I made my way out of the central chamber and I ducked behind one of the taller bushes to listen.

"Where was she?" Father asked.

"At the hot springs. I followed her for a while but she did not appear to know where she was, or where she was going."

"But you are certain she is not under his influence anymore?"

"I do not believe so. She asked after Alexis and their daughter almost immediately."

"Where is she now?"

"Gathering her armor."

"Good. I shall do the same and meet you at the stables. We need to get to Alexis quickly; Ares has already had too much time with her as it is."

I leaned forward so I could see them, watching as Father headed for the barracks and Thaddeus for his apartment. I was glad Father knew where Alexis was, just as I hoped he would, but he not would be making the journey with me when I was done with him.

I started across the courtyard towards my father, keeping out of sight as I circled around behind him. I emerged from the garden near the andron at the same time as Agrias appeared in the walkway to my right. When our eyes met, I knew there was no chance of retreat and, not wanting him to call out and alert my father to my presence, I stepped in his direction, embracing him when he held his arms out.

"Thank the gods. I was so worried. Are you well?" Agrias murmured as he released me. I cast a glance back along the veranda catching sight of my father turning into the walkway that would take him to the barracks.

"I am," I replied.

"You have heard Alexis is missing?"

"Thaddeus told me," I nodded. "He and Father want to join me to search for her."

"I could think of no two better men to aid in bringing her back safely."

"Normally I would agree with you but Ares' influence was swift over her, as it was me. I think it best if I go alone."

"Do you think that wise? What if Ares is able to influence you once again? You still wear his amulet," the king noted, pointing to the necklace.

I tucked it beneath my tunic. "He holds no power over me any longer. This is nothing but a piece of jewelry now. I broke the line, that is why I have been gone so long," I lied.

"Thank the gods," he said again. "Now there is only Alexis to be returned and perhaps then you and your father can begin to mend your broken relationship."

"I hope so. You know the depth of my love for Alexis and you know what I have always wanted; to keep those I love and care about safe. Allow me now to do that. You and my father have a close friendship – I am certain he shared with you the path he would take to find her. Tell me so I can do what I must to find my wife and free her from Ares as I once freed her from Melanthios and his brothers."

Agrias reached for my hand and I took it. "Since the day you entered our lives, you have fought for my daughter. I trust you to bring her back. She travels towards Epirus." I opened my mouth to speak but he squeezed my hand and I kept quiet. "I have not seen her since … since the day the army came, but your father and Moeris searched every day for both of you. They only found her once and in their brief conversation, she told them she was returning to Epirus. Leandros told her Andreas was dead and attempted to convince her to return to the palace but she would not. She insisted the Molossian tribe was her home. That her child must be born surrounded by their fierce nature, that it was the only way she would be safe from …"

"From me," I finished for him.

The king nodded. "I am sorry to speak the words, I know they must cut deeply. But you must understand what Ares has done to her, and her words *must* come from him because he appeared before your father could convince her to return to the palace with him and Moeris."

"Do not spare my feelings, if I find her, I need to know what she is feeling. Did she say anything else?"

"She said she wanted to honor the alliance we had with the Molossians. She would agree to become the wife of whoever took Andreas' place. Please, I cannot bear thoughts of her there again. Not now. Not when she is with child. *Your* child."

"Did she take Calla?" I asked, wondering how many days it would take me to catch her up.

"No, she is on foot. In her condition, I cannot imagine she has reached the Thessalian Plain yet."

I frowned. "When my father and I came here from Stratos, we took a path over the Evrytania Mountains and Mount Tymphristos, but Alexis once told me she and Basileios travelled over the Othrys Mountains to get here from Epirus. Is that the path you believe she has taken?"

"It would make sense as it is the only one she is familiar with."

"Show me the way on the map you keep in the Throne Room. It shall only take me a few moments to memorize the way and then I can go."

"Are you certain you do not want to tell your father you need to go alone? I could speak on your behalf and he would listen to me."

"No. Every moment I waste attempting to convince him of my reasons, is another moment Alexis draws closer to Epirus. And if Ares aided her when she saw my father, then who is to say he shall not assist the Molossians against me if she reaches them?"

Agrias hesitated before once again nodding in agreement. "Of course, of course. Apologies. I forget you are skilled in making quick plans for attack. Come, I shall show you the way."

I stepped back and allowed him to lead the way to the Throne Room. Agrias spread the map out on the table behind the thrones. He lit another torch, bringing it closer as he pointed out the rivers Melas, Dyras and Spercheios, all of which I would need to cross before I reached the Pass of Coela and the Othrys Mountain range beyond.

"You can find fresh water for Skotos at Lake Xynias. Take the northwest path around the lake. On the other side, the Apidanus River shall lead you the rest of the way through the mountains and out onto the Thessalian Plain. If you have not caught up to her by then, you must follow the base of the Pindos Mountains north until you reach Gomphoi."

"From there we shall have to go west into the mountains. Shall our horses be able to remain with us?" Father's voice interrupted.

I turned, meeting his stare and attempting to suppress the anger the sight of him brought. "*You* shall not be travelling anywhere. I shall go alone to find Alexis," I corrected.

"You need me," he countered.

"Leandros, perhaps it is best i–"

"For Alexis' sake, our quarrel needs to be set aside," my father cut over the king. "The past cannot be changed but now we must work together to bring her back. So, the horses?" he added, looking to Agrias for the answer.

"If they are used to mountain travel, then I see no reason for you not to take them into the Pindos Mountains, though I dearly hope you do not need to journey so far to find my daughter."

"As do I," Father agreed.

"You are not coming with me. Only *I* know what to do to release Alexis from Ares' influence. And it does not need an audience," I growled. I turned my back to him, tracing my finger along the route Agrias had indicated.

"Tell me how you plan to do it then," Father needled. "You were able to free yourself from Ares' hold. I would be interested to hear how you did so."

"There shall be time for stories when I return," I replied, keeping my back to him. I compared the length of the path with previous journeys, determining I could be at Lake Xynias within four or five candlemarks, depending on Skotos' willingness to travel quickly in the darkness.

"You are *certain* you do not wish for me to join you?"

"It is not necessary," I replied, anger at the repetition of his questions tightening my jaw and hands.

"Then take my cuirass. You should not be without protection."

"I do not need such flimsy protection. The amulet shall give me whatever I need," I replied, committing the map to memory.

"You still have the amulet …?" my father murmured, realization hitting him at the same time it did me.

I reached for my sword but Father was faster, the hilt of his weapon crashing into my skull and sending me to Hypnos' realm before I could defend myself.

34

I woke, coughing. Cold water streamed down my face and throat, choking me. I wrenched my head to the side and attempted to suck in more air than water. My father stood, throwing aside a water skin, regarding me as I took in our surroundings, and my predicament.

I sat on the ground. A long length of rope bound my hands, the other end tethered to the tree at my back. Skotos and Skaris were nearby, munching at the grass either side of the dirt path.

"Where are we?" I asked, struggling to my knees. "And how long was I out for?"

"We are at Lake Xynias and it is now morning, so a number of candlemarks," Father replied, pointing behind me. "I believe Alexis is not far ahead. Remains of her fire are still warm. She cannot be gone more than half-a-candlemark."

"Then why are we still here?"

Father crossed his arms over his chest. "Why are you so eager to see her again? You lied to Agrias and Thaddeus; you are still loyal to Ares."

"Untie me and maybe I shall tell you what you want to know."

"I think for now I shall keep you tied up. I am not eager to meet Hades today, and I imagine Ares would love to see you punish me for keeping you from him all these winters."

"I doubt you even cross his mind. You are nothing in what is to come. It is the child who matters now," I sneered, unable to keep the words inside as I pushed myself to my feet and stepped forward as far as I could.

"Indeed?" Father murmured, his eyebrows rising. "And why is that?"

"Because she holds the power of the Chosen One and when I find Alexis, I shall kill the child inside her and take back the power for myself."

Father took a step forward and slapped me. I reeled but remained on my feet. "Do you hear yourself? You have never sought power, and you would *never* kill a child. Especially not your own."

"What I may or may not have done in the past is over. I am destined to be the Chosen One and I shall do whatever I must to ensure I am."

"When you see Alexis again you shall remember just how much she means to you and you shall not harm your daughter, or your wife."

"*That* is your great plan? To reunite us and expect I shall just *remember* what you think I have forgotten? You are a fool, old man. Alexis and I have seen one another since I engulfed the army in Trachis in flames and she wanted nothing to do with me. It is no loss, for soon I shall have any mortal or goddess I choose, it has been proven to me already."

"You would turn so easily from the greatest love you have ever known? You would not fight to keep Alexis by your side and revel in something more than the solitary life we led before we came to Thermopylae?"

"Perhaps I have always been destined to walk alone. Without the need to call any other my own, I am free to do what I must, and what I choose."

"And yet you allow Ares to place thoughts in your mind about what you are to do."

"Ares has no part in my thoughts. He led me to the amulet and its power, but he does not control my choices any longer. He discarded me. He shall find out what a mistake that was."

Father advanced. I backed up until I felt the tree behind me again. "You shall remember who you truly are this day. I shall ensure it is so," he rumbled, tugging at the rope holding me to the tree. It remained tight and with a nod he crossed to Skaris. "When I return, we shall finish our conversation," he promised.

"Release me. Now," I demanded, struggling in the bonds.

Father ignored me, encouraging Skaris forward and taking off down the north-west path beside Lake Xynias.

I screamed and kicked at the dirt, frustrated he had been able to tether me in such a common manner. Again. I tugged and writhed in the restraints, the rope shredding the skin at my wrists. It was no use, my father was well skilled. I consoled myself with the knowledge that at least he was foolish and misguided enough to be bringing me exactly what I wanted; the child I would kill.

*

I was not certain how long it took for my father to return but when he did,

Alexis was with him. She sat atop Skaris and I noticed her hands were bound in front of her. I smirked; obviously he had told her he was taking her to me.

Alexis caught sight of me and resisted as best she could when Father lifted her off his horse. He was too strong and brought her close enough that we could touch each other if we wanted – not that either of us reached out. The amulet warmed beneath my tunic but I left it where it was, I doubted he had told Alexis I believed the child was the Chosen One.

"Leandros, please, you must allow me to continue on my journey to Epirus. That is my home now, as it has been for winters."

He stood between us, shaking his head. "I cannot allow it to be so, and neither shall Skylar. She fought so hard to free you from the Molossians and ensure you were always safe from their fearsome ways."

"And yet she is just as ruthless," Alexis countered. "You know she tortured Melanthios before she killed him. She enjoyed watching him suffer. Perhaps she did the same to the rest of his brothers before she came for me. And now Andreas is dead. Who do you suppose saw to that? He had a legitimate claim to me, but he stood in Skylar's way to get what she wanted. She does not love me, she merely wishes to possess me for herself, to have everyone know she is better than another. She has often said she would have stopped at nothing to have me. She relishes the opportunity to kill to have what she wants, more than anyone else – even you – knows."

I grinned and took a step forward, forcing Alexis to take one back. "And I always get what I want. Was it not you who suggested it was so when I told you the story of how Skotos came to be mine?"

"Stop it, both of you," Father growled, stepping further between us. "Ares has turned you against one another. He has filled your heads with lies and twisted the truth. Please, you must forget what he has told you." He took Alexis' hand, addressing her. "Skylar freed you from the Molossian tribe by killing the sons of Andreas, that is the truth, but did you not yearn for it? Did you not encourage her to do so?"

"You accuse me of being as she is?" Alexis asked, eyes wide.

"I am simply reminding you that without Skylar you would be back in Epirus now, suffering at the hands of Melanthios. You would not be carrying the child the two of you created through your deep love for one another."

"You saw what she did to that army. She is nothing more than a killer. She uses others for her own pleasure, regardless of their wants or desires."

My smile widened. "You cannot tell me you did not enjoy our time in the flames."

"It was a mistake to ever go to you that day. Were it not for you, my life and that of my unborn child would not have been in danger. They came for me to provoke you. Ever since you arrived in Trachis I have been in danger. My family and the people of our town lost friends, sons, husbands, fighting the Illyrians and Molossians because you wanted me for yourself. I am glad I saw you use that amulet, for now I know who you truly are."

"Enough!" my father yelled. "Skylar saved you once again from a soldier who would do you harm. She ensured you and your child were safe at her side. Even when she did not know who you were outside Trachis, she fought to free you from your bindings. She takes other people's struggles and troubles personally, she does not shy away from aiding where she can." He grabbed both of our hands, mashing them together as he continued. "Ever since Skylar was twelve winters old, she has gone out of her way to help those who need it. It is part of who she is. That is the part of her you first fell in love with, you told me so."

The amulet heated further at my chest, the familiar orange glow visible beneath the material. Calm flooded my veins and my back prickled.

"Release me," Alexis insisted, attempting to shake my hands free from hers.

"No. The two of you *must* remember how much you love each other. Only together can you overcome all that stands in your way. This is not the first time you have had to do so, and it shall not be the last. But you are stronger together."

I threaded my fingers through Alexis', ensuring she could not get away.

The itching at my back intensified. My wings broke through my skin far less painfully than they had the first time. Father was knocked backwards, but Alexis' hand remained in mine and I drew the power from the child.

With my free hand I drew my sword. "You are right when you say I kill to get what I want. I shall kill the child inside you and, with her death, take back what is mi–ah!" My shoulders burned hot as fire. I screamed and released Alexis as I dropped to my knees. My sword landed in the dirt beside me, covered almost immediately by my thick wings. Blood slipped off the black ends and I could feel it trickling down my back as well. A wave of nausea washed over me. My head throbbed.

Ares. Dianthe. The army. The amulet. Every conversation. Every thought and action since I had met my grandmother in the agora replayed itself in my mind. Faster and faster the images flipped, faces merging from one to another. The pressure in my head increased. I grabbed at it, my stomach also threatening to erupt even though it must have been a moon since I last ate. The words I had spoken to Alexis, how I felt about her, how she feared me. Hated me. *How could I have thought of her as meaning nothing more to me than someone to take to bed whenever I wanted it?* It was so far from the truth. I retched noisily.

A loud rumble echoed off the lake. The Pindos Mountains shook, four massive boulders tumbling awkwardly down the steep side. Two came to rest at the edge of the water, half submerged beneath the darkness, a small gap between them. The other two were larger and landed closer to the path. If I was to stand between them, the path in either direction would probably be hidden from me. But I was in no condition to even consider standing. My entire body ached. I felt as though I had been fighting a brutal enemy for days. I collapsed forward, closing my eyes against the pounding in my head and the bright light reflecting off the water.

35

"What did you do?" Ares boomed, his feet crunching across the ground beside me.

"What I had to," my father replied.

The pain in my head was beginning to fade. My stomach settled and I opened my eyes again. The amulet still glowed faintly but it was cooler against my chest. My thoughts were clear. I no longer had any want to be Ares' Chosen One. I did not want to hurt the child inside Alexis or take any power she possessed. My child. Our child. The one Hera had helped us to create ... Alexis. Had she been broken from her hating thoughts as well?

I rolled onto my side and pushed myself to my feet, my legs shaking against the movement. She was crouched on the ground nearby. "Alexis," I whispered.

She met my gaze and I saw her confusion. Thankfully, there was no fear or anger beneath that. She allowed my father to help her up and I took a step towards them. Ares stepped between us, his frown deep across his brow as he searched my face. I met his stare, and he quickly realized that I was no longer loyal to him, or wanted to be ruled by him, as I had been.

Ares growled low in his chest. I shoved past and stumbled across to Alexis, taking her in my arms. She wrapped her own tightly around my waist, hot tears and breath combining against my chest when I kissed the top of her head.

Ares rounded on us as my father spoke. "It appears that I, a lowly mortal has once again bested the God of War." Ares' frown deepened but he did not sweep my father aside or strike him down as I thought he might. Nevertheless, I rested my hand on the pommel of my sword, knowing the god would be faster than me if he decided to attack.

"You believe you have won, old man, but you have not. You cannot stop what is fated. When it is time to bring your granddaughter into the world, you shall not be able to stop me. To stop us. You shall learn just how weak you are."

"At least you cannot use my daughter to make it so. Without wings she cannot belong to your number."

"You fool. It is not her wings which hold the power, it is the amulet. And when I need her, she shall come to me without hesitation." He turned to Alexis and me, and I drew my sword, keeping him at length. He grinned, pushing the blade aside but remained where he was. "Your daughter, the child I gifted the two of you with shall be far more powerful than you. The Keres bloodline is strong in her veins. *She* is the one I have waited for. I can feel it."

"You shall never have her. Just as *my* parents denied you of me, so too shall Alexis and I keep her from you." My voice trembled with the words but it was from exhaustion rather than fear.

"And me," my father added, placing his hand on my shoulder.

Ares laughed. "You all speak with such passion, but you cannot change what has been promised to me. We shall see one another again soon, I promise you that." He laughed again, the echo of it lingering even after he disappeared.

I collapsed to my knees once more, head spinning and throbbing. The intense agony of the separation of my wings had dulled, but I could feel the blood pouring from the wounds and taste its metallic tang at the back of my throat.

"We have to stop the bleeding," Father said.

"I shall fetch some tinder and wood," Alexis replied.

I closed my eyes and lay down on the hard ground, listening to the two of them as they prepared a fire, the familiar crackling of wood and the smell of pine needles drifting through my nostrils.

"Can you hold her?" Father asked.

"Yes," came Alexis' reply.

"I shall do one at a time but if you cannot hold her, we shall have to swap." Alexis did not reply, but their hands manipulated my body to remove my tunic and lay me on my stomach. I knew the only way to stem the flow of blood draining from my body was to heat it, searing the skin so it could begin to repair itself. Alexis straddled my thighs, her cool hands resting on my forearms. "Ready?"

"Yes."

I drew a deep breath and held it, willing myself not to react when my father pressed the hot metal onto my flesh; I did not want to hurt Alexis when he did so and I hoped I was strong enough to remain still.

Heat emanated from what I could only assume was my sword, or my father's, a moment before he held it against my skin. I cried out, my fingers digging into the dirt as I struggled not to fling Alexis from atop me. When he finally lifted it away, the unmistakable stench of burning flesh filling my nose and I fought the wave of sickness that washed over me. Alexis stroked my hair, whispering words of comfort before settling herself atop me again.

My father pushed the fire-heated metal to the second wound, the sizzling sound worse than the smell. When he took it off again Alexis lifted herself from my body, her fingers still stroking my hair and arm as she sat beside me. As the pain at my back and in my head began to lessen, I slept.

When I woke, Father and Alexis were talking quietly. I attempted to roll onto my side, Alexis crossing to my side to help me sit up when she realized I was awake.

"We should burn the wings and return to Trachis," my father said, immediately including me in their conversation.

I drew a long breath but nodded as Alexis draped my tunic over my shoulders and down my body. Father stood, dragging the feathered lengths to the fire and throwing them on top. The flames resisted momentarily, suffocating beneath the denseness before roaring to life again and engulfing the wings, reducing them to ash. A sudden breeze drew it high into the air and when it faded from sight Father extinguished the fire with the last of the water in his waterskin. He led Skaris over and placed Alexis on his back before returning to my side. I attempted to push myself to my feet but I was still too weak.

"Allow me," Father murmured, lifting me from the ground and laying me across Skotos' back to protect my injuries. He took both sets of reins and led the horses back towards Trachis.

I wondered how any of us would be able to forgive each other for what we had said and done since the army arrived in Trachis but I was too tired for any such conversation at the moment. I closed my eyes, sucking in a breath as Skotos' every step reverberated through my back and shoulders.

36

Ares stood in his palace, awaiting the arrival of the Valkyrie who had requested to speak with him. It had been countless winters since he had seen any of the fair-haired women who had aided in the creation of the amulet and he was curious as to why she wanted to see him now. He wondered if she would confirm that the child growing inside Alexis was indeed his Chosen One.

At length, Dianthe showed her in and Ares recognized Eir immediately. The Valkyrie aged as little as his own Keres – Eir looking just as she had the last time Ares saw her; an attractive face framed by long, wheat-colored hair which hung far past her shoulders and down her back. Brilliant, white wings extended from her shoulder blades, extending through specially made holes in the back of her golden chest plate. Her high, full breasts were as prominent as ever, though Ares barely glanced at her womanly figure; such was his intent to hear what she had to say.

"Ares, it is good to see you again," the Valkyrie nodded.

"And you, Eir," Ares replied, acknowledging the nod with one of his own. "To what do I owe the pleasure?" Dianthe left them alone again and Ares indicated Eir join him at the black marble table which dominated the room.

"Since last we spoke, much has changed in the north lands," Eir began, taking a seat across from him. "Back then, we lived in a Golden Age where our deities lived, for the most part, in peace."

"It is not so now?"

"It is not. Do you know much of our ways or our gods?" she asked.

"No," Ares replied with a frown, hoping she would get to the point of her visit quickly.

"We have always had two races of gods – the Aesir and the Vanir. The Aesir are the warriors, the Vanir, the fertility gods. A battle began between the two, and the Vanir destroyed the walls of Asgard, home of the Aesir. In retaliation, the Aesir brought down the walls of Vanaheim where the Vanir live. The fighting raged long, until the leaders of each side realized that neither could gain decisive victory; they were too well matched, though their gifts were very different. A peace was agreed upon, the result an alliance of war and fertility gods living amongst one another with relative calm."

"I can only guess you belong to the Aesir," Ares noted.

"I do," Eir agreed. "My master is Odin, Father of all, greatest of all our gods. He is akin to your father, Zeus, in his role over our deities. It is he that sees me here with you now."

"Oh?" Ares asked, sitting forward in his chair.

Eir nodded. "We Valkyrie have always stood at Odin's side, tending his needs and healing injuries to our Aesir warriors. Until recently that is. Lord Odin has the gift of foresight and he speaks of the Ragnarök and the role we Valkyrie must play in preparation for it."

"Ragnarök?"

Eir nodded again. "It shall be the Twilight of our Gods. A fierce battle where few shall survive and for those who do, the world shall not be as it once was. Many among our number believe it is something to be feared, though Odin urges us to think of it as simply a re-birth."

"And what is the role of the Valkyrie?"

"We have been charged with gathering the most heroic and fearsome warriors of our northern lands. We take them to Valhalla where they await the Ragnarök by further training and feasting. Only those warriors who honor themselves and our gods by falling in battle are chosen for Valhalla. When the final battle comes, they shall rise again to fight beside Odin."

"So why have you come to me?"

"When Odin spoke of needing all the best warriors to stand beside him, I thought of your Chosen One – the woman I spoke of so many winters ago when I created the amulet for you. I have not followed your future particularly closely, though I see you have not yet taken the place of your father. This leads me to believe that your Chosen One has not been born to the line yet."

"Not yet, though I know who she is. Her power has revealed itself. Her birth shall come about within the mortal moon."

Eir raised her eyebrows. "She is not born yet? Have you somehow glimpsed her mark though she is inside her mother?"

"No, but I am certain she is the one I have waited for."

"How so?"

"The amulet you gave me reacted when she and her mother were put in danger, though the wielder could not call forth more than one element."

"I do not understand, was her mother not attempting its use for you?"

"Not the woman who shall birth her, no. Just as you predicted, the Chosen One shall be different to all the others. Her creation and parentage is only part of that. Perhaps one day we can speak of the specifics, though for now know that she shall soon be born."

"Show her to me."

"Now?" Ares asked.

When Eir nodded, he exhaled loudly, but stood, offering his hand to her as they prepared for travel together.

Within moments, Ares and Eir arrived in Skylar and Alexis' apartment in the palace at Trachis. Both slept deeply but Ares was careful to keep himself and Eir hidden in case they woke.

Eir approached the sleeping form of Alexis, placing a hand on her rounded belly. Alexis murmured, but did not open her eyes. "You speak true, God of War. This is certainly the child you have waited for." She grinned, moving her hand across the surface, both watching as the child within followed her movements with its own hand or foot. "There are many differences with this child; that I am certain of."

"Such as?" Ares prompted.

"The mark she wears. It is not the same as the others before her."

"How can you be certain? Can *you* see her skin beneath the body that holds her?"

"No, though I too am somewhat linked to the amulet and being so close to both it and the Chosen One, I am able to know much I did not before."

"Tell me," Ares insisted.

"Rather than a single, three-sided shape, it shall be two opposite one another, with the bottom line removed on both."

"Show me," Ares frowned.

Eir knelt, dragging her finger across the stone floor to reveal what she had seen.

Ares joined her, eyes following the lines, his thoughts fixed on just how many differences his Chosen One had to the others of the line.

"The design of your mark has evolved," Eir noted.

"Perhaps to incorporate all the elements in the amulet?" Ares murmured. "There are four points, one for each."

"I believe so," Eir nodded. "It unites all the elements in the amulet, not just the one for fire, which the Delta is known to represent."

"I thought the Delta was *my* symbol, that it represented change."

"It does, but have you never wondered why it was always the fire element the women of your chosen line were able to call upon first?" Ares only shrugged in reply, knowing there was one who was different. He should have realized then that the time was nearing. "This symbol shall represent them all; Fire, Water, Wind and Earth. It shall be known as the Completed Mark." Eir stood and the design she had drawn faded.

"When the child is born, you shall find it on her skin and you shall know your time as a subservient master to your father is passed."

"You are certain of this?"

"I am. She is the one you have waited for."

"Good."

"Now that we have confirmed her lineage, would you be prepared to agree to an alliance between our two clans?"

"What sort of an alliance?" Ares asked, pushing himself up and crossing his arms as he regarded the Valkyrie.

"When it comes time for us to fight in the Ragnarök, would you lend your Chosen One to us? With her at our side, we would be victorious."

"Can you give your word that she shall not be killed?"

"Of course. Master Odin did not speak of her death in the Twilight."

"I suppose I do owe a debt to you for the creation of the amulet, and for confirming the child here is who I believed," Ares mused, his hand straying to his chin. "If, by the time your Ragnarök arrives, I have taken my father's title then I shall allow her to join you."

"Good," Eir nodded. "Would you allow me to add a symbol of our own to your Chosen One to bind our agreement?"

"Now?" Ares asked again, eyebrows raised.

"No. Once she is born and you have seen the Completed Mark for yourself."

"What is it you want to put on her?"

"The Gungnir. It is the name of Odin's magic spear, known to never miss its mark."

"And what would it look like?" Ares asked. Once again, Eir dropped to one knee and drew on the stone floor.

"By adding Odin's spear to your mark, all Norse and Greek gods who see it shall know she is protected and loyal to us both."

"Very well," Ares agreed with a nod.

"After she is born, send word via your Keres and I shall place our mark over yours. Our fates shall see us twined together by not only our words, but by the black on her skin."

Ares nodded, his fingers stroking the hairs at his chin. "It appears it is time I brought the child into the world. Her mothers shall be struck down if they dare stand opposed to me again."

"Do not be so hasty to take her parents from her. Not yet at least. For now, she is of no use to you, but you can shape her into who you need her to be by acting from afar until she comes of age."

"And if I do not? If I wish to take her and raise her with my Keres immediately after she arrives?"

"You shall do as you see fit, as you always have," Eir shrugged. "But in this I would advise you to heed my words."

"I shall take it under advisement."

"As you wish," Eir conceded. Ares began to brighten, but Eir placed a hand on his arm to halt his departure. "Perhaps if you have not killed all your kin already, you would choose those you consider friends and join us and your Chosen One at the Ragnarök?"

"Perhaps," Ares nodded.

Eir removed her hand, allowing the God of War to vanish in a flash of bright light. She turned, watching the sleeping mother and the woman beside her. Eir placed her hand on Alexis' stomach again. "We shall see great things from you and your kin, child, of that I am certain," she whispered. She grinned as the pressure against her hand increased and as she left the palace in Trachis she wondered how long it would be before they met again.

37
13th Moon Full, Gamelion

"Welcome home," Alexis said as I entered our apartment. "I was just about to go to the baths, do you want to join me?"

"I cannot. I need to get to the training area, see how the recruits are doing," I replied, wishing I had gone there directly instead of to the palace.

"Skylar please, do not go yet. You have been away over half a moon. I missed you. *We* missed you." She reached out and took my hand, placing it on her stomach.

I drew my hand from her again and quickly swapped my dirty chiton for a clean one, stepping towards the door. "I am late. Sander and the others shall be waiting." Alexis was everything to me but I could not deny that it had been something of a relief not to have to see her every day the past few weeks.

Alexis blocked my path. "It has been a moon since we were freed from Ares' influence and you have avoided every attempt I have made to talk about what happened when we were apart. You could not volunteer quickly enough when Leandros asked for company south to bring the metalworkers back to Trachis just so you did not have to face the conversation you know we should have. Did you keep your silence with him as well, or did the two of you repair your rift?"

"I said very little to him. I do not know what you want me to say – Ares believed I was his Chosen One, then he did not. I could not use the power of the amulet after that first time. We are free of that. It is done." I did not tell her the rest of what I thought, or feared, would come to pass with our daughter, of who she may become; Ares had said he needed all the Keres to assist in her birth, and I had to presume that still included me. Without my wings though, I would not be as strong as the others. I would not be as loyal to him. Perhaps without them, our daughter's birth would kill me, just as I had always believed I had killed my mother. Alexis would lose us both if that was the case. Our child would belong to Ares. I could not bear such devastation to befall Alexis, not with all she had already suffered in her life and I did not know how to stop it.

"And what about what *I* went through? What if it is something I need to talk about?"

"You have Hesper, I am certain she would listen if you asked her to."

"I do not want to talk to Hesper about this. I want to tell *you*, share it with *you* as my wife, my partner in life. I want to tell you how it was for me the day you destroyed that army, why I believed Epirus was the best place for me."

"Later then," I shrugged, attempting to step around her.

"No. Enough, Skylar. I shall not allow you to sweep my questions aside. Not today."

"Look, it is done, neither of us can change it. We can only move forward, and I can do that without talking about it. Now get out of the way."

"No," she insisted, hands on hips. "You appear to have forgotten that to move forward with our lives and get the child we wanted, we had to share everything we had previously kept from each other."

I blew out a quick breath, but stepped back, crossing my arms over my chest. Clearly she had worked on the speech while I had been away and I would get to the training area faster if I allowed her to just tell me. "Fine, go ahead."

"When you used the amulet to destroy the army, I felt what you did – the calm strength and power – as well as the feelings of overwhelming lust. Just as you were, I too was drawn to the carnage, the bloodlust you could create. I wanted it. I knew you were powerless to stop the feelings. That you did not want to stop them. You felt unstoppable with so much power running through you, through us both – but for me when the wall of fire surrounding us disappeared, so too did those feelings. I was left with a deep repulsion and an intense desire to be far away from you."

"I know," I growled. So many thoughts had plagued me since our return, though the knowledge of how much Alexis had hated me and how easily I would have thrown away what we had, haunted me as much as the thoughts about our child.

"Ares made me forget what you truly meant to me. He twisted the truth of our time against Melanthios and his brothers. Deep down I felt his words were lies but when he was near, I believed everything he said. He wanted to turn us against each other, and perhaps he has succeeded. You speak no words of love or comfort to me. You do not lay hands upon my stomach or talk to our daughter as you did before."

"Because I am not certain she should still live," I muttered, the words slipping out before I could stop them.

"What?" Alexis whispered.

"I have to go," I said, attempting to get around her to the door handle.

"Oh no. No way," she growled, grabbing my outstretched arm. "Is that why you are running from me all the time? Tell me everything that is going on in your head."

"Alex–"

"Everything, Skylar. Now. I mean it."

I closed my eyes for a long moment. "You do not know what you ask."

"I know there are things you do not want to share with me. While we were apart, Ares convinced me that you would harm me and our baby. He was insistent that you did not care for either of us. He may have been right then, but do you still want to hurt her and take her power?"

I rested one hand on the pommel of my sword. "I do not want her power, I have told you that."

"But you want to hurt her?"

"It was Ares who ensured she was created, knowing that how can you want her to be born?" I asked her instead. "She is the Chosen One and we should break the line while we have the chance: before she is even born," I managed, the words making me sick to my stomach to say, even though I meant every one of them.

"Skylar, no ... how can you say that about our child?" Alexis stammered.

"You are carrying a child who shall cause nothing but destruction and pain in the mortal realm. Can you truly tell me you are willing to allow such an infant to be born? To hold responsibility for the damage she shall cause?"

"You still believe Ares so easily, as you did Dianthe when she first spoke with you."

"What reason do I have not to? You saw what I was able to do when I was *not* his Chosen One. Imagine what she could do if she is. I felt the power in the amulet, in myself, just as you did. Her power would be so much more destructive than that."

"Our daughter is not the one," Alexis insisted.

"I believe she is," I murmured, dropping my gaze from her.

Alexis moved swiftly, knocking aside my hand and drawing my sword from its sheath, holding it awkwardly above her belly. "Then go ahead, take your sword and drive it through my stomach. Kill us both, for that is the only way I shall allow you to end her life."

"Alexis," I began.

She shook her head, tears spilling down her cheeks as she pushed the handle towards me. "Go ahead. If this is what you want then push your blade into me and see it done."

"Alexis," I said again, my fingers closing automatically around my weapon. "You are being ridiculous."

"Do it," she screamed, pressing the tip against her stomach, the material of her dress ripping with the pressure.

"I shall not. This is not the way," I roared, pulling my sword from her chiton and slamming it back into its holder. Before she could stop me again I turned on my heel and pulled open the door, half way through when I crashed into Thaddeus.

"Skylar!" he managed, stumbling backwards. I grabbed him before he hit the ground. "Is Alexis with you? Hesper finds herself filled with the pains of our child's arrival."

"I am here," Alexis answered, subtly wiping the tears from her face as she emerged from our room.

"The boys are excited to stay with you until their new brother or sister is born," Thaddeus grinned, addressing me again.

"Er … I am not certain I should look after them today," I murmured.

"Oh? Are you unwell?

"No, it is not that …"

"Please, Skylar. They miss you; they have barely seen you lately."

"And you gave your word you would take them when the time came," Alexis said, keeping her eyes from me.

I exhaled a long breath. It was true – I had hardly spent any time with his children since I returned from Ares and Lake Xynias, and I had not given Thaddeus a reason for it; not that he had asked for one. I did miss the boys but what they represented – family, children – was difficult and I did not want to treat them unkindly for an issue that was mine, not theirs. "Where are they?" I finally asked.

Thaddeus smiled again and stepped out of the central chamber, motioning to them with a wave of his hand. The three boys raced towards us, stumbling and pushing one another in their quest to be first. Tritonos claimed victory and attached himself to my leg, the older two boys merely tagging me before stepping back with wide grins beneath their pink cheeks.

"I am going to the training fields, are you happy for me to take the boys along?"

"Of course, of course. I trust you to keep them away from the pointed ends of the swords and spears. Take Lysistratos as well."

I nodded in reply, lifting Tritonos into my arms and collecting Lysistratos from his house in town on our way to the plain beyond the

Melas River.

The recruits were sweating hard when we arrived and were grateful for the interruption of the younger children. Pamphilos, Tritonos and I sat at the edge of the Melas; Pamphilos drawing patterns in the soft dirt at the bank and Tritonos lying contentedly against my chest, his fingers twirling the ends of my hair which hung down beside him. Nikomachos and Lysistratos attempted to complete the various tasks, Kleitos helping his younger brother in the target practice, though in truth, Lysistratos did not need much instruction. He was gifted with weapons already and it confirmed my belief he would join the soldiers of Trachis as soon as he was old enough. I could not help grin as I thought what a powerful army Trachis would have one day. Dedicated, skilled warriors who would fight proudly to keep their home and their loved ones safe.

Eventually I called Nikomachos and Lysistratos back and we headed into Trachis where I told the boys they could purchase a gift each for Hesper and the new baby. Tritonos fell asleep at my shoulder as we walked and Pamphilos took the opportunity to hold my hand, happy to watch his older brother and Lysistratos run ahead. They fought one another with long sticks, only stopping when we reached the first houses and dropping back to walk with the rest of us.

In their company, it was easy to forget the argument I had had with Alexis before I left the palace. But I had not forgotten the fear and anger in her eyes when she held my sword against her stomach. I knew that look would stay with me, and haunt me, for a long time yet.

"Good day, Skylar," Ophelos called as we neared his stall.

"Ophelos," I nodded in return.

"Wine?" he asked. I nodded again, taking the skyphos he offered. "What brings you to the agora this day?"

"My mother is birthing our brother or sister," Pamphilos replied proudly.

"Is she indeed? Well, that is cause for celebration."

"Indeed," I murmured, handing the cup back. "We should continue on, boys. We are searching for a gift for Hesper and the baby."

"Do not allow me to keep you then. I shall see you again soon," Ophelos waved as a customer approached and ordered three amphorae.

"Thank you," I nodded, taking Pamphilos' hand again as we made our way to the next street over.

*

A candlemark later saw the gifts purchased – a blanket, some perfume and several large pieces of charcoal, courtesy of Pamphilos, who wanted to ensure the new baby kept warm and survived its first winter.

"Skylar," Father called, waving when I turned. "Hello boys. Do you have time to come back to Ophelos' before returning to the palace? I have a gift for you."

I hesitated. Even though Father and I had travelled south together alone, it had taken us a long time to broach the subject of Ares and what had happened at Lake Xynias, and we did not speak of it for long; neither of us eager to dwell on what had occurred, and neither of us able to offer solution as to how to keep the amulet's power from passing to the child when she was born.

I had not spoken of the only solution I had come up with; I was afraid he would not understand. But more than that, I was afraid he *would*, and would aid me to snuff out the life within Alexis. If it came to that end, I knew neither of us could remain in Trachis. We would not be welcomed even by those we were closest to and it was too hard to even consider that.

"We shou–"

"A gift? What is it?" Nikomachos cut over the top of me.

"*Please* can we go?" Lysistratos added.

I shook my head, but grinned, gesturing my father lead the way.

"Perhaps it is a sword," Nikomachos suggested.

"Or a bag of coins," Lysistratos countered; both aware that Father was not only a warrior but worked with metals as well.

Nasrin and Aspasia met us when we arrived, fussing over the children and taking Pamphilos and Tritonos, who had just woken from his sleep hungry and agitated, to the kitchen. Father climbed the ladder to the first floor and returned with a covered package. The older boys and I trailed him to the metal workshop – the middle room on the ground floor to the left of the entrance.

"I told you it would not be a sword," Lysistratos crowed, pushing at Nikomachos' shoulder. "Skylar's is still sharp. No soldier gets a new sword unless their old one is broken in battle."

"It could have been," Nikomachos shrugged as they both crowded around my father.

He handed me the gift and I opened it, revealing a leather cuirass in exactly my size. I held it up.

"Wow," Lysistratos murmured.

"Yeah," Nikomachos agreed.

"I thought perhaps it was time for a new one in a different material to the last," Father explained.

"It is perfect," I grinned, noting the thick layers of leather stitched together which would give the cuirass strength, and me good protection.

"What happened to your bronze one?" Nikomachos asked.

"It was getting old. Skylar needed a new one," Father replied before I had the chance to find a sufficient explanation. Father handed me a second package. "Beeswax," he advised when I freed the pyxis from the paper. "It protects the leather and keeps it supple."

"Thank you," I said, smiling again. I placed the pyxis on the workbench and Father helped me pull the new cuirass over my head.

"I was closest then," Lysistratos announced. "A cuirass is armor and a sword is a weapon."

"Were not," Nikomachos insisted. "It is made from leather, not metal." The boys continued to argue as Father tied the leather lengths at my shoulder.

"What did Gnosidicus say when you saw him?" he asked quietly.

"I am healing well enough; he took the bandaging off and said I should be able to begin training in the next few days, though not as much as I was. Not yet anyway," I replied.

"That is to be expected."

I nodded again, thankful that my sword would soon be more than just a weight around my waist as it had been for the past moon. I had no doubt that what Father had done for me at Lake Xynias had ensured a quicker recovery – without the heat of the metal against my flesh, I could have died from the loss of blood before we even reached Trachis again.

"Thank you," I muttered as he tied the last of the leather. He nodded in reply and we both knew I spoke of more than just the gift of the cuirass.

We remained with my father for the evening meal, returning Lysistratos to his house afterwards as the rest of us continued to the palace. My father carried Nikomachos and Pamphilos and I held Tritonos, all three children asleep by the time we reached the entrance way.

38

Thaddeus paced outside his apartment, joining us when he saw us come in. "It shall not be long now," he said. "Gnosidicus says within the candlemark."

I nodded. "I shall put the boys to bed in our apartment. You can collect them in the morning."

"Are you certain? What about you and Alexis?"

"We can sleep in her old room," I replied.

"When I have news, I shall send Hesper's mother, she can stay with the boys until they wake."

I nodded again and Father and I made our way to the room, settling the sleeping children into the large bed and leaving one torch burning low so they had light if they woke and wondered where they were.

"I must get back. You shall send word when the child arrives?" Father asked.

"Of course," I replied, wrapping my arms around his waist. "Thank you for the cuirass."

"A soldier must remain protected," was his only reply.

We released one another and I watched him leave before opening the door to the room intended for our daughter. I set about lighting the torches and placing a blanket on the bed, hanging my new cuirass over the back of the chair.

Alone again, the memory of Alexis holding my sword to her stomach assaulted me with its intensity. To hear her goad me to push it through her and into our child, had frightened me. Perhaps as much as I frightened her by suggesting I take our child's life in the first place. I knew the conversation was not finished – how could it be when we were both so determined to have our way? But I did not know how to continue it without hurting Alexis with my words. With only a few moons until our child was due to be born, I knew I had avoided the conversation for too long – perhaps it was already too late to stop her arrival without killing Alexis as well.

I sighed, half-filling a cauldron and placing it over the flames, warming the water inside. Alexis would need to bathe before she went to bed after assisting as she had, and I lay down to await her arrival, attempting to calm my thoughts, and find a solution to what lay ahead.

I was almost asleep when Alexis came in, bringing the news that Thaddeus and Hesper had a daughter. Her chiton was soiled and I helped her remove it, tipping the heated water into a basin and wiping the blood and sweat from her body with a length of soft material.

"We should talk," I murmured when she was clean again, knowing it had to be me who began the continuation of our earlier conversation. I placed my hand beneath her chin, lifting her eyes to mine. "I cannot lose you. We can have another child, but I could never find anyone I love as much as you. You understand that, do you not?"

"I do not want you to lose either of us," she murmured. "I am sorry for what I did earlier, for what I said. I was … frustrated … scared I had lost you, that we would never be the same."

"I am sorry too. Sorry I made you feel that way. You have not lost me. I am here but I cannot allow Ares to use our daughter. I shall not. I see no other way to deny him of her than to … stop her being born in the first place."

"We have to find one. I do not want to lose her or you either. At Lake Xynias Leandros said we are stronger together. We always have been. But you need to stay with me and help me find that way. Please."

I drew a deep breath. "We do not need part of me to be in our child, I will love it regardless because it came from you. Perhaps … perhaps we should consider what once I was not willing to. With Thaddeus."

"No," she replied, taking my hand. "It is time we faced this together. Please, can you do that for me? For us? We *can* find a way to deny Ares what he wants. I truly believe that."

"I want to. I promise I do but I have sought answers from the gods, from Hera, I have prayed for guidance and a solution and none has been given to me."

"You do not enjoy when you have no answers to a question," she said with a slight grin. "I saw it with Melanthios and when I first spoke of wanting a child."

"I do not enjoy being unable to provide you with everything you need or want," I corrected. "I am torn by the thoughts in my head. I wish for nothing more than to share the birth of our child, to share her first laugh, her first step, her first everything. But those images war with the ones of what Ares could do with her as his Chosen One. What she would feel if she used the amulet. Against him, against her, I could do nothing. For all my strength, I would be weak. I could raise no army, no defense that would win against them or the amulet. And what about when Ares spoke of using me to bring her into this world?"

"There is much we do not know about what is to come. We cannot know it. But this is *our* daughter. Not his. We are not getting rid of our baby, Skylar."

"Bu–"

"No," Alexis insisted, squeezing my fingers and silencing me. "She is *not* Ares' Chosen One. I would feel it just as I felt the power running through you when we touched. You are wrong. They are wrong. She is ours. We can protect her from him. From them."

I drew another long breath. My parents had once thought the same, and they too had been denied. I did not repeat my thoughts out loud. "I hope so," I murmured instead, drawing Alexis close and pressing my lips to the top of her head. "I think when the time comes and you find yourself with the pains of birth, we should do it alone – without Hera's assistance. Without *any* god or goddesses' help."

"Yes. We should go through it as any other mortal – with only us and our healer."

"As Hesper did," I nodded. With one arm still around Alexis, I led her to the bed, settling her beneath the blanket and sliding in beside her. I placed my hand tentatively on her stomach, relieved when I felt no heat or pull of power coming from within – just a tiny hand or foot pushing up to meet mine.

Alexis smiled and covered my hand with her own. "See? She has missed you. The amulet is still dark, there is no power in her. She is simply just ours."

I only nodded, realizing just how much I had missed the quiet moments in the nights before Ares arrived when Alexis was asleep and I lay as we were now, my hand to her stomach and our daughter pushing hers to mine. It was something special we had shared and I had told no one else about it, wanting it to be just for the two of us.

"Do you want to hear of Hesper and the baby?" Alexis asked after a few moments. I nodded, sliding my fingers across the skin of Alexis' stomach and watching as my daughter mirrored the action. "They are both well. She is such a combination of Thaddeus and Hesper. She is beautiful, just as our daughter shall be."

I met her gaze, bringing my hand to her cheek. "I hope she has your green eyes," I smiled, tracing her cheekbone.

"Perhaps she shall have your blue ones," she replied, closing her eyes and kissing my palm. "I have missed you so much. This. Us," she murmured.

I leaned forward and kissed her. "Me too."

We were quiet for a long while, eyes closed, foreheads touching, hands entwined on Alexis' stomach. "Hesper and Thaddeus intend to name their daughter Eumelia ... I too have been considering some names for our daughter," Alexis finally said.

"You have one you favor most?"

"Sophia," she nodded.

"Sophia," I repeated. I had not heard it before. "What does it mean?"

"Wisdom ... if she is who you and Ares think then she shall need wisdom to choose the correct path. The one that Ares does not offer her."

"It is a fine choice," I nodded, considering it. "Moons ago, before Dianthe and Ares arrived, I came up with a name too," I admitted.

"Oh?"

"I thought we could name her Ava."

"That was the name of Nasrin's daughter, was it not?"

"It was," I agreed. "I have learnt much about Ava since last I saw her; who her father was, what she and Nasrin had to endure to leave Persia and come here. And if Darius ever dared come to Greece, I would ensure he was met with force, for I too now call him my enemy."

"You favor a name that belongs to the daughter of an enemy?" Alexis frowned. "How close did you and Ava become as you travelled together? You said until Kuria you had never ... been with a woman before, but did you want to be with Ava? Were you ... attracted to her?" Alexis kept her eyes from mine as I studied her face.

I heard the jealousy in her question but I also heard her fear. Even after everything we had overcome, there was still part of her that feared my past. I understood how such thoughts could invade and take over at inopportune times and I did not hold it against her.

I raised her chin and she met my gaze. "I would give our daughter the name for no other reason than to honor the memory of my friend. That was *all* she was to me; a friend. I give you my word."

Alexis exhaled, her cheeks darkening beneath my stare. "I am sorry. I am tired an—"

"It is alright," I smiled. "But hear me when I tell you that friendship was all Ava and I ever shared, just as it is for you and Hesper. Indeed, until you, she was the only friend I really ever had." Alexis nodded and I leaned forward to press my lips against hers. "It was just a thought – I would be more than happy to name our daughter Sophia. It is beautiful, just as she shall be when she arrives in a few moons."

"Yes," Alexis agreed, a yawn taking her over.

"You need to rest," I grinned. "Come here." Alexis inched over, laying her head on my shoulder as she blew out another long breath.

"It has been a long day," she murmured. I closed my eyes as her arm rested across my stomach, reveling in the feel of her in my arms.

"I love you," I whispered.

"You too," Alexis replied sleepily as Hypnos took us both into his realm.

39

Father and I stood in the metalworking area of Ophelos' house, the area lit by the fading light outside and the clay bloomery dominating the south-west corner of the room. The heat of the furnace was a comfort as the winter evenings settled in but I wondered how stifling it would be in the summer. Father had brought back a number of metalworkers to assist with the production of weapons and armor, but we had found no Celators willing to leave their current positions when we travelled south together. Instead, the two of us were attempting to teach the metalworkers to craft coins as well.

We had been toiling away inside the room all day, extracting the metal we needed from the heated ore inside the bloomery. Lengths of wood and charcoal kept the furnace hot, one man responsible for pumping air in through the attached clay pipes with bellows (a bladder of sorts made from the skin of goats) while the other two confirmed the progress, adding whatever was needed, or removing the slag from the bottom of the furnace when it was ready.

Flans of silver lay on the workbench at the opposite end of the room. Father and I had spent candlemarks and candlemarks creating the flans the past couple of weeks. They began as lumps of silver which we heated until it liquefied before pouring it into two-sided clay molds and allowing it to cool. When we took them from the molds, they were blank discs of varying sizes and weights. We wanted them to weigh the same as the Athenian coins; otherwise they would not be accepted for payment when they were exchanged for goods our traders wanted. All we had to do now was put our pictures on each of the flans to identify where they came from.

The metalworkers joined us at the workbench so we could show them how to do so. Father held up a die which had a sword and the picture from my shield carved, in reverse, into it. "The obverse of each coin is created by this block of bronze, called a die," he told them. "The design for the reverse side is carved into the anvil die."

He pointed to a second block of bronze which was counter sunk into a log, the underside of which had been smoothed until it was flat, rather than rounded, ensuring its stability on the ground. The picture in the anvil die was more intricate; the palace as seen from Trachis looking back to the eastern and northern balconies but with the Malian Gulf behind it, rather than Mount Oetaea. Father and I had argued about the Gulf being included – mainly because it was not an accurate portrayal of the town and area itself. I had lost the argument, Father insisting it did not have to be accurate, merely suggestive of what was in Trachis.

Father took a hammer from beside the anvil and passed the first die to me. "Now, watch what happens when we place this silver between the dies," he instructed. I positioned the die on the flan, ensuring the center of the carved picture was in the center of the silver.

Father caught my eye and I gave him a nod. He brought the hammer down hard on the end of the bronze I held, punching both pictures into the coin. I lifted the die and allowed my father to show it to the men. I grinned as they peppered him with questions, and attempted the technique themselves, frowning when their grip slipped and half the picture was lost off the side of the flan. Father told them it did not matter if the design was not perfect; it was the weight that mattered. Silently I disagreed, if we were to be taken seriously as a coin minting town, then our coins should be of the highest quality in both weight and design.

As the last of the light outside disappeared, the door to the room opened. The amulet flared momentarily beneath my cuirass. "What is wrong?" I asked, frowning at the look on Alexis' face as I crossed to her.

"I have been having pains for the past few candlemarks. I … I think our daughter is ready to meet us."

"That is not possible," I said, taking her hands and finding them cold to the touch. "Come, stand by the furnace," I added, leading her to the flames.

"I agree, she is not due for over two moons but when I described the sensations to Hesper, she told me she believed it was time."

"Why did you not send Thaddeus to find me? You should not have come. Especially not alone."

"I am scared, Skylar."

I wrapped my arms around her as though that was all it would take to protect her and our daughter. "I know," I murmured, my heart beating fast and my thoughts spiraling out of control.

My father herded the metalworkers out and closed the door behind them before joining us. "What is it?" he asked.

"Alexis believes our daughter is coming. Now. Today," I stammered.

"It is too early," Father frowned.

"Oh, it is exactly the right time," Ares' voice announced a moment before he appeared. I swept Alexis behind me and drew my sword as Father did the same.

Ares was not alone; Dianthe stood beside him, grinning. "When I first laid hands on Alexis I felt she was seven moons along rather than the four you expected her to be, so she is exactly on time."

"That is not possible," I murmured.

"For a child of the Ker line, it is," Ares shrugged.

"Children birthed too early never survive," Alexis whispered, her voice wavering with the words.

Ares neared, ignoring my sword as he reached out and stroked her cheek. "Do not fear for your daughter. My blood runs through her veins. She is my Chosen One. She shall arrive strong and healthy."

"Until she is old enough to learn to use the amulet, she is useless to you," I growled, slapping his hand aside. "I was not ready until I was nineteen winters, for her it may be even longer; she is *full* mortal, not half-mortal, half-Ker as I am."

Ares shrugged again and stepped back. "True enough. But the sooner I can begin making my preparations for the future, the better."

The amulet at my chest was dark again but I took it off and held it up. Ares' gaze fell on it almost immediately. "You told us it was not the line that was powerful, but the amulet, so what is to stop me destroying it? Our child would never have it, never attempt to use it. Your plan would be finished."

Ares laughed. "Oh, Skylar, do you truly think it would be that easy to destroy? That the Keres and Valkyrie would have allowed it to be so?"

"You cannot destroy it without releasing its power," Dianthe cackled, silencing when Ares raised his hand.

"If the amulet is cracked or broken, the elemental powers it holds will find their way to the closest being and then … well the fun shall begin."

"If that is true, then why have you never broken it open before? Why wait for a *Chosen One* to be born?" Father asked.

"Now, where would the fun be in that, old man?" Ares grinned.

"What would happen to that person if they were not of your line?" Alexis asked.

"There is no way to know if they can achieve what has been predicted with the Chosen One. Only *she* can ensure our victory, for anyone else … the outcome is unknown."

"Oh no, Dianthe, I *know* what would happen: they would be killed. But their body – the vessel – would still be immensely useful to me."

"Perhaps you are just saying that so I do not destroy it," I countered.

"Go ahead – see what happens if you do," Ares taunted. I swallowed but did not take him up on his offer. "I thought not. Now …" He rubbed his hands together. "It is time we went to the palace. We have a child to birth." Without waiting for anyone to object, Ares grabbed one of my hands, and one of Alexis' and took us from Ophelos' house.

I regained consciousness when my feet touched solid ground. Ares still held Alexis and me but we were not alone in the palace courtyard; at least twenty Keres stood around a spit in the middle of the garden, the carcass of a boar roasting above the flames.

"What … What are they doing here?" I stammered.

"They are drawn to the power of your child – they are here to ensure she arrives safely. You shall help too."

One of the women approached, her eyes on Alexis' rounded stomach as she addressed Ares. "Is it time, Master?"

"Yes," he grinned. With a sweep of his hand, the doors to the palace slammed shut – the front ones as well as those at each of the walkways – their locking device falling into place. "Now no one can disturb us," Ares said. "Gather around, all of you. It is time the Chosen One was brought into our midst."

At his words, Alexis' knees buckled. I rushed forward, but Ares was faster, gathering her in his arms before she reached the ground as two Keres held me in place. "Give her to me," I demanded, struggling in their taloned grips.

"You have a role to play but it is not to hold your lover's hand as she delivers the one I have waited for."

"What then?"

"You shall join your kin in an unbroken circle and chant the ancient words we have always uttered when one is born to the line."

"And then?" I prompted.

Ares grinned again. "You are going to die. Without your wings, the power of the Keres flowing through you shall be too much. But do not fear about Alexis raising your child alone – we shall take your daughter as soon as she is born and keep her with us until her time comes."

"No! You cannot have her," I insisted, uselessly fighting against my captors.

Ares turned toward our apartment, addressing Dianthe over his shoulder. "Ensure Skylar is part of that circle. She is still powerful and we are far fewer in number than we once were."

"Of course, Master," she replied.

"Ares!" I screamed, kicking out as something heavy collected me in the side of the head and everything went dark.

40

Pressure at my forearm pulled me from the darkness. Hot fingers gripped me, nails digging into my skin. "I have only just found you, you changed my life. Do not make me walk alone in this world. I cannot do it again. Come back to me, Skylar. Please, I beg it of you. I cannot do this without you."

Alexis. Fear laced her pleas. I opened my eyes, panic fluttering in my stomach. My neck ached. *How long was I unconscious?* My chin rested against the smooth leather armor covering my chest, my vision impeded by long strands of hair. My arms were bound tight against a wooden chair and I could not move. Pain stabbed at my shoulder blades, reminding me what was about to happen.

Ares. The Keres. The baby.

I fought against my bindings, my hair swinging out of my eyes and revealing the circle of Keres. We were no longer in the palace courtyard, but in the room Alexis and I shared.

The women all had their eyes closed. Hands clasped together, fingers of the two either side of me wrapped around my upper arms to form an unbroken circle. Their black wings flapped silently, moving the fire-warmed air in the room.

Alexis sat within the circle, grimacing in pain.

The Keres chanted words, almost melodic in their repetitiveness; soft, encouraging. I did not understand the language, but I knew the meaning; they were bringing our daughter into the world. The power swirling about our bedroom intensified. It would not be long now.

The amulet heated my chest but I felt none of its power or that seductive calm flowing through me.

I bucked against the ropes, finally breaking free of them, and the hands holding me. I jumped to my feet. Alexis screamed, grabbing at her swollen belly and, though I had said we would ask no goddess for help on this particular day, I sent a prayer to Artemis to protect Alexis, as well as our child, as she entered the world. *We may need your help too, Goddess Hera,* I added. I unsheathed the sword at my thigh, driving the metal blade into the Ker to my left. Her eyes grew wide as she grabbed at her injury, dropping to the floor as I wrenched my sword from her suddenly lifeless body. I had no sooner retrieved my weapon than Ares was beside Alexis, his face a mask of concentration as he continued the chant of the Keres. He shouted the foreign words as though attempting to mask the loss of the Ker I had slain.

I turned to the next Ker, slicing her head from her neck in a spray of blood. Ares' voice heightened in response. I rounded the circle, cutting and slashing at the monstrous women before they could mount a defense. I had counted twenty back in the courtyard, but that number had swelled considerably. Sweat trickled down the back of my neck as I drove my blade into body after body, stopping only when Alexis cried "No!"

I turned. Dianthe held a small, pink child in her arms. She stared in surprise at the bare patch on its left shoulder. Ares too, looked on in disbelief, taking the baby and inspecting every inch of her. My baby girl.

The wispy smattering of hair on her tiny head matched the dark shade of my own. She cried at Ares' rough treatment and I sheathed my weapon, crossing to them in two strides and snatching my daughter from him. Her howls quieted as I drew her to my chest.

"She is not one of you. Leave this place. Do not return. Ever," I growled.

"She does not carry your mark. She is not your Chosen One," Alexis panted, reaching her hand up to me. I helped her across to the bed, handing her our child and settling them both on the covers.

"She does not wear the completed mark," Ares murmured.

"It must be there. Eir told you she would," Dianthe replied.

I turned and drew my sword on Ares and my grandmother. "Get. Out," I snarled.

"She is powerful, Granddaughter," Dianthe said. "With your tainted blood and lack of wings, you may not have felt it, but she is of the line. She *is* the one."

"No!" I screamed. I charged at Dianthe and slammed my sword into her stomach. Blood spilled from her mouth, dripping to the floor to pool with the blood from the wound. I retrieved my weapon again as she grabbed at her insides, choking on the mucus in her throat before she fell to the ground.

I levelled my weapon at Ares, but he only howled in response, disappearing in a flash of light and leaving Alexis and I alone in the room with the bodies of my kin. I put away my sword and returned to her side, taking our daughter and checking for the mark myself. There was no three-sided shape on her shoulder as there was on mine. No indication at all that the blood of the Keres, of Ares, ran through her.

Her eyes matched Alexis' in their greenness. She looked up at me with those familiar orbs, innocence and openness written across her small, pink face. I smiled. My daughter. Our daughter. Strong and healthy.

How could I have wanted to end her life before she could show me that she did not belong to them; that she belonged to us? No matter what Ares believed, what *I* had believed, I would always protect her from him, teach her to be strong and resist whatever he offered her. She would know what I had not when she was old enough.

I kissed her forehead and handed her back to Alexis, crossing to the door and lifting the timber lock. Father and Thaddeus burst into the room, swords and shields in hand, eyes wide as they surveyed the scene in front of them.

"Where is Ares?" Father asked.

"Gone," I replied.

"You killed them all?" Thaddeus added, kneeling beside each Ker, searching for signs of life.

"Yes."

"Even Dianthe?" Father queried.

"Yes," I said again, pointing out her lifeless body.

Father's eyes held mine for a moment before he turned his attention to Alexis. "Are you alright?" he asked. "The child?"

Alexis managed a smile for him. "I am well. Come, meet your granddaughter."

The smile that split my father's face could have lit the room on a dark winter's eve. He dropped his weapons and crossed to Alexis, taking the child and wrapping her in a long length of material when Alexis offered it to him.

His eyes found her shoulder, as ours all had, and his grin widened when he saw she bore nothing there. "My darling girl," he crooned, drawing in the smell of the small child as he cradled her against his large body.

"How are you?" Thaddeus asked quietly, a hand on my arm.

"Alive," I replied. "Go see our child," I added, gesturing in Alexis' direction.

One side of his mouth lifted in a grin and he gave me a curt nod, making his way to the rest of my small family.

With the three of them occupied with the child, I slipped out of the room. Leaning against the cold stone wall, I blew out a deep breath.

"She is perfect, Alexis," Thaddeus said, his voice carrying through the still-open door. "Welcome to Trachis, sweetheart."

Welcome indeed, I thought. *What shall await you as you grow, daughter of mine?*

"What name have you chosen to give her?" Father asked.

"Ava," Alexis replied. I raised an eyebrow at her response. We had not discussed names again since Eumelia was born two weeks ago, though I had believed that when the time came, we would choose Sophia.

A flash of light announced Ares' presence beside me and I rested my hand on the end of my sword. "You lose," I murmured. "She is not who you thought she was."

"It would appear that way now, but I felt her power. I know who she is." I made no response, and he did not appear to need one before he spoke again. "I approve of her name. Ava. A good, strong Persian name. I have always admired the Persian way of fighting. It is fitting for my chosen warrior."

"She is not yours," I muttered, exhaustion beginning to creep into my body.

"Not yet. But I shall return for her when her time comes."

He began to light up again the way he always did when he disappeared, but I reached out and placed a hand on his arm. "Wait. Dianthe spoke of Ava's quick growth inside Alexis, do you expect her to continue to age faster than other children?"

"I cannot say," he shrugged. "Nothing about her has been as I expected."

"No," I agreed, releasing him and turning my head as he departed. I took a deep breath and returned to the room, taking Alexis' trembling hand when she offered it to me. "You named her Ava?" I whispered.

"Nasrin told me in Persia it means voice or sound and I think that suits her – she has already had much to say about our lives, and I am certain her voice is one that many others shall hear in winters to come," Alexis grinned.

"I can only imagine," I nodded, leaning down and kissing Alexis' dry lips. "I shall never allow Ares to hurt you or Ava. I give you my word."

"Thank you," she replied.

"We shall take our leave," Father said. "I shall tell Agrias and Melina that their newest princess has arrived."

"Thank you, Leandros," Alexis smiled.

He nodded and bent down, placing a gentle kiss on Ava's forehead. "Welcome, my darling. Sleep well and I shall see you soon."

Thaddeus joined us and stroked her dark hair. "If you are feeling well enough tomorrow, I know some very excited boys who shall want to visit. I am certain they shall be just as protective of their youngest sister as they are of Eumelia, even if they never learn of their kinship to her."

I gave him a tight grin. "Thank you, Thaddeus."

When the door closed behind them, I considered pulling down the locking device so the three of us could have some privacy, but I knew Agrias and Melina would be eager to meet their first grandchild and I would not deny them of that opportunity.

"Our sweet girl," Alexis crooned, her finger tracing the contour of our daughter's face.

Carefully I sat beside her on the bed and drew Alexis' lips to mine wishing, not for the first time, that my touch, my kiss could explain everything I felt but did not know how to say. "I am sorry I ever wanted to deny us of this day. Of our daughter," I whispered when we parted. "The two of you are everything to me, you know that, right?"

Alexis' eyes held mine and she smiled. "I do and I thank you for loving me … us so completely."

I kissed her again, thankful that she was alive – that she had survived the birth of our daughter. But more than that, I was certain that had she not woken me from my Keres-induced sleep that I would have died as my daughter was born. Her unwavering love had ensured that did not happen and I would be eternally grateful to her for it. With Alexis' help, I was able to ensure I kept both of them safe from those who would do them harm. As I always would.

"Do you want to hold her?" Alexis asked. I nodded, taking Ava when Alexis passed her to me and hugging her to my chest. Alexis lay back, her head propped against the pillows, eyes drooping.

I placed our child on the bed beside her and stretched out so Ava was between us, my head resting on my hand. I smiled as Ava yawned widely and closed her eyes, a strand of my hair in her tiny fist. "I love you, Ava," I whispered, looking up to find Alexis watching us. "And you," I added with a grin.

"I love you too." I reached for her hand and twined our fingers before laying my head on the bed, exhausted.

I realized that the amulet had gone dark once again and I briefly wondered if it would ever light up again. For now, that was not important. All that mattered was that my daughter was here. Safe. Ours. She had no mark that signified she was Ares'. He had been wrong and so had I. She would grow as the Princess of Trachis, the Princess of Thermopylae, surrounded by those who loved her until her days in this world were done, and I could not wait to see who she became as she grew.

The soft breaths of my wife and daughter lulled me towards sleep. "She is everything I could have hoped for. You both are," I murmured, asleep mere moments later.

41

"Thrax, show yourself," Leandros demanded.

"What is it, old man?" the God of War asked, appearing beneath the tree, ankles crossed as he skipped a stone across the surface of the Eurotas River.

"You have followed me here to Sparta so I presume you know why I have come?"

"Your son," Ares replied with a shrug. "I understand why you were not happy to learn Skylar had shackled Trachis to Sparta."

Leandros nodded. "He is of no interest to you, not as Skylar was, is he?"

"Why should he be? He carries none of my blood, nor Zita's. He has a great future ahead of him but only if he remains here."

"I have no intention of making myself known to him, nor asking him to come to Trachis."

"Do you intend to tell Skylar about him?"

"One day. Perhaps when Cleomenes passes into the Underworld Leonidas shall become king. Perhaps that shall be the time."

Ares regarded Leandros. "You mortals are strange beings. Did you learn nothing from what you kept secret from Skylar these past winters? Should she not have a chance to meet her brother and know what it truly is to have a family with parents *and* siblings?" Leandros exhaled but said nothing. "Her alliance with the Spartan King may see them meet before you have the chance to speak of it," Ares warned.

"You threaten to tell her?"

Ares shrugged again. "Only if it served my purpose. For now, there is no need."

Leandros shielded his eyes, just able to make out the form of his son as he trained in the distance. "Perhaps you speak with truth. Perhaps it is time to lay bare all of my secrets. If I do so now, perhaps Skylar's wrath shall not be as severe as before and she may forgive me quickly for keeping it from her," Leandros murmured, though it was more to himself than to the god beside him.

"If I know you, Leandros, you shall speak of this with her only when you must. As you have with everything related to your history and Skylar's."

"Indeed," Leandros replied, noticing that, for once, Thrax spoke without taunting or contempt for him, and that he had used his actual name. Perhaps there would be many changes in the coming winters between the two of them.

42

A res watched Ava as she slept fitfully in Skylar's arms, Alexis beside them, the exhaustion of the past week written on her face even as she slept. The room was warm, heat emanating from the fireplace on the opposite wall to the bed. His Chosen One suffered with illness, as many of the children in the town of Trachis had this particular winter, and he wondered if he would once again have to intervene to keep his line alive. If it came to that, he knew he would not hesitate, just as he had not with Skylar when she first arrived.

Ava's dark hair was already past her shoulders, though Skylar and Alexis often plaited it to keep it from her face as she rushed about the courtyard and palace, the lengths easily tangling when left undone. She was barely two winters old, but was already full of fire and energy, and a number of other traits Ares recognized from those in his line.

She shivered violently and opened her eyes as he appeared to her in the dimness. She smiled, her fingers reaching out to him when he returned it. He neared, the amulet at Skylar's throat beginning to glow. The women continued to sleep, unaware of the God of War, their daughter's wakefulness, or the amulet's reaction to both.

Ares touched his hand to Ava's and her smile widened. "Hello, my Chosen One," he whispered.

"Hello," she replied.

Ares placed a hand to her forehead, unsurprised at the heat he found there, and the power running between the two of them. She closed her eyes again as the amulet's orange light intensified. She reached for it, drawing it into her palm. She sighed in contentment, the hint of a smile still on her lips as her breathing evened out and her dangerously high temperature cooled. Within moments she was back in Hypnos' realm, her slumber no longer erratic, or fraught with danger of death.

Ares raised his eyebrows at the obvious pull the amulet already had on her and the smile returned to his lips. He removed his hand, knowing she would wake with barely a cough or sniffle in the morning, though no one would know how it came to be. No one except the two of them. "You may not have the *Completed Mark* as Eir said you would, but I feel my blood flowing strongly through you. When it is time, I shall return. You shall be everything I have waited for, and I shall be all you ever need."

He pressed his lips to her forehead and disappeared in his familiar, bright light, returning to Aphrodite, and his palace on Olympos, to await the day when he returned to Trachis for Ava.

For his Chosen One.

ABOUT THE AUTHOR

Belinda Harrison was born and raised in a country town in North East Victoria, Australia. She spent some time experiencing 'big city life' in Melbourne and Sydney in her twenties where she held jobs in a packaging company, an online gaming firm, various temp positions and a hair loss treatment center before the lure of the country recalled her.

She joined her family's business in the world of retail plumbing and appliance sales - which is when she started writing the Thermopylae Bound Series - before deciding to leave the familiar and join another well-respected local firm in the Real Estate sector where she worked in the Commercial Property Management area.

Belinda then decided it was time for another change and moved across the road to the local newspaper where she looks after Circulation and Distribution. She fits in writing after hours and during lunch when the mood strikes her.

Belinda holds a Certificate IV in Multimedia and currently lives in 'the best part of Victoria' with her wife Renee, their daughter Ava, Charlie the dog and cats Caesar and Max.

She is working on the final books in the Thermopylae Bound Series, as well as a number of other adult and middle-grade novels, not all of which are set in the Ancient World!

www.ingramcontent.com/pod-product-compliance
Lightning Source LLC
Chambersburg PA
CBHW031725170626
46808CB00005B/1887

* 9 780648 372165 *